a (not so) lonely planet

a (not so) lonely planet

karina
kennedy

CLEiS
PRESS

Published in the United States by Cleis Press, an imprint of Start Midnight, LLC, 221 River Street, Ninth Floor, Hoboken, New Jersey 07030.

Printed in the United States
Cover design: Jennifer Do
Cover image: Shutterstock
Text design: Frank Wiedemann

First Edition.
10 9 8 7 6 5 4 3 2 1

Trade paper ISBN: 978-1-62778-312-5
E-book ISBN: 978-1-62778-525-9

Table Of Contents

for my mother,
who first explored Italy with me
and is not allowed to read this book.

Chapter 1

How Not to
Seduce a Man

Ristorante La Brezza, Positano, Italy:
Tuesday, 11:26 p.m.

The dynamic lesbian duo I meet on the train from Rome to Positano are full of wing-woman potential. I'm traveling alone, so the refined, blonde Parisian one who reminds me of a beautiful wood nymph invites me to join them for dinner with her friends. Her saucy British girlfriend, more nympho than nymph, orders me to come. I accept out of curiosity and fear of insulting the Brit, who was clearly Wicked Spice, a sixth girl, kicked out of the group for bad behavior. Anyway, I didn't just come to Italy to research a book. I came to meet people and have adventures. This qualifies as both. Positano is a sleepy, gorgeous town near the Italian Riviera, and the warmly lit *trattoria* is right on the blue-green water. I have no idea *he* will be there. Dinner is *eccellente*. Dessert does not go as planned. If you are ever traveling on your own Italian-love-cation, here are some things I learned.

HINTS FOR NOT BEING "TOO AMERICAN":

1. Espresso is to be enjoyed after dessert, not with. (What are you, a hedonist?)
2. *Fragola* and *Limoncello* are digestive liqueurs. Not shots. Trust me. (You don't want to be cleaning your own strawberry-lemon smoothie off the floor of your *pensione* bathroom at 2:00 a.m.)
3. Italians don't do doggie bags. (Even if they were the best meatballs you ever had in your life, don't try to put the last three in your purse.)

The meal is finishing up.

AT THIS POINT, IF: you've been playing footsies with the sexy photographer across from you, only to realize it's actually the female Alitalia pilot or the leg of the table ...

YOU SHOULD: start the Escher-esque climb of steps back to your *pensione*.

DO NOT: do what I do now.

I take a slow look around the table so it doesn't seem like I'm looking at *him*. I know him. He's a certain half-French, half-Italian photographer from the Roman fountain last week. The cocky, handsome stranger had pissed me off, and I'd taken the high road, instead of a ride in his sports car. Since that day, I'd distracted myself pretty fantastically, but Frantonio (I'd decided to call him this since I never got his name), kept slipping back into my mind.

Tonight when we were introduced we both pretended not to recognize each other. Now, he sips espresso, listening to his friend talk about football while staring at *me*. Is it hot in here? When we met in Rome, he had the upper hand. I decide now that tonight will be different. Seduction is a fine art to be practiced by masters. Rembrandt. Degas. Renoir. Me, I'm more of a Pollock. It's definitely hot in here.

I fill my glass with ice from the Prosecco bucket, lift my hair, and roll the glass gently against my neck, willing him to watch me. How sexy is this? Unfortunately, I've forgotten the bright red "Luscious Passion" lipstick on my glass, and I now have red smears on my neck as if I've been recently strangled. Sadly, I am unaware of this. Seeing that I've got his attention, I shift my weight so the neck of my dress drapes open enough for the lace of my bra to show. Glancing down, I then remember my one sexy bra had smelled like a gladiator in the Colosseum after he'd been beaten and buried for thousands of years. Tonight I've worn my sensible, once-white-now-gray-and-fraying Target bra. I quickly sit up straight again. Or at least what I think is straight. The pictures on the wall opposite all slope downhill as if I'm on a cruise ship. I'm sure it has nothing to do with all the wine I've had.

I know he recognizes me also. How could he not? It was only a brief encounter, but I remembered every inch of him. I allow my eyes to wander over his nicely shaped forearms, his dirty blond, perfectly ruffled hair, the graceful arc of his collarbone, his strong jawline peppered with stubble, and the firm curve of his lip. But what's been creeping into my dreams are those eyes, framed by his glasses—deep brown with hints of gold and playful, curling lashes. He is gorgeous. Here's a second chance to see what's behind door number one. It's now or never. I rise slowly. I'm not a person who passes up risky potential for a safe bet. As I walk toward the hall that leads to the bathroom, I throw Frantonio a sexy smile. *Andiamo.* Let's go.

IF YOU'VE MADE IT THIS FAR, FOLLOW THESE INSTRUCTIONS:

1. Quick pee and hand wash.
2. Cleavage hike.
3. Breath check.
4. Pit sniff and pit wipe.

5. In the hall, drape yourself against the wall and channel your best Jessica (Biel, Alba, Simpson, for me it's Rabbit).
6. Wait.

DO NOT: reapply previously mentioned "Luscious Passion" red lipstick.

Back hallway, *Ristorante La Brezza*, Positano, Italy: Tuesday, 11:45 p.m.

I don't have to pretend to check my phone too long before I hear footsteps.

"Waiting for someone, *chèrie?*" His accent is a musical mash up of nationalities.

"My phone isn't working," I lie.

"We meet again," he smiles. "A force of nature pulls us together, *peut-être?*"

"Yes, we both had to pee," I say coolly.

"Very funny. Come now, you can't deny, there is some kind of . . . magnetism."

"I think that's called lust."

"Well, une rose par tout autre nom—?" He laughs.

"Why does everything sound sexier in French?" I ask.

"Because, it's the most powerful language in the world," he winks. "First Rome, now here. Surely you can feel the energy between us even now?" He smiles. I wet my finger, hold it up, like a sailor testing for wind.

"Hmmmm . . . not really getting anything," I say with a straight face. This coolness with men was taught by my mother, who'd been abandoned by my father. It was reinforced by my Catholic school nuns, and finally perfected out of self-preservation as a nerdy teen who hid behind romance books and took teasing to heart. Later in college, I slowly began to grasp my own natural sex appeal and use this coolness as an ambush instead of a barrier. Now, it takes all my self-control to act indifferent when Frantonio takes my finger and puts it into *his own mouth*. This is definitely gross, yet somehow sexy at the same time, as I immediately imagine how his tongue and lips would feel elsewhere on my body.

"*Adesso?*" he asks. "Now can you feel it?" He takes a step closer to me. "Is it like a woozy, sloshy feeling? Because I'm definitely getting that. I thought it was the wine and that very rich sauce on my meatballs . . ." I trail off as he leans in even closer. I can feel the heat from his body. He reaches out and fingers the tiny star I wear on a delicate chain around my neck. This was made in high school from one of my father's bowling trophies after I found his soldering iron and started permanently sticking things together in his office (my revenge for his extended absences). I wear it because it reminds me to look up, aim high, and navigate with confidence. Right now, with my heart thumping like an overloaded washing machine, I'm faking every ounce of confidence.

Frantonio slides his hand behind my back and pulls me toward him. His other hand brushes my hair from my shoulder as his warm breath and stubble tickle my neck, sending an uncontrollable shiver down my legs. He kisses me first lightly and then harder. I kiss him back and run my fingers through his perfectly ruffled hair.

AT THIS POINT, YOU SHOULD: step back, blush beautifully, let him ask you out.

I DO NOT.

My Jessica Rabbit morphs into Sharon Stone as I lean my head back for him to kiss my neck, and then arch my chest up so that he can bend down to kiss my breasts. I slip my hand into his shirt between the buttons as I slide one knee up his leg. Here, my other foot suddenly slips on the Travertine marble, sending my thigh smashing into his crotch as I fall to the floor, my arm still caught in his shirt, ripping it open like the Incredible Hulk. My ass on the cold tile, I watch Frantonio lean against the wall, moaning in pain, glasses askew, "Luscious Passion" smeared down his chin and chest, swearing in both French and Italian. Fuck! (Right now you're thinking, *I wouldn't fall.* Probably not. But, I'm the klutziest person I know, with the exception of my mother. More on this later.)

Quickly, if not gracefully, I scramble to my feet, run through the kitchen, smash into a guy hauling garbage, and escape through the back with spaghetti on my arm. I don't stop until I'm crawling up the last of the eighteen flights of steps to my *pensione* at the top of the hill. It is here that I realize the designer purse-that-turns-into-a-clutch my friend Sarah gave me is no longer clutching *anything.* It's come open somewhere along the way, and now everything is gone, including my room key. Fortunately, I've left my window open. Unfortunately, my room is on the second floor.

IF YOU: find yourself in this situation, DEFINITELY DO NOT:

1. Cry.
2. Vomit outside your neighbor's window.
3. Attempt to climb a thirty-year-old rose trellis.
4. Fall, ripping your dress open.
5. Tell the old man who runs the place you thought there was a fire.
6. Silently freak out like a coked-up mime because you lost your wallet and phone.
7. Forget you're dripping with sweat and your mascara looks like Courtney Love's.
8. Get out your tablet and video call your best friend, who is also your ex . . .

. . . and still in love with you.

Introduction

You're probably thinking, "Introductions go at the beginning of books, not after the first chapter." You're right. But you would have skipped it. We all do. I think it's best if we're properly introduced before you see me with my pants down . . .

"My mother is a fish." It's a line from *As I Lay Dying,* one of my favorite books, and also what my father told me on one of our little fishing trips. I hated fishing, but Dad was a chartered yacht captain who sailed off for weeks, so I took any time I could get. He said he'd fallen in love with a mermaid long ago on one of his journeys. They'd lived together on a beautiful island in the South Pacific and had a baby. But fish are not like people. They don't mate for life. One day, she swam away, leaving him with me. When my father returned to Key West, Rosalie, the innkeeper's daughter, took pity on us and invited us to live with her. She and my father eventually married.

Of course, this was all a silly story. Probably. It's just always been hard for me to reconcile how two people as different as my parents got together. Dad's traveled the world and Rosalie's never even left the country. Also,

I'm probably more like a mermaid than I am like my mother. Also, I love the water. Being in it, on it, around it. Like me, fish don't swim in a straight line. They're impossible to hold onto. The tighter you grasp them, the more likely they are to slip into the sea and disappear forever. Rosalie never understood this. Each time my father came home from a voyage, she would try to hold on tighter and keep him from leaving, but he always did. During those longer and longer trips, she would then grip *me* more tightly. This made me want to swim away too.

My name is Nativity Marina Taylor. Rosalie wanted something biblical and Dad liked nautical. Despite my Sunday school and Catholic school education, Jesus and I are still figuring out our complicated relationship. When I was nine, I stopped answering to Nativity and claimed Marina. I grew up in a place other people escape to, but I wanted to escape from. Florida is the country's fun, sticky, dangly part that should be kept in its pants. Swamps and beaches, guns, drugs, gators, theme parks, tourists, retirees, rednecks, politicians, immigrants, millionaires, and homeless people. It's a schizophrenic tropical paradise where heat madness is a valid legal defense. (A good thing to remember when you move back in with your mother after college.)

I feel like Rosalie and I are polar opposites. She watches every flavor of CSI while quilting things to raise money for charity. I watch raunchy comedies and adventure romance films for the cute meets and the sex scenes. (I never bother with the endings, they're all the same.) Mostly Rosalie and I do not enjoy each other's company. But we do have one thing in common. My father abandoned us. So up to this point, we've been stuck together like barnacles. But now, I've got a get out of jail free card. My friend Mike who works for an airline has given me a buddy pass. A super cheap, open-ended ticket to Europe! I feel like Charlie with his golden ticket to Willy Wonka's Chocolate Factory.

Not so long ago, a woman traveling alone was seen to be of questionable moral character. But you've read the first few pages of this book, so any questions about my moral character have already been answered. I am a writer and a restless spirit. Remember *Choose Your Own Adventure* books? At the end of each chapter you're given a choice. Depending on your choice, you turn to a certain page, read, make another choice, etc. I loved and hated those books. I kept my fingers stuck in different places so I could look at all the options, change my mind, choose again. Who wants *only one* adventure?

My plan has always been to save up money after college and go abroad, to research my first book. I'm taking a creative non-fiction essay I wrote as an English major and expanding it into a book. This will be a noble contribution to the world of literature. Never mind that I grew up reading more adventure romance novels than noble contributions to the world of literature. And, never mind the real reason I want to go to Europe is to have exotic lovers and awesome adventures. The point is, now I can go!

As an intrepid explorer, I am unwilling to miss out on a memory, willing to bend the rules, unafraid of my own beauty, and ready to share it with those who deserve it. Men get to roam the world with London, Kerouac, and Larry McMurtry. Have gun—will travel. Women get to stay home with Austen? Fuck that. Have pen and pussy—will travel.

I want to date like a man. Unapologetically. Confidence must be faked until it is found. Openness must be practiced until it eclipses ego.

The book you're about to read is NOT the one I traveled to Italy to write. Yes, I planned to write about admirable women to inspire other women. Here's the problem. Every good story needs drama and conflict. Enter me: B-side to admirable women everywhere. So, this is a travel diary for romantic readers, with notes on inspirational women and the misadventures of a not-so-inspirational one. This time, we'll start at the beginning.

WARNING: This book may be unsuitable for: children, my mother, judgy Catholic school friends, Italian greyhounds (they already shake too much), and bold young ladies with poor judgment (like me) who think things like naked bungee jumping or moonlight surfing sound fun.

Chapter 2

How Not to
Say Goodbye

Harbor House B&B: Wednesday, 3:23 p.m.

My plane to Rome leaves tomorrow at 1:45 p.m., and the following night, I'll be at an exclusive wine release party. As soon as I posted on social media about my upcoming trip, my friend Nadya, an Italian sommelier I'd met in Miami, invited me. My version of good wine is whatever's on sale at Costco, and I have no idea what a release party is, but exclusive is definitely in my vocabulary. My plane leaves in less than twenty-four hours, so of course, instead of packing, I'm outside cleaning fish.

Many of you won't know the special, stinky hell of one-hundred-and-three-degree heat with eighty-nine percent humidity while scraping off scales and skin, cutting off tails, and yanking out bones and guts—all while haunting eyes give you a death stare. But my family owns a bed and breakfast, and paying guests don't clean their own fish. This has been my job since my father left. I do not eat fish. (I'm part fish, after all.) Sadly, the poetic tragedy of forcing me to scrape the flesh off my brethren has always failed to move Rosalie. As

I mop sweat from my brow, smearing fish guts on my forehead, my phone buzzes in my pocket. I pull it out (with slimy hands) and check the message.

WILL:
When do you leave?

ME:
Not soon enough.

WILL:
I have something for your trip.

ME:
I'm already packed.

WILL:
Won't take much space.

I'm not actually packed. I start to answer him, but at this moment a devious seagull (with whom I have a checkered past) goes for one of the fish filets. Was that bastard bird sitting there waiting for me to clean a fish for him? As I dive forward, flailing my arms to block him, my phone flies out of my slippery, slimy hand, into the air, hits the wooden deck, and skitters over the edge into the water. Fuck.

WHAT TO PACK FOR YOUR ITALIAN-LOVE-CATION
1. Old cell phone that was supposed to be your back-up phone (1).
2. Cute sundress (1–2).
3. LBD (little black dress) for wine release party and other fancy events (1–2).
4. Comfortable sandals or flip-flops (1–2) and ridiculously uncomfortable stilettos (1).
5. Comfortable underwear (6) and uncomfortable sexy lingerie (1).
6. Bathing suit that shows off your assets (1).
7. Sarong to cover up your assets (1).
8. Birth control pills and condoms (can't be too careful).

My Boat on Stilts, Harbor House B&B: Wednesday, 11:15 p.m.

The twenty-six-foot sloop my father never got around to fixing has been my "bedroom" since I tried to run away at age fourteen. Rosalie and I compromised, and I got my own space. The obvious irony of living in a boat, up on stilts, in my mother's backyard, that was never going anywhere ever again, never occurred to me.

AT THIS POINT, IF: it's almost midnight on the night before your first adventure abroad, and you're still lying in bed awake, you probably shouldn't have had that double espresso. And latte. And cappuccino. (Rosalie's new machine for the B&B needed testing.)

YOU SHOULD: do a mental autopsy of your luggage. The dinner purse you packed is too big. You can't use it for dinner. Instead, pack the purse-that-turns-into-a-clutch that Sarah gave you. That one is beautiful and functional. You won't be sorry. Remove the stilettos. They'll get stuck in the cobblestones. Get out of your bunk, open your new Swiss Army suitcase with the super strong zipper (guaranteed for life), switch the purses, sit on your suitcase, and zip it back up.

DO NOT: accidentally zip the bottom of the oversized T-shirt you're wearing into your suitcase, jamming the super strong zipper (guaranteed for life), so you have to crawl over to the table, dragging the bag behind, break your letter opener in the super strong zipper, grab the scissors, and chop the end of your shirt off, along with the part of your knee that was bracing the bag.

My Boat on Stilts, Harbor House B&B: Thursday, 2:08 a.m.

I'm lying in my little berth bed, still awake, icepack on my newly bandaged knee, listening to the rain outside. Suddenly I jump. Something hit the deck above me. I stand up and slowly poke my head out of the hatch.

Rain pelts the deck. To my relief, the raccoon that's been harassing me for weeks by knocking rocks against the deck until I toss cookies out the hatch is nowhere in sight. I know this sounds cute, but this fierce trash panda is actually a pirate. He limps, is missing one eye, and breaks into my boat to eat my tropical fish. He's not cute. He's a dick. I lie back down, but then . . .

"Marina?" a voice calls from below. I slide the small curtain back and look down. There, standing in the rain, is my sweet, sexy, soggy ex-boyfriend. What's he doing here? I throw on a raincoat.

"What the hell, Will? It's the middle of the night," I call down.

"Sorry. I said I had something for you." He holds up a book, in a Ziploc bag.

"You drove all the way from Miami, in a storm, to give me a book?"

"Yeah, you need it for your trip."

"Bullshit, Will. The only thing you're missing is a boom box and a trench coat." Will's always been the hopeless romantic waiting patiently for his movie ending. I, on the other hand, know there is no *happily ever after*. You must find your own happy. Over and over again.

"What happened to your leg, Marina?" he asks. I look down. The rain washes blood from my knee down my leg. "You're always bleeding."

"Will, *you're* the one who said only messages and emails after we broke up."

"I know. Just come down, please," he says. I pitch the rope ladder over the side and climb down. Water drips off the brim of the straw cowboy hat he's worn for years. The guys on the police force tease him, but Will's not the sort that cares. He grew up near Ocala, looking after a ranch full of cattle. Now he works as a cop in Key West, looking after an island full of misfits. I try not to notice that his favorite blue shirt is soaked and now plastered to his well-sculpted break-up bod.

"Will, you can't stop me. I have a cheap ticket to Europe, an invitation to an exclusive wine release party, a book to research, and a mother who's driving me crazy. I can't stay here cleaning fish and making key lime pies for *other* people who left home to explore new places. I have to get the fuck out of this boat, out of this town, and out of this state."

"I know, Marina. You got ants in your pants." He always said that. I used to say, "And you're jealous of those ants," but tonight I do not. "Besides, how can you be a great writer if you never have any worldly experiences?"

"Exactly," I say, surprised and disarmed. There's an awkward moment filled with only the sound of the warm rain around us. I stare at my toes, wiggling them in the mud.

"Have you read this?" He hands me the book.

"*The Alchemist*? No."

"Okay, good."

"Thanks." We both stand there, silent again. It's been months since we broke up. But, then there was that "one last time" on his sailboat during the fireworks on the Fourth of July. Now, as he leans in to hug me goodbye, I smell the sweet, earthy scent of his rain-soaked hair and I flash back to that night.

The silhouette of his perfectly shaped nose was lit by soft, distant flashes of light as he had leaned in to kiss me. The boat had gently swayed, pressing our bodies together. The cool salt breeze had tickled the glass mermaid wind chime as the stubble of his day-old beard tickled my neck, sending goose bumps racing down my arms and chest. I could feel his heart racing, pounding against my wet T-shirt as I gripped his hair and kissed him hungrily. I could never get enough of those strong, confident kisses. I could kiss this man for hours.

Our bodies had swayed rhythmically with the boat. It was like we were dancing . . . although, I never dance to slow songs. His hands had cupped my ass, pulling me into him, tighter, closer. As I felt him harden for me, my desperate fingers had tugged at the strings of his board shorts as my forehead pressed against his abs. He'd lifted me easily up onto the cabin bunk and peeled off my wet T-shirt. The fireworks had flashed from afar, illuminating his beautiful face as he'd smiled and untied the string on my bikini. His gentle, strong hands on my breasts, his thumb stroking my nipple—

"You're getting all wet," Will's voice breaks through my memory. No shit. Here, now, in the dark and the warm rain, I want him so badly, but I simply lean in and kiss his cheek. He hugs me tightly. It feels good, too good, even though rainwater pours off his hat into my hood, and down my back. I peel myself out of his arms. I have to. We want different things.

"Bye, Cowboy."

"Have fun, Mermaid," he says. "But not too much fun." I get a glimpse of his one slightly crooked tooth that only shows when he smiles. Will gets into his old Bronco and drives away. Back in my boat, I reopen my new Swiss Army suitcase with the super strong zipper (guaranteed for life) and stuff in the book. Then, to counteract the weight of old relationships with the prospect of new ones, I also cram back in the ridiculously uncomfortable stilettos.

Chapter 3

How Not to Fly

My Boat on Stilts, Harbor House B&B:
Thursday, 6:49 a.m.

"Marina!" My mother's voice slices into my Ryan Gosling dream like a buzz saw, but it's actually a relief. Moments ago, I'd been waiting patiently in the extra large, first-class plane bathroom stripped down to my purple *La Perla* lingerie, waiting for Ryan to induct me into the mile-high club. But then my dream had taken a sharp nose-dive. Ryan bashed the door open from the outside, brandishing a gun and his US Marshalls badge, seizing my oversized bottle of perfume. "It's over three ounces! Everybody get down!" Screams of horror, as passengers assumed the crash position.

"Marina! Get up now if you want a ride! I need help with breakfast, and we have to drop some guests at the Hemingway House on the way to the airport shuttle." A radio squawks by my head. It's a system we rigged up so Rosalie could communicate with me from the main house at any time. Biggest mistake I ever made. I blink at the clock. Shit.

Kitchen, Harbor House B&B: Thursday, 7:12 a.m.

"You've already read that crap to me once, Rosalie!" I fry the bacon as she, AGAIN, reads me the State Department's web page of safety precautions for citizens traveling abroad.

"They update it daily. You can't be too careful. Don't call me that. *Know before you go.*" She problematically reminds me that I've chosen a country with, "gypsies and gigolos everywhere."

"Why do you think I picked it?" I reply. I know her real beef with gypsies is that my father insisted on naming their Romanian Gypsy friend my official godfather instead of her brother. Rosalie never quite understood dad's fascination with this resourceful, nomadic culture. I, on the other hand, loved visiting their cigar-scented home, with sparkling crystal chandeliers, plastic-covered furniture, and neon palm reader signs blinking proudly. As I said before, Rosalie isn't the wandering type. The fact that she's never been out of the country doesn't seem to bother her at all. I flip the bacon. "Stop worrying. We'll video chat weekly, if you can remember how to use the app I downloaded onto your not-so-smart phone." She reaches over me to get her coffee and her arm grazes the sizzling frying pan.

"Oh!" She winces, drawing back quickly. I immediately examine it and, yanking a bag of frozen peas out of the freezer, sit her down with her mug of coffee. Rosalie is prone to accidents causing herself bodily injury. (Okay, we have two things in common.)

"Relax. I'm the one that's leaving the country, Rosalie."

"I said don't call me that." She hates this, which is why I do it. "How long will you be gone?" she asks, her voice pained, but it's not her arm that's bothering her.

"Until my money runs out or I get arrested, whichever comes first," I joke. She doesn't smile. "I'll be fine. I've got Dad's survivalist instincts." At the mention of my father, she bristles.

"That's what I'm afraid of." She looks away, annoyed and trying not to let me see her nervous tears welling up. I know what's worrying her most. I hug her with my spatula in hand. "I'm coming back. I promise."

"You're dripping bacon juice on my blouse."

"It smells better than your perfume."

Miami International Airport, Florida: Thursday, 1:07 p.m.

I'm late to the airport, but apparently when you're traveling on a buddy pass, they don't care if you show up at all. Buddy passes are inexpensive standby tickets from friends who work for the airline. You're a seat-filler. If you're lucky, you'll get out on the first flight. Extremely lucky, you'll be put in first class. I am neither.

Gate 24A, MIA: Thursday, 1:48 p.m.

The jetway door is closed. Only one standby passenger got a seat. The rest of us are "rolled over" to the next flight, leaving in two hours from gate 56B. I kill time in the bookstore looking at magazines I won't buy. Cate Blanchett is playing mother, daughter, and grandmother in the same film? She is so talented.

Gate 32A, MIA: Thursday, 5:36 p.m.

The next flight also left without me. I'm starting to get nervous that I won't make it in time for Nadya's exclusive wine party. But there are three more flights to Rome tonight. I start to make friends with the other "leftovers." It feels like the rapture, watching others get whisked away to paradise. There is a list on a screen. Your name moves up or down, depending on who shows up that outranks you. Currently, Ruby Johnson is directly ahead of me on the list. She is over eighty, uses a wheeled, floral backpack for a carry on, and is on her way to see her new great-grandchild in Rome.

"I do yoga every day at sunrise for an hour and eat a vegan diet," she informs me proudly. Halfway through the blanket she's knitting, Ruby has been here since 5:00 a.m. "This will be my fourth trip to Rome. My granddaughter served in the Peace Corps and is now the assistant to the US Ambassador of Italy. What do you do?"

"I'm a writer. I'm going to Italy to research a book."

"Wonderful! Like *Eat Pray Love?* Or *Under the Tuscan Sun?*"

"No. It's not about middle-aged women eating gelato and falling in love while growing basil gardens. It's about Italian women of influence."

"Sounds more like a college term paper."

"It's the first in a series I'm going to write. All over the world," I retort.

"Oh, your first book. *I see,*" says Ruby. She does? What does she see?

"Well, I'm only twenty-four."

"My granddaughter is twenty-four," she says smugly. "Speaking of basil, my uncle once had a dog called Basil, he was British you see, and that dog, he was a border collie. They're very smart you know. He used to pull his own sled up a hill, the dog, not my uncle . . ." After an hour of stories, sage advice, and vegan farts worse than a goat's, I excuse myself to get a coffee. Note to self: never let my mom go vegan.

Here I should explain an unpopular opinion. I'm not a fan of old people. I grew up surrounded by retirees who have a sense of entitlement. My ex-best friend Laurel used to say, "Their give-a-shitter's broken." Oldies write checks and use coupons on their more than fifteen items in the express grocery line. They drive ten miles below the speed limit in the fast lane. Old men get away with sexist or racist comments because you can't scold a senior.

When I return to the gate, I choose a seat next to a man wearing a rumpled sports jacket. This is Helpful Jack. He's actually trying to get to Paris, but those flights are even more crowded and he's been here for thirty-six hours. He tells me the carpeted alcove next to the Cinnabon is a good place to sleep—they don't vacuum there at night. Another man, Nervous Neil, smells homeless and his eyes never focus in one place. Nobody knows how long he's been here. I think I've seen him on an episode of that forensic murder show my mother likes. As the next flight begins to board, I start to wonder if waking up with a petrified raisin stuck to the side of my face is worse than the scream of an industrial-sized vacuum cleaner for six hours.

Halfway through the boarding process, two women stroll up, with large diamonds, lots of makeup, and inflatable neck pillows. They check in at the gate and suddenly everyone on the standby screen bumps down two spots. Fuck! Pilots' wives? I don't care if they're astronauts' wives! They should be home drinking Chardonnay in their hot tubs. Nobody wants them here. Not me, not Ruby of the Vegan Goat Farts, and certainly not their husbands' Italian mistresses! I'm coming unhinged. I'm reminded of the movie *Terminal* where Tom Hanks plays a refugee trapped inside the airport for weeks watching everyone come and go from exotic places. A shudder of horror runs down my spine. I'd rather be stuck on an island talking to a volleyball. At least I'd get a tan.

Chapter 4

How Not to Get Arrested at the Airport

HELPFUL HINTS FOR BUDDY PASS RIDERS:

1. When your mother tries to pack you a sandwich, take it.
2. Make friends with your fellow leftovers, but don't get too close.
3. Don't stand on the chairs to reach the volume switch of the television—even if you're afraid you may snap and start hurling luggage if you listen to the same Fox News story for the thirtieth time.
4. Don't ask the man in the massage stand if they have "free samples."
5. Offering the octogenarian (Ruby) ahead of you on the list a bottle of water every half hour, hoping she'll be in the bathroom when they call her name, is wrong. Right?

Gate 51C, MIA: Thursday, 10:23 p.m.

The next flight has now left without me. But Helpful Jack won the lottery. There were cheers, tears, and applause among the leftovers, hands slapping five as he ran for the jetway like it was a closing time portal. Ruby and I are next on the list. There is one last flight. If I don't make this one, I'll have to try again tomorrow, and I'll miss Nadya's party. This cannot happen. I can't miss out on meeting the rich, handsome, recently divorced Italian underwear model I've already decided will most certainly be seated next to me at the event. I move closer to the counter and casually mention to the agent with the hair beehive like a Hindu temple that my sister works for UNICEF.

"She was airlifted to Rome yesterday after she was shot trying to save a baby elephant from a poacher. Her condition is critical."

"Italian elephants?" Ruby snorts. "What malarkey!" This causes a coughing fit.

"Do you need your oxygen tank, ma'am?" I ask Ruby. Then I whisper to Hindu Hair, "Maybe she shouldn't fly?"

"Nonsense, I'm an eighty-two-year-old with the body of a seventy-year-old!" snaps the old bag as she heads for the bathroom, again. (My evil plan is working.)

Gate 32B, MIA: Thursday, 11:03 p.m.

Everything is closed except a twenty-four-hour doughnut shop. As I wait for my "hot now" doughnut in the microwave, I notice the electrical outlet next to the cash register. I study the young girl behind the counter. She doesn't look like the type to watch porn on my tablet if I leave it with her for fifteen minutes to charge.

IF YOU: need to charge a device and find a nice doughnut girl to leave it with.

DO NOT: do it.

Gate 32B, MIA: Thursday, 11:39 p.m.

There is one last seat, on the last plane tonight. "Passenger Ruby Johnson," calls Hindu Hair. Ruby got the seat! Fuck. Goodbye wine party. The recently divorced underwear model is going to be showing someone else that trick he does with his tongue. "Passenger Johnson?" the agent calls again. I look around, surprised. Where is Ruby? The agent calls her name again. No answer. She wouldn't have left. Did she have a heart attack in the bathroom? Is she at this very moment lying face down on the cold tile with her eye open like Janet Leigh in *Psycho*? Faced with this horrible thought, I suddenly jump up and yell:

"She's not here, I'm next!" Hindu Hair peers at me with a tired expression. Her hair temple leans sideways as she looks around, careful not to make eye contact with the other leftovers, who are staring like shelter dogs hoping to be adopted.

"Passenger Taylor, Nativity Marina Taylor," Hindu Hair announces into the microphone, even though I'm fifteen feet away seated on the floor.

"Yes! Me!" I scramble to corral the belongings I had spread around me to mark my territory like a hermit crab. She hands me a boarding pass. Seat 54B. I can hardly believe it. That's when it happens.

"Wait, I'm here!" Ruby of the Vegan Goat Farts appears, out of breath.

"It's too late!" I say. "I'm getting on the plane."

"That's my seat. I was in the bathroom!"

"You snooze, you lose," I say. Ruby starts to cry.

"I'm eighty-four, I've got to see my great-grandchild before it's too late." She moves between me and the jetway.

"You've got the body of a seventy-year-old, remember?"

"No respect for your elders," snaps Ruby.

"You're three times my age. You've had your adventures. It's my turn!" I say. Without warning, Ruby tries to snatch the boarding pass out of my hand. I react, and tug back on it. Suddenly, she's grabbed my arm, with a look right out of the exorcist on her face. I grab her hand and the wrestling match is on, each of us trying to take the boarding pass without ripping it.

"Ladies, please! Don't make me call TSA," says Hindu Hair, without much intention of actually doing anything. Obviously this is not her first standby skirmish.

"This isn't a geriatric wrestling tournament—the seat is mine!" I shout. But now Ruby's twisted my arm around her body and is leaning forward so it looks like I'm grabbing *her* and not the ticket.

"Help! This woman is attacking me!" she yells.

"What?!" I yell. "That's not—" I try to snake my arm out, but she's got me.

"Let her go," says Hindu Hair to me.

"I'm not—she's the one that—" but I'm cut off by Ruby's lung-filled yell.

"Help! Attacker! Call 911!" Now, literally everyone is looking as Ruby throws her arms up, thrusting her ass back into my stomach (a move she's certainly learned in her self-defense for seniors class at the American Legion) and karate chopping my shoulder as she kicks my shin. I yell in pain, and the weight of my backpack pulls me onto my butt on the floor. Boarding pass in hand, Ruby grabs her bag and runs into the jetway.

"Get back here, you mean, lying, very strong—old cow!" I get to my knees, about to give chase, but she's gone. "I hope your oxygen mask doesn't work!" I yell. Big arms wearing blue shirts suddenly grab me, lifting me to my feet.

"Hold it there, or you're under arrest!" The arms belong to two big, muscly TSA guys. SHIT! But then, suddenly I see a face I know. Mike!

"Oh dear God! Marina? Don't worry, sweetie, I've got your pills!" Mike, my good friend, a flight attendant, is suddenly shoving spearmint Tic Tacs into my mouth and pinching my nose. "Swallow!" he commands. I stare at him with bewildered confusion. "She's a fly-polar-phobic. Her fear of flying alters her brain chemistry. Hold still—" He checks my eyes and puts his wrist on my forehead. To me: "Your pulse is low. Hold your arms up in the air." To the guys: "I've got to get some cranberry juice in her, STAT. Thank you boys, I'll take care of this." He peels me out of their grip. "Wow, aren't you strong?" Mike shoots a flirty smile at the TSA agent as he hauls me to a door marked "No Entry." As we disappear through the door, he calls over his shoulder, "Keep up the good work brave men in blue."

Employee Hallway, MIA: Thursday, 11:47 p.m.

"Are you trying to get me fired?" Mike is furious.

"No!" I'm tearing up.

"Remember when I said be on your *best* behavior because anything you do is a reflection on the employee who gave you the buddy pass? That's me, you asshole!"

"I'm so sorry, Mike! I just snapped! They called *my* name, Mike. That geriatric bitch took my spot! They called my name." I sob.

He suddenly smacks my face lightly. I glare at him, shocked.

"Get it together, sister," he says. "The whole idea of a buddy pass is flexibility. Can you be flexible, Marina?" Mike asks.

"I've been like double-jointed hooker flexible, Mike! This is the last flight tonight. If I don't get on it, I'll have to sleep on your couch in South Beach!"

"Well, I just got off a triple shift and haven't seen my boyfriend in a week, so that is *not* happening," he says. I grab his blue vest.

"Then get me on that flight!"

Flight #632: Thursday, 11:58 p.m.

Yes! Wine party here I come. Mike has worked some voodoo magic and found an extra seat somehow. The plane is pushing back before I've buckled my seatbelt. It's a middle seat in the last row, in front of the bathrooms, right next to . . . Ruby. But my feeling of dread begins to fade as the first announcement in Italian is made over the PA system. *"Tutti i dispositivi elettronici devono essere spenti ora."*[i*] I'm going to Rome, at last! I'll just call my mother and let her know.

---

i * Translation: All electronic devices must be switched off now.

Chapter 5

How Not to Get Picked Up

Fiumicino Airport, Rome, Italy: Friday, 3:56 p.m.

WHAT TO EXPECT WHEN YOU LAND
1. Men with machine guns walking around the airport.
2. The beautiful white noise of language soup.
3. Lines in the bathroom.
4. Cigarette smoke, everywhere.
5. A half-hour wait for your luggage.
6. Body odor, lots of it.
7. Lines in customs.
8. Lines in passport control.
9. Nuns in habits.
10. Lines at the bar (where you buy your *caffè latte*).

Piazza Della Repubblica, Rome: Friday, 5:40 p.m.

I have taken the train to Termini station and changed into a sundress and floppy hat, cute and ready for adventure. Outside Termini, I haul my stuff past buses, taxis, trinket stands, and a group of Chinese tourists squeezing into a bus at the same time. I pause on the edge of the busy traffic circle. In the middle, the fountain stands in full glory and splendor. A stream of cars and scooters flow around it. Backlit water gleams like liquid fire in the late afternoon sun, cascading off the backs of the four beautiful nymphs of the lakes, rivers, oceans, and springs. A strong wind sweeps through buildings that are hundreds of years old and over the surface of the fountain, sending a light mist all the way to where I'm standing, the droplets kissing my bare arms and legs. Could I take a selfie from the safety of this vantage point? Yes. Do I? Of course not.

I have two false starts, edging my way out timidly into the traffic circle, only to be scuttled back onto the sidewalk like a pigeon by angry taxi horns. Finally, I decide to just go for it. Halfway across, a scooter swerves around me, someone curses me in Italian, my rolling case flops over on its side, and the wind rips my sunhat off my head, launching it into the air. Dragging my little suitcase behind me, I make it to the safety of the fountain . . . and see my hat floating toward the center. I could tell you now that it was my favorite hat, but the truth is I needed little excuse to go in. After all, I am part fish. It was not *Fontana di Trevi* and I was not Anita Ekberg, but I was going to have my *La Dolce Vita* moment.

The water is cold. I wade quickly toward my hat, slip on the scummy bottom, and go down on my ass. (I'm not the most graceful, we've already established that.) I scramble back up, my heart pounding, endorphins coursing through me. Suddenly I'm laughing uncontrollably. I'm thousands of miles away from the place I've always been. I'm far away from anyone who knows me at all. I'm in ROME! In a fountain! Alone! I'm whomever I want to be, each new moment, deciding for myself. And, in this moment I choose to frolic. I jump. I dance. I splash. I scream with joy.

Then, I see *him*. I freeze. Seated in a red vintage Alpha Romeo convertible is a man, with a camera, and a long lens . . . aimed at me. He's watching through the telephoto lens and snapping away. What's he getting close ups of? My wet hair stuck to my face and neck? My soaked sundress plastered to my body like a glove? My heaving chest and wet breasts, out of breath from dancing? The open buttons of the top of my dress slightly exposing my left nipple? The wet, floral skirt of my dress stuck into the crack of my shapely, supple, perfect ass? How dare he? I'm flattered, embarrassed, and enraged. Who does he think he is? And more importantly, do I look like a model from the *Sports Illustrated* swimsuit edition?

I flip him off. He grins and shoots another photo. This is not what I expect. He shrugs and points. I look over and see the busload of Chinese tourists, also shooting photos. Oh. That's. Wow. Not good. Suddenly I'm not whomever I want to be. I'm the crazy American girl breaking the law, disrespecting history, and getting hepatitis C from pigeon poop water. I will now appear in no less than twenty-seven family slideshows of their vacations in Europe. I look around for my hat. Fuck it.

Wading to the side of the fountain, I quickly haul myself out, put my shoes on, and collect my things. The Alpha Romeo pulls up right in front of me. The man hops out of the car, holding a new hat he's purchased from a tourist stand.

"*Bonjour belle sirène.* If you're done with your swim, would you like a ride?" His accent is strange and adorable. His hair dirty blond, skin a very dark tan. His beautiful light brown eyes are hiding behind glasses. And his smile is cocky.

"You can't just take photos of people without asking," I say, trying to hold onto any shred of dignity I may have left.

"*Je suis désolé,*" he smiles. "I'm a photographer. When I see something interesting, odd, or beautiful, I must shoot it. It's an addiction."

"Odd?" I give him a look. "What the heck does that mean?"

"It means bizarre."

"I know what it means!"

"*Étrange,* and full of *joie de vivre,*" he grins.

"It doesn't make it okay if you say it in French." I narrow my eyes.

"Sure it does. French is the most powerful language in the world," he smiles. "Everything sounds nicer in French. You're alone?"

"No. I'm independent."

He laughs as he lifts my suitcase effortlessly into the back seat of his car. "Exactly where are you going, independent girl?" He opens the passenger door.

"Exactly nowhere with a presumptuous, rude stranger who sounds like a language experiment gone wrong." I step over and grab the handle of my suitcase, and (not effortlessly) yank it back out of the car.

"My mother is Italian. My father is French Moroccan. I am generous. I'm offering a ride. None of the taxi drivers will take you dripping wet."

"But *you* will in your midlife crisis car with leather seats?"

"I like wet American girls," he tilts his head and grins. He is standing very close to me and I feel my stomach lurch as he raises his eyebrow at his own innuendo. Oh dear. I am definitely not getting into his car now. No matter how much I want to ride in that beautiful car, or how handsome he is.

"Well I don't like creepy Euro guys who take photos of me with my dress plastered to my ass!" His glance slips down my body, and I take a step back.

"But it's such a beautiful one," he smiles. Does he mean my dress or my ass?

"Delete those photos!"

"I'd sooner blow up that statue." He stares at me. I stare back. Neither of us blinks. Water drips from the tip of my nose. Mist forms a glistening sheen on his dirty blond, wavy hair. The wind frees my wet skirt from my legs, sending it out around my legs and up like Marilyn Monroe. A sudden chill up my body, goose bumps rippling up my arms. I tremble. He catches this.

"*Chair de poule*! You have the goose bumps. Last chance, *chérie*," he says. "*Viens*. Let's get you out of these wet clothes. Come with me."

"So you can abduct me, take my passport, and sell me into sex slavery? I've seen that movie. It doesn't end well," I sputter. He laughs.

"*D'accord.*" He plops the hat on my wet head and hops back into the convertible. Then, a siren. I look over to see *Carabinieri* veer into the traffic circle, blue lights flashing.

"Wait," my convictions crumble.

"*Bonne chance*, independent girl," he calls as he drives away. Dick. The police car stops in front of me. SHIT.

IF YOU: ever find yourself in this situation DEFINITELY DO NOT:

1. Cry. They don't care.
2. Laugh. They're not amused.
3. Pretend you only speak Danish. You don't.
4. Ask if they've seen *La Dolce Vita*.
5. Offer money.
6. Offer "some other kind of arrangement."
7. Say you have a rare skin condition and will dehydrate if you cannot fully submerge yourself in water every twenty-four hours.

Istituto delle Suore Della Virtù Santa, Outskirts of Rome: Friday, 7:16 p.m.

I have decided to put Frantonio out of my mind. This is what I've named him. Yes, I could have gotten into the car and had a fantastic Italian tryst with a handsome French-Italian stranger on night one. But I also could have been kidnapped and ransomed back to a mother who won't even pay full price at a garage sale. I've chosen wisely. No regrets. I won't think about Frantonino anymore. Ever. Really.

The "clean, safe, and affordable" place to stay with a "stunning view" that my mother's friend Donna recommended turns out to be an actual convent on the top of a very tall hill, just outside of Rome. It's a twenty-five-minute bus ride from the center of the action. This must be where the Vatican sends its nuns post-retirement, because there is no way any of these ladies are under seventy. One wheels her oxygen around with her, which is decorated with a hand-stitched depiction of the crucifixion, resurrection, and ascension of Christ. My mother would love it. This is just her sort of place. Perfect. And here I was thinking I'd left all the retirees back in Florida. But it's too late now to find another place. I had eagerly taken my mother up on her offer to pay for lodging my first week in Rome, so now I'm stuck. The nuns don't speak much English, but the youngest of them (sixty-three) is able to use her computer to access the Comune Di Roma website and help me pay the fine I'd been given by the Carabinieri.

Soon, I'm in my room, unpacking by upending my entire bag onto my bed. Apparently, *"Senz'aria condizionata"* is not a brand of air conditioning unit. There is only a small fan near my bed that stops and starts randomly when you use anything else electric in the room. But the place is clean and cute. By this point, I have only a half hour to get ready for the wine party and catch the bus back down the hill into the center of town.

I grab my little black dress and stilettos and suddenly I realize my tablet is gone. Seriously? My mother was right? I've been in the country less than six hours and I've already been robbed? Where and when? The train station? What should I do? Call the police? I run out of my room, find the nearest nuns, and launch into a terrible charades routine trying to explain. I've never been good at charades, but thankfully these ladies are. I'm miming the word "tablet," which they somehow get. They're likely trying to decide whether I need aspirin or I'm a drug addict, when I suddenly remember. The doughnut shop, Miami airport.

VIDEO CALL

Call - WILL - No Answer	7:36 p.m.
Call - WILL - No Answer	7:38 p.m.
Call - WILL - No Answer	7:39 p.m.

INSTANT MESSAGE

WK:
at work, what's up?

> **MT:**
> need your help.

WK:
you okay? something happen?

> **MT:**
> I'm ok. my tablet is at MIA

WK:
missing in action?

> **MT:**
> Miami airport.
> doughnut shop. T2.

WK:
you kidding?

> **MT:**
> no, can you get it?

WK:
and?

> **MT:**
> Fedex it?
> (long pause)

WK:
I'm busy

> **MT:**
> come on, cops
> love doughnuts

WK:
(middle finger emoji)

MT:
please

WK:
I'm working

MT:
doing what?
(pause)

WK:
drug bust

MT:
BS

WK:
serious

MT:
really?

WK:
you worried?
(long pause)

MT:
yeah, about my tablet

WK:
(double middle finger emoji)

MT:
officer cowboy can
take care of himself

WK:
true

MT:
Will, there are photos on it

WK:
so?

MT:
sexy ones

WK:
seriously?

MT:
yeah
(pause)

WK:
for who?
(long pause)

MT:
Will, please

WK:
this is a boyfriend ask

MT:
I know

WK:
I'm not your
boyfriend anymore

MT:
I know
(long pause)

MT:
please, Will

WK:
send me your address

MT:
thank you

WK:
keeping the photos.

Chapter 6

How Not to Impress Your Friend's Friends

Rooftop Garden, *Hotel De' Ricci*, Navona, *Roma*, Rome: Friday, 8:35 p.m.

String lights illuminate a long table elegantly decorated with flowers, fine china, and many, many wine glasses. Waiters in black jackets buzz in and out of a catering station. Apparently, an exclusive wine release party is a wine tasting and dinner party, held at a swanky, boutique hotel for wine lovers. Just off Piazza Navona in the center of the historic district, the hip Hotel De' Ricci is a stark contrast to my stoic convent east of Eden. The party gives the vintner an exclusive backdrop to unveil the latest and greatest wines of the season to Italians wearing shoes more expensive than my college car. The little black dress I'm wearing is indistinguishable from the ones the cocktail waitresses are wearing. The only difference is the amount of cleavage they're all displaying. So far three people have asked me where the bathroom is and one ordered a drink. At least I think that's what he wanted. They're all speaking Italian.

Nadya is radiant in a backless, powder blue halter dress and silver stilettos. Her blonde hair, piled "carelessly" atop her head, sits magically in place, tiny ringlets cascading onto her shoulders. Two or three well-dressed Italian men hover around her, like attendants to Titania, the Shakespearean fairy queen. My dirty airplane hair pulled into a ponytail doesn't quite have the same effect, but I didn't have time to shower after the tablet drama. I'd asked for a key as I rushed out of the convent to catch the bus, and the nuns had explained to me that there was no key. The convent is open until midnight. After that, I will be locked out. A curfew? My first night in Rome? I'd decided to worry about this later.

As soon as we are all seated, Nadya introduces the first wine. It is indeed better than anything I've ever bought at Costco. As I sip the fine red nectar of the gods, I find myself thinking again about Frantonio. What nerve. I guess rich, attractive Italian men with sport cars are used to having women fall into their arms. His *were* nice arms.

"*Un bel vino rosso,*" Nadya's voice breaks through my daydream. She's seated next to me. "Plums and cherries on the nose, well balanced with just a whisper of coffee and cocoa on the palate, you taste? *É fantastico, no?*" Yes, it is fantastic. By the third wine we sample, I have realized that drinking with Nadya is like test-driving a classic sports car. You quickly find yourself in a love you can't afford. "*Amarone Classico,*" she tells me. "She's like the princess of the Italian wine aristocracy. As we eat, I'll introduce you to the king and queen." I smile with anticipation and make a mental note to take it easy so I'll last.

Nadya introduces me to everyone as her "talented American writer friend from Miami." This gives me instant street cred. Not the writer part . . . the Miami part. "Have you ever been to Pharrell Williams's house?" and "Are there really alligators in the sewers?" they ask. I tell them the best drag shows in the country are in South Beach, and *Topolino* (Mickey Mouse) isn't my favorite neighbor. When I explain that I only went to college in Miami and actually live in Key West, a strange island of misfits, their eyes glaze over. But then, "Hemming-way?" asks a voice from behind me.

"Yes, exactly!" I smile, turning around, pleased that someone knows something about Key West. It's one of the young waiters. He's got a bashful smile with a dimple in his left cheek. "He's one of my favorite writers, despite the fact that he was a little sexist and a lot drunk."

"You've just described the national character of this country," says the German ex-pat across from me with a chuckle. I'm glad not to be the only non-Italian.

"I like *Sun Also Rises*, and *Old Man and the Sea*, but most of all, *For Whom the Bell Tolls*," the waiter smiles. "I'm reading him for school," he says enthusiastically as he sets down a huge plate of roped *mozzarella di bufala* for an appetizer, and my mouth begins to water. The table conversation slips back into Italian. But I've been using my Italian study app diligently, so I listen carefully. Soon, I deduce the following:

1. The girl with the green blouse either works as a flight attendant for Alitalia, or at a meat packing plant.
2. The man with the hat hates Tom Cruise movies and is allergic to eggplant.
3. The German lady has a parrot that swears like a sailor. Or her father is married to a sailor.
4. One of the guys at the end of the table has just parachuted with a koala. Or he's just graduated from hairdresser school.

"Ernesto Hemingway" returns with our *primi piatti*. When he sets my plate down, I thank him with a polite *grazie,* tacking on this new nickname, and he is delighted. His lovely green eyes flirt with me as he cleverly describes the octopus salad in front of me as "A Farewell to Arms." But I don't laugh. In fact, I'm horrified.

"Oh, no! I can't eat this, I'm sorry, Ernesto," I say.

"*Perchè?* You are vegetarian, *bella?*"

"No, it's just that octopuses are highly intelligent and have individual personalities. They can solve complex puzzles and they have three hearts." Ernesto is now bright red, and I've attracted the attention of everyone around me.

"*Tre?*" He exclaims. I have only one heart and I break it often!" he winks. "*Mi dispiace molto, bella.* I will change it for you *subito.*"

"Change mine too please," Nadya saves me. "I can't eat something smarter than I am." Everyone laughs.

"Having a best friend who is a marine biologist limits your diet considerably," I explain.

"I'll bring you the green salad," Ernesto smiles. "The pasta is rigatoni with cheese and mushroom—is this okay?"

"Oh, yes! I adore rigatoni," I say, eager to show everyone I'm not actually difficult. For some reason this elicits chuckles. Later I find out that *rigatoni* is sometimes a euphemism for oral sex, thanks to a famous Italian TV commercial. Who knew?

Piazza Augusto Imperatore, Rome: Friday, 11:50 p.m.

My fantasy rich, handsome, recently divorced underwear model must have had a prior engagement in someone else's fantasy, because he never showed. All of the other men there were either with dates, older than my dad, or government officials facing charges of corruption. I'm pretty sure I'm the only one leaving the wine party early to catch a bus so that nuns won't lock me out of my room. Even worse, I'm pretty sure I've now missed the last bus. There's nobody else here at the bus stop. The schedule is written in very blurry Italian. The only souls in sight are some teenagers who have wandered down from *Piazza di Spagna* after a night of singing and drinking and making fun of tourists. I'm just about to ask one of them if there are any more buses, when a scooter pulls up.

"*Signorina Polpo!*" the rider calls to me. I move a few steps away. He pulls off his helmet, and I'm pleased to see it's Ernesto Hemingway, the adorable waiter. I smile and walk over. "The buses are finished. Only the night buses over at *Piazza Venezia.*"

"Perfect. The nuns are about to lock me out."

"Nuns?"

"At the convent where I'm staying. There's a midnight curfew."
Mezzanotte? It's too soon. I will take you." He grabs an extra helmet from the compartment inside his scooter. "We must hurry." I stare at the helmet, then at him. Really? He seems harmless enough. This is for sure my only small chance of making it back to my room in time. *"Bella donna, vieni*!" says Ernesto, earnestly.

"Okay. *Grazie.*" I take the helmet, jam it onto my head, and throw my leg over the back of the scooter. Ernesto cranks the scooter. My heart races. *Andiamo*! Let's go! Yes! I will seize the opportunity this time. I will throw caution to the wind. Together we will zoom up the hill to the convent, and arrive just in time!

Chapter 7

How Not to Discuss Hemingway

Outskirts of Rome: Friday, 11:59 p.m.

Or not. These visions quickly vanish as we putter and sputter up the steep Roman hill at the pace of a senior division marathon runner. There is absolutely no way we're going to make it in time. As the Romans say, *"Non c'è trippa per gatti"* (no tripe for cats, or, no hope in hell). But the view is beautiful, and I have plenty of time to enjoy it as we make the slow climb. *Roma* is beautifully sprawled out below us with her twinkling lights, like a drunken prom queen passed out on the floor in her sparkly dress. Ernesto points out buildings and monuments as we go, but I can't hear over the angry wasp sound of his scooter. Our bodies are sandwiched together, secure and comfortable.

The wind whisks a cacophony of kitchen smells off his clothes and hair, filling my nostrils: basil, fish, onions, wine, garlic . . . lots of garlic. I close my eyes and feel the cool wind on my face. Somewhere along the way I stop worrying about getting locked out of my room, about the fact that I'm vertically spooning a complete stranger, about everything. This is the real magic of Italy. Italians have mastered the physics of slowing time down. The minute you stop thinking about what you just did, or what you're about to do . . . the moment you're actually in comes into sharp, delicious focus.

Istituto delle Suore Della Virtù Santa, Outskirts of Rome: Saturday, 12:14 a.m.

The gate is locked. Punctuality is a godly requirement. "To every thing there is a season, and a time to every purpose under the heaven" (Ecclesiastes 3:1). In high school I had a notebook filled with that one scripture, written over and over in detention. The Byrds were probably inspired by the same punishment in Catholic school.

The stone wall surrounding the convent is higher than I remembered. I stand, staring up at it. Maybe if he gives me a boost, I can pull myself up and over. Ernesto thinks this is a bad idea, but when I kick off my flip-flops he relents, bends his knees, and forms a basket for my foot with his hands.

"*Uno, due, tre!*" he whispers as I jump, and he hikes up my foot. I grope the wall, but slide back down, into his arms. We laugh awkwardly. We try again. *Uno, due, tre* . . . grunting noises . . . laughing. Each time, I almost grab the top, but slide back down into his arms. We are both trying desperately not to make noise, but now laughing so hard we can barely breathe. On the fourth try, I manage to catch hold of a crack in the wall and hoist an arm over the top.

"Yes!" he cheers a little too loudly as I dangle triumphantly above him.

"Shhhh! (*grunt, umph*)" I manage to throw my other arm over the top of the wall, fight for every inch, and pull myself up. I straddle the wall, panting. Ernesto is doubled over with laughter. "You have the alligatori dancing ballet on your pants?" he sputters. I blush. Rosalie has given me silly animal socks and underwear since I was a kid. We both love animals doing crazy things. (Fine, three things in common.)

"I didn't expect anyone to be seeing my panties tonight, okay?" I whisper-shout back. I look down over the other side of the wall. Shit. It's a long, hard drop. There's a tree I could climb down about fifteen yards away, but getting to it involves walking the wall like a circus performer, standing up, and leaping. The ground on the right side drops to steep hillside. I doubt I could even do it sober, which I am not.

"It's too far down. I'll break my leg or something," I whisper-shout down to him.

"*Allora* come down. I will take you somewhere," he whisper-shouts back.

"What? Where?"

"To hang out. We will have *del vino o gelato*. To talk about Hemmingway."

"You want to discuss Hemingway at midnight?"

"*Mezzanotte a Roma* is early, *bella*," he laughs.

"Maybe I can make it to that tree." I point, knowing I can't.

"*No, dio mio!*" He stops laughing. "*Bella*, jump down. I catch you." Ernesto opens his arms. I size him up. He's a short, skinny Italian guy. I'll crush him into the ground like a nail into a board. He smiles up at me. "Kick your feet up when you jumping. *Alligatori* pants first!" He grins, his dimple winking at me. What a goof. He's seriously adorable. I bend my knees like I'm on a diving board. "*Uno, due . . .*"

WHAM! He does catch me, but I'm heavier than he realizes and we both land in a heap on the ground. Our heads knock together on impact. I'm still on top of him as he sits up. My wrist throbs, my head spins. I see blood on my hand. I freak out.

"Oh, God, I'm bleeding. I broke something." I frantically search my hands, arms, nothing. Then, I see blood on his upper lip. "*You're* bleeding! I broke you! I knocked your teeth! Oh God. I'm so sorry. This is my fault." Then, suddenly, I'm crying.

"No, *no tutto bene, bella*. I'm fine. Just my nose." He sniffs a bit and wipes the blood from his nose. I cup his chin in my hands, trying to examine his nose through my tears. "I'm fine. *Tutto bene*. See?" Ernesto wipes my face and then—he's kissing me. Warm, soft, salty kisses. He wraps me in his arms. His lips gently pry mine apart as his kisses grow deeper and his tongue meets mine playfully.

Sitting in his lap with my legs on either side, I relax into his embrace, kissing him back. My breathing slows but not my heart. I can once again smell the garlic and sweat on his skin. Garlic never smelled so damn good. It's earthy and sensual and comforting and sexy. I want to swallow him up. I can feel his heart beating hard against my chest, which is pressed tightly to him. Ernesto is a well-practiced kisser. He runs one hand through my hair, the other down my back, and then he slips it under my ass, squeezing me gently. Feeling his grip on my ass, I automatically tilt my hips into his. He slides the strap of my little black dress off my shoulder, and I feel his hot, quick breath on my neck, and then my chest. His lips gently brush just the top of my left breast, teasing me. Then, lying backward, he pulls me down on top of him, still kissing me, my legs straddled around him. His tongue owns my mouth. His hand slips into to the top of my dress, and I feel his warm fingers around my breast. My whole body tingles. I want more. My hands find the snap on his pants and then—

"No fornicating on holy ground!" shouts a voice from somewhere deep inside me. It's Modesty. How did she find me here? Who invited her on this trip? She is my mother's bestie, not mine. But the damage is done. I am no longer tingling all over.

"Wait, we can't." I sit suddenly up.

"Perché?" Ernesto sits up too but continues kissing my neck. That feels good. He kisses my breast. Oh God, that really feels good. God? Right. I'm sitting outside a convent! Definitely not *buono.*

"This is holy ground." I pull my shoulder strap back up. He pulls it back down with his teeth, grinning at me. He is seriously adorable. "Aren't you Catholic?" I ask.

"Così così." He blows hot breath down into my cleavage, sending a shiver through me. Okay, I really don't want to end this party. But we can't get into my room.

"Why don't we go to your house?" I suggest.

"Why?" He laughs. "You want to meet my mother?"

"You live with your mother?" I slip my strap back up.

"My whole family," he says. "Don't you?"

"Actually, yes. I do live with my mother now. I graduated college last year."

"I am just twenty-three."

"I'm twenty-four," I say.

"Come, I will show you a beautiful place." Ernesto stands and reaches down for my hand. "Then we can sleep under the stars." I consider this. What else am I going to do? Curl up on the doorstep of this convent like a stray cat? If you're going to sleep under the stars in Italy, why do it alone?

Villa Aventine Hill, Roma: Saturday, 12:51 a.m.

We pull up next to a Cathedral of *Santa Maria del Priorato*. Another church? He seems to have misunderstood. The point was to get *off* of holy ground before fornicating. But, in Rome, that may be hard—there are over nine hundred of them.

"This is the priory for the Knights of Malta. But we don't go in." Ernesto takes me by the hand and leads me down a dirt path along an ancient wall. We come to a closed door. It looks like an ordinary wooden door, with big circular knockers.

"Look through," my Italian Hemming-way says with the expectant joy you have when you're waiting for someone to open a present. I notice the worn areas in the wood and highly polished brass around the keyhole. Many hands, noses, and cheeks have been here before mine. I smile and bend down to take a look. It's a postcard perfect view of St. Peter's and Rome, perfectly framed by the garden bushes on the other side and the keyhole itself.

"Wow. That's amazing. Like a tiny snow globe without the snow," I smile. Ernesto smiles proudly. "What a perfect gift on my first night in Rome."

"Your first night?" he asks. I nod. "Ever?" he says incredulously. I nod again. He smiles bigger. Taking my hand, he leads me around into the *Giardino degli Aranci* through a different gate. Now all of Rome, with her lit domes, shadowy stone monuments, and red rooftops, is visible, stretched out between her seven hills. He pulls me to him, wraps his arms around me, and with his face close to mine, points things out in the distance.

"*Piazza Navona, Circo Massimo* where the chariots were, by the *Colosseo* and *L'Arco di Costantino, Vaticano, e Lungotevere* . . . along the Tiber River. This white one is called 'wedding cake.' It is *Altare della Patria,* for Victor Emmanuel, but this is new."

"New?"

"Middle eighteen hundred."

"So new," I laugh. "It took Rome a long time to get her shit together, huh? This makes me feel better about myself." Ernesto laughs too.

"In Roma we say: *Roma Capoccia!* This means, Roma is the head."

"Of the country?"

"Of the world," he smiles.

"Oh really?" I tease him.

"*Sì.* Roma is the Eternal City," he says. "She is older than time, but even still more beautiful. She is envied, *e fraintesa* . . . misunderstood, and hated but *amata da sempre,* always loved. She has fallen many times, but will never die." He smiles. I'm impressed. Ernesto is a poet after all.

"*Roma capoccia,*" I practice.

"*Perfetto,*" he smiles proudly. This is clearly his favorite word.

"You speak like a writer," I say. "A few moments ago I was still an outsider peeking in, seeing only the tiny, tourist postcard of Rome. But now, I feel like I know her." His eyes gleam. He loves this.

"*Benvenuta a Roma*, Marina."

"*Grazie*, Ernesto Hemingway." Ernesto takes me in his arms and kisses me sweetly.

Villa Pamphili, Lago del Belvedere, Roma, Saturday, 1:17 a.m.

Ernesto parks his scooter under some trees on the banks of the beautiful little lake that rests in the middle of this huge, gorgeous park—away from the hustle and bustle of the city. I try to put visions of thieves camped in the bushes out of my mind and focus on the soothing gurgle of an unseen fountain and the sounds of crickets. Ernesto lithely climbs one of the nearby trees. I hope he's not expecting me to join him—I've had enough climbing for one night. A bag lands on the ground next to me. He swings down and lands like Tarzan, smiling at me in the moonlight. Sexy little devil. Next he unzips the bag and takes out a blanket. He unrolls this blanket to reveal a bottle of wine.

"You've done this before?" I ask.

"*Sì*, many times," he replies.

"This is where you bring all the American girls you pick up?" I tease, a little surprised. He had seemed so innocent.

"No! *Bella*! I just like to read here. And drink. See." Ernesto reaches into his bag and pulls out a copy of *A Farewell to Arms*. My heart melts. I'm even more attracted to him. He spreads out the blanket and pats it.

"Sit." He smiles. I do. "The opener is in the bag." I pull out a corkscrew and pass it to him. "*Perfetto*," he says. I decide this is my favorite word too. Inside the bag I also see: a candle, matches, and some condoms. Cheeky monkey! I guess I'm not the only girl he's brought here, but somehow, that doesn't seem to matter. And I actually feel safer. If he's slept out here before without wolves or Romulus and Remus (legendary twins who founded Rome) tearing him limb from limb, then we should be okay. Ernesto lights the candle and then hands me the book.

"Will you read to me?" He smiles. Read? That's not exactly what I thought we were going to be doing on this blanket, but how can I say no to that dimple? I open the book and begin to read. He listens for a few moments, and then I feel his hands gently guide me to my back. I stop reading, waiting for his lips to find mine. "No. You must not stop," he says. He wants me to keep reading? Seriously? Okay. So, I keep reading. Soon, I feel his fingers unbuttoning my dress . . . all the way down. Exposed to the night air, my breasts quiver beneath my black bra (thank God I wore the sexy one).

I keep reading. His fingers slide beneath the lace. His thumbs circle my nipples, which are now standing at attention in the moonlight. My breath catches in my throat as his strong lips wrap around first one nipple and then the other. "Keep reading," he whispers. My body tingles. My tummy trembles as he runs his tongue down it, ever so slowly, finding my navel. My breath quickens as I struggle to read. And then, his hands find my alligator panties, pulling them gently from my hips, down my legs, and completely off. My heart is thumping hard. I can feel my blood racing around my body and my groin aching for him.

"*La tua figa è come un fiore*," whispers Ernesto. I stop reading and sit up on my elbows, watching him over the fast rise and fall of my breasts.

"My what?"

"Your *figa*—" he plants one soft, gentle kiss on my pussy. "Like a flower." A shudder runs down my aching body. My *figa* wants more. He looks at me. "You wish me to stop?" he asks quietly.

"No. Don't stop," I say, my heart pounding. "Please."

"Then keep reading," Ernesto grins. "*Perfavore.*" Seriously?

"What is this? Some sort of oral book report?" I ask.

"*Esattamente,*" he laughs. So I continue. And so does he. The climax of the book is reached on page two. Hemingway is just that good.

DURING ORAL BOOK REPORTS IN PARKS WITH ITALIAN BOYS, DO NOT:

1. Lose all self-control, grabbing his shirt and yelling out as you orgasm, knocking the candle over and catching the book on fire.

2. Try to smother the flame with the blanket, catching it too on fire.

3. Jump up and drag the blanket into the lake, half spilling the bottle of wine.
4. Leave your wine-soaked shoes near the blanket to attract an ant block party.
5. Pick a bush nearby to pee because it's dark and you're afraid to go too far.
6. Remain silent as you notice your urine trickle downhill toward the blanket, because it's already wet, burned, and soaked with wine so he won't notice.
7. Rub ANY unidentified leaf on your "soft, delicate *figa*" (vagina).
8. Let the conservative, Anglo-American ideas about sex with strangers that your mother worked hard to instill in you get in the way of your good time.

Chapter 8

How Not to See Roma like a Tourist

Roma is simply too historical, too beautiful, and too big to see in four days—unless of course you have a handsome boy on a scooter shuttling you from vista to museum to his personal favorite pizzeria, *Est Est Est*.

SUGGESTED ITINERARY FOR YOUR ROMAN HOLIDAY:

1. Follow a paid tour around the Forum until you're noticed and then find another one to follow. (Repeat.)
2. Kiss in the senate where Julius Caesar was murdered. Make out behind a row of columns and get your *figa* tickled.
3. Walk around the Colosseum.
4. Kiss in the prison where Christians were fed to the lions.
5. Eat gelato while watching the *Gattare* (old cat ladies) feed stray cats in *Largo Argentina*.
6. Kiss in the sunlight beaming through the ceiling of the Pantheon.
7. Eat gelato on the Spanish steps and make fun of the tourists, pretending you are not one.

8. Peddle around the Villa Borghese on one of those stupid bike carriages.
9. Sneak in the back way to the Baths of Caracalla to watch the second half of the opera *Carmen*, then make out under the bleachers like you're in high school.
10. Go to a Roma football game and get him to teach you the songs. Celebrate Roma's victory by sneaking him into your convent room.

Enoteca Antica: Monday, 7:42 p.m.

While Ernesto works, I sit in the back, drinking free wine and eating free mozzarella while I do research for my book. For my first Italian woman of influence, I decide on one everyone knows.

NOTES ON ITALIAN WOMAN OF INFLUENCE: Sophia Loren

1. Born in 1934 as Sofia Villani Scicolone, in Rome.
2. Her mother was a piano teacher, father an engineer of noble descent who abandoned them both, leaving Sofia to live in poverty for the first fifteen years of her life—shy, lean, and nicknamed "Little Stick."
3. Met her father three times: ages five, seventeen, and forty-two (at his deathbed).
4. Spotted in the Miss Italia beauty pageant at fifteen by film producer and future husband, Carlo Ponti, her acting career promptly began.
5. Starred in Hollywood films opposite Cary Grant, Frank Sinatra, John Wayne, and Clark Gable, among others.
6. In Vittorio De Sica's *Two Women*, 1960, she portrays a mother protecting her twelve-year-old daughter in war-torn Italy. She herself had been hit by shrapnel during an Allied air raid.
7. This performance won her the first Best Actress Oscar ever awarded for a foreign language performance.

8. Her memorable striptease for Marcello Mastroianni in *Yesterday, Today and Tomorrow* was paid homage to in the film satire *Prêt-à-Porter* by Robert Altman.
9. She is a record holder of six David di Donatello awards.
10. She is the mother of two boys, Carlo and Edoardo Ponti.

Wow, imagine going from "Little Stick" to internationally famous film star and sex symbol. I close my eyes and try to picture her on that warm day in Naples, in September, 1950, as she prepares to step on stage for the pageant. Is her mother there fixing young Sofia's thick mascara and hoisting her daughter's fifteen-year-old breasts up in her padded bikini top? Does the destitute piano teacher, desperately hoping she will change her daughter's future, have any idea what is about to happen? And now I find myself wondering, were there any moments after my father left when my mother thought to herself, "How the hell will I raise this child alone?" If there were, I never saw them.

ON YOUR LAST NIGHT IN ROME, DO NOT:
1. Worry about what to say to him before you leave.
2. Drink so much that you end up in another fountain.
3. Pretend that you'll email or message each other. Neither of you will. This romance is for the here and now. Enjoy it.
4. Go to sleep before 5:00 a.m. You can snooze on the train to Naples.
5. Forget to say *Grazie mille*.

Chapter 9

How Not to Ride in Coach

Stazione Termini, Rome, Italy: Tuesday, 7:20 a.m.

A NOTE ABOUT EUROPEAN TRAIN STATIONS:
1. You will see people smoking beside no smoking signs.
2. Wear your backpack on your front, no matter how dorky you look.
3. Your train will not be posted on the automated board until an hour before it is scheduled to leave.
4. Your train will also not be posted on the automated board if you're not actually at the right train station. (Most cities have more than one.)
5. Do not sit down on your bag and rest your eyes, "just for a second."

Stazione Tiburtina, Rome, Italy: Tuesday, 8:25 a.m.
When I woke in a panic and realized that I was not even at the right station, I opted for a taxi instead of calling Ernesto. It cost me almost as much as the train ticket. But I wanted his last images of our short but

glorious romance to be: sexy, American vamp blowing twilight kisses through a convent window. Juliette of Verona. Not: crazed American bimbo, puffing on her asthma inhaler and knocking children over with her rolling bag as she races to her train only to be left behind, crumbling to the ground in sobs as if auditioning for a Pasolini film. Nobody needs to see that. Now I'm in a very long line, hoping to exchange my original ticket for one on the next train, which leaves in an hour.

When I was dating Will, he was the one who always kept me from screwing up, or from freaking out when I did. He's got a calm strength that's impossible not to feel. That's why I call him Cowboy. Not because he grew up in Central Florida on a farm, which he did, or because of the straw cowboy hat he always wears, but because Will's demeanor is like Sam Elliott's voice doing yoga: alluring, irresistible, comforting. Will is solid. But this is also the challenge. There can be a tempest inside him and you won't see a ripple.

He signed up for that narcotics task force right after we broke up. Apparently, meth heads and smugglers are easier to deal with than I am. They're more predictable, he says. They know what they want, he says. Jerk. I know what I want. I want things I've never seen, never experienced, never dreamt of. Will's the guy who orders the same thing every time at a restaurant. I'm the girl who tries a new restaurant every time. He's just doing drug busts to make me worry about him. It won't work.

I get out my tablet to pass time. It arrived yesterday, thanks to Will. I've sent him messages to say thanks, and photos of myself at various landmarks (alone). Now I'm realizing he may wonder who was taking those photos. On my tablet, I decide to delete the sexy photos I'm still hoping the doughnut girl didn't sell to anyone. In the trash folder, I catch sight of an old photo of Will. He's standing on *top* of his kayak, perfectly balanced in a crystal clear river, trying to reach his straw hat that I tossed in the tree. I took the photo expecting him to go over. He did not. I stare at the photo. He looks good with his shirt off. I hope he's not getting shot today. I drag the photo out of the trash.

YOU WILL KNOW YOU'RE IN FIRST CLASS IF:
1. You see a 1 on the outside of the train car.
2. You see large, clean seats that recline.
3. You see nice folding tables between them.
4. You see electrical outlets.
5. You see signs for Wi-Fi.
6. You hear soft classical guitar or whimsical accordion music.
7. You smell hints of leather and honeysuckle in the air-conditioned air.
8. People around you are smiling.

YOU WILL KNOW YOU'RE IN SECOND CLASS IF:
1. You see a 2 on the outside of the car.
2. You see small seats you suspect have been repurposed from prison transport vehicles.
3. You smell old urine and vomit.
4. You hear the banging of a bathroom door that doesn't latch.

Train, Roma to Napoli, Italy: Tuesday, 9:24 a.m.

This is where my ticket is. *Perfetto*. I pick a window seat, five rows from the bathroom with the swinging door, three rows behind a mother wearing a leopard print scarf and her son in a Spider-Man tee, and two rows in front of a man with a beard who is already snoring loudly. I secure my rolling bag under my seat, tucking my backpack between the window and myself. Leaning my head awkwardly onto the backpack, I close my eyes.

Ten minutes later I'm awakened by the train conductor, asking for my ticket. My neck now stuck at forty-five degrees, I rummage through my bag and hand him the ticket, looking like a very curious dog. I go back to sleep. Twenty minutes later, I'm reawakened by my small intestine hosting a Zumba class in my abdomen. Three espressos and no food was not good planning. The bathroom is small enough to feel cramped, but somehow large enough that when seated on the cold, metal prison cell potty,

I must lean completely forward in order to reach the tiny knob and hold the door with the broken latch closed. Every time the train goes around a bend, I must lean with all my might the other direction, to keep from falling off the toilet. Every time the train slows, I lurch slightly forward and the door opens a few inches until I manage to slam it shut. Finally I'm finished. There is no toilet paper left. Minnie Mouse grins maniacally at me from the kids pack of tissues I fish out of my backpack.

"Thanks Min."

Back in my seat, I'm just drifting off again when I feel a tap on my shoulder.

"*Scusami. Mi dispiace. Parli Italiano?*" The Italian woman with the leopard scarf is leaning over the empty seat next to me. I shake my head.

"Sorry. I'm American, I only speak English and Emoji," I reply.

"Oh, okay. I just wondered, is there any way, could you by any chance, just for five minutes, watch my son while I go to the smoking car?" Of course she speaks fluent English. She points to her boy, who is wearing headphones and playing a game on his iPad. "He's nine, almost ten. He's fine, but I don't want to make him come with me—the smoke, you know? I'm sorry to ask, but we've got almost two hours," she pleads, embarrassed but desperate.

"Sure, no problem," I say. Leopard Lady smiles, relieved. I watch her walk back to her boy, speak to him in Italian. He doesn't reply. The woman disappears.

A few moments after she disappears, a very cute, petite blonde woman in a floral romper enters the train car and goes into the bathroom. I wonder how she's going to reach the door from the toilet. Her arms are shorter than mine. About a minute later, another woman enters the train car. She's tall, dark skinned, and wearing a crop top to display a black snake tattoo that winds around her stomach like a belt. Her wild mane of black hair is harnessed behind her ears by a bright silk scarf. She enters the bathroom also. Naïvely I think it's a mistake, that she'll emerge immediately, embarrassed. She does not. Shocked and fascinated, I wonder what's about to transpire. Drugs? Sex? Maybe the blonde just needed help with the zipper on her romper? I don't wonder long. As the train sways, the door swings open, and slams closed. Apparently she needed help with her zipper, and her bra, and her panties. As the door swings open and slams closed again, I am mesmerized. I cannot look away.

> **FLASH:** hair and elbows.
> SLAM.
> **FLASH:** tongues.
> SLAM.
> **FLASH:** tongues in mouths.
> SLAM.
> **FLASH:** naked shoulders.
> SLAM.
> **FLASH:** breasts.
> SLAM.
> **FLASH:** lips on breasts.
> SLAM.
> **FLASH:** hips, moving.
> SLAM.
> **FLASH:** naked asses.
> SLAM.
> **FLASH:** hands on naked asses.
> SLAM.
> **FLASH:** knees in the air.
> SLAM.
> **FLASH:** full frontal *figa*, nicely groomed.

It's like a French, flip-book style porno, the kind they used to show in the penny arcades and nickelodeons. My brain suddenly snaps out of this sensual reverie with a rapid connection: nickelodeon→ kids→ nine-year-old I'm supposed to be watching. *"Corruption of a minor!"* shouts a voice from inside. It's Modesty again. I look over and indeed, the boy is watching the same show I am. I jump up, fling myself in the direction of the bathroom, misjudge the momentum of the train, and slam into the door as I close it. I expect this to stop the action inside. Nope. Apparently that train too has left the station.

Standing next to the bathroom, I can hear moaning and groping. I hold the bathroom door closed and smile at the boy. He does not smile back. Right now, I am his very least favorite person on the face of the planet. In fact, the man with the beard is also now awake and also not my number one fan. As the sounds of satisfaction grow louder and more satisfied inside the bathroom, I continue to hold the door, turning away from the man and boy, pretending to examine my nails (I have none). I begin to sing the first loud song that comes to mind: "La Bamba." I know about one third of the words, can't carry a tune, and don't speak Spanish.

After what seems like the loudest, longest orgasm I've ever heard (making me slightly jealous), things quiet down inside the bathroom. Then a shriek from the train car. I turn back around to see Leopard Lady entering through the back door as her son, now standing in his seat by an open window, is smoking a cigarette. SHIT! Where did he even get that? The woman shoots me a look. But before I can say, "Where do you think he learned it?" there's a push on the bathroom door. I release it and out comes the brunette.

"Couldn't see from your seat, mate?" she says, not a hint of embarrassment.

"Actually, we all had a pretty good view," I say, pointing to the boy. The petite blonde emerges. Seeing the boy, she looks horrified. She chastises her girlfriend in a flood of angry, whispered French.

"I am so sorry," the blonde says to me. "Thank you for holding the door. It's my girlfriend. I told her to wait but she is very insistent and hungry for me all the time."

"Clearly," I reply. The brunette winks at me.

"And now I'm thirsty," the brunette says. Her accent is British, but not snooty, starchy crisps British. It's fat, greasy chips British. "Come on. I've got a bottle," she says. It takes me a second to realize she's talking to me.

"Me?"

"*Oui*, come have a glass of wine with us. We owe it to you," the blonde smiles. I look over my shoulder and see Leopard Lady still staring daggers at me.

"Three cars up," says the brunette, holding the carriage door for her girlfriend.

"In first class?" I ask.

"*Oui*," smiles the blonde as she exits.

"And you came back here to . . . use the bathroom?"

"Course, mate. Not looking to get kicked out of our posh seats, are we? How barmy would that be?" She begins to hum "La Bamba," and winks as she exits, the train door slamming closed behind her.

"Right," I say.

Chapter 10

How Not to
Earn a Nickname

Train, Roma to Napoli, Italy: Tuesday, 10:43 a.m.

**HELPFUL TIPS FOR BONDING WITH INTERNATIONAL
GIRLFRIENDS:**

1. Tell them you're Canadian.
2. Don't guess where they're from by deciding which actor they sound like.
3. Don't try to hug them. They'll know you're American.
4. Don't try to imitate their accents.
5. When they figure out you're American and ask about the last election, tell them you were in a coma.
6. Don't ask to see their passports. They have WAY more stamps than you.
7. Don't ask why Europeans don't wear deodorant.

I'm now seated comfortably in first class next to my new international friends, Yin and Yang. Complete opposites, they seem like they'd fall apart if separated. By the second plastic cup of wine, I begin to understand why. Yin is a delicate, blonde, Parisian fairy. She attended *Surval Montreux*, an elite girls' boarding school in Switzerland. Yang calls it the princess academy because it's literally a storybook castle on a hill. Here, Yin learned four languages and seven ways to orally pleasure another girl. By contrast, Yang grew up in Brixton, a colorful, rough neighborhood of London, where she went to public school and played rugby. Yin depends on Yang to interpret any pop culture references of the last fifteen years. Yang depends on Yin to tell her when her shirt is inside out or needs to be washed. Yin's a people pleaser. Always second-guessing others' needs, she's got a menu of options. *Par exemple:*

"Marina, do you want to sit in the middle so you can talk to both of us? Or maybe you're more comfortable by the window, or you like the aisle better? We are having *un petit pique-nique*. Do you like rosé wine? We have some red also if you prefer. It goes well with the cheese. Do you prefer cow or goat? Maybe you're not hungry? Do you prefer the window open?"

"Just give me the fuckin' bottle." Yang doesn't give a shit what you want. You're getting red wine. Yang's tough and toned, but not a bruiser. She's smart but not as knowledgeable as Yin. She drinks too much but doesn't do drugs. Yin's tried every pill on the black market. Yang likes the spotlight. Yin doesn't. Yang likes reggae and raves. Yin likes opera and orgies. Yang reads comic books to Yin and explains them. Yin reads poetry to Yang and explains it. The Brit can cook. The Frenchie cannot. The irony doesn't end there. Yang likes black and white, French New Wave films. Yin likes Guy Ritchie.

Yin's mother, a world-renowned human rights lawyer, never has much time for her. Yin's father, the head of an NGO, is in prison for embezzling 5.5 million euro. Yin needs to be wanted, desired, needed.

Yang's the daughter of an alcoholic Irish bartender from Brixton and a beautiful Afro-Spanish Flamenco dancer. Cliché right? Wrong. Her father's the dancer: sensual, expressive, and passionate. Yang's convinced he's a sex addict. Her mother's the bartender: high school drop-out and perpetual student of human behavior. Yang learned to cook from her father, who believes that food is a spiritual way to access your body's pleasure receptors. Yang's mother taught her how to make a dirty martini when she was eight.

Yin is quiet and sweet. Yang is brash and unapologetic. She likes to fuck with you. *Por ejemplo:*

"Don't think I don't know what you're after, mate," Yang growls at me when Yin leaves to get us lunch from the dining car.

"What?" I ask, nervously. Yang is suddenly in my face, nostrils flaring like a bull.

"You were on your way to that bathroom before I got there. That's why you came to sit with us. Even now you're waitin' to get her on your own."

"No! I swear to God."

"I see you lookin' at her. Checkin' out that tight little ass and those perfect little titties." Yang leans closer and closer to me. "I know you're thinkin' about kissin' 'em. Lickin' 'em. Suckin' 'em. You wanna slip your finger down her—"

"I don't! I'm not—I am *not*," I say, horrified. Yang smiles.

"Yeah, I know. I'm just fuckin' with you, mate," she laughs. "Cause if you were, I'd have to take that wine bottle and shove it so far up your ass I'd get a stool sample and then I'd make you suck it out of the bottle." She wasn't smiling anymore. WTF?

"I don't—" Words fail me.

"Got ya! You're too easy. Just takin' the piss, mate. I'm not really the jealous type. Yin either. We're givers. Unity and community. She's got mad skills, and I got like this rockin' body, yeah. Would be a shame not to share. Check out these tits, see?" Suddenly she's hiked her top up, revealing a red lace bra two sizes too small, overflowing with beautiful, brown breasts. "Go on, give 'em a squeeze. They're like grapefruit." She grabs my hand and shoves it into her cleavage.

"Oh! Very nice. But I'm straight," I whisper, reclaiming my hand. Yang smiles.

"Yeah, I know, mate," she laughs. "You're like so straight it's like comical."

"Comical?"

"Like obvious, mate. When that muscly guy with the suit and tie helped you put your bag up in the rack, you looked like you were ready to offer him a blow job as a thank you."

"I was just flirting. He was cute."

"Yeah. You love dick. It's like somebody drew an arrow on your cheek pointing to your mouth: *insert dick here.*"

"Well, I do enjoy the male body." I blush.

"Yeah you do. You'd like, eat a dick sandwich for lunch every day. Dick, egg, and cheese. Grilled dick sandwich. Barbeque dick sandwich."

"Um, no." I can't help but visualize these and I'm kind of disgusted.

"French dip dick. Nutella and dick sandwich. Dick and pickle sandwich."

"Definitely not."

"Oh, right. You're American. You like peanut butter and dick sandwiches," Yang snorts.

"Well who doesn't like *those*?" I laugh. Yin enters with a tray of food.

"Anyone want a sandwich?" she smiles brightly. Yang laughs even harder.

"Do you have a DLT?" I ask innocently. Yang loses her shit, doubles over with laughter, tears in her eyes. Yin looks at me. I shrug. "Just takin' the piss, mate."

Train, Roma to Napoli, Italy: Tuesday, 11:15 a.m.

"So what's the deal with you, DLT?" asks Yang. She's latched onto this nickname like a pit bull on a Pomeranian. "Why you travelin' alone? Get in a fight with your man and leave him at the train station?"

"I don't have a man. I came to Italy alone to travel around and research a series of books I'm writing. *Herstory: Women Who Changed the World.* The first book will be Italian women. That's why I'm here, for my research and inspiration." Yang pretends to snore loudly. Yin smacks her.

"Nobody's going to buy that book. Do people even buy books anymore?" Yang asks.

"*Ne sois pas aussi grossière!*" scolds Yin. "Sorry, she gets like this when she doesn't get enough sex."

"It's been like an hour since the bathroom," I say, surprised.

"Exactly. You know how some people have low blood sugar," Yin says. "It's like that."

"It's my da's fault. He's a sex addict."

"*I* would buy your book, Marina," Yin says apologetically.

"She would," agrees Yang. "But she's got a shelf of books she's never read."

"I've got one in my suitcase," I tell Yin. "Haven't even cracked it open."

"Who are the women for your book?" asks Yin. I open my journal and show them my list.

"Trotula of Salerno?" Yang asks. "Artemisia Gentileschi? Eleonora Pimento Cheese? Who the hell are they? What about Lucrezia Borgia? You gotta have sex in the book, DLT. This is Italy."

"There are already enough sexploitation books about women."

"Then what's that? I can see the words 'firm cock' right there!" Yang points at a page in my journal. I close it quickly, embarrassed.

"That's just my own travel diary. I'm using the same notebook for book notes."

"Well, that stuff is what people want to read, DLT! If you don't want to sex-ploit the historical ladies, sex-ploit yourself."

"*Don Quixote* isn't about sex and it's the most popular book in history," objects Yin. "Over five hundred million copies sold."

"What about *Lady Chatterly's Lover?*" asks Yang. "I'm telling you, it's got to have a lot of sex in it. Like two hot lesbians on a train—wait, hold on a tick, is that what you were scribbling before?"

"What?" I squirm.

"Are we in your travel diary, DLT?" Both girls look at me.

"No."

"You lying?"

"Yes." I jump up from the seat. "Please don't shove the bottle up my ass."

Chapter 11

How Not to Stick to an Itinerary

Castel Sant'Elmo, Napoli: Tuesday, 1:35 p.m.

I've convinced my new friends to come with me to see the medieval fortress that overlooks the city of Naples. It was built in the fourteenth century but was seized and changed hands many times over the centuries. In 1799, the people of Naples, inspired and led by revolutionaries like Eleonora Pimentel, gained control of the fortress. But when the republic fell, the fortress was used to jail those same people. She was imprisoned here until she was hung. Unfortunately, it's Tuesday, so the museum is closed. But the grounds are open. As we meander down ancient walkways, I read Yin and Yang some of my research notes.

ITALIAN WOMAN OF INFLUENCE: Eleonora de Fonseca Pimentel

1. Lived from 1752–1799 (only forty-seven years!).
2. Italian poet and revolutionary.
3. As a child, she wrote poetry and read Latin and Greek.
4. A pen pal of Voltaire.

5. Beaten by her husband, which caused two miscarriages.
6. Imported values of the French Revolution to Italy.
7. A leader of the Neapolitan revolution that overthrew the Bourbon monarchy and installed the Neapolitan Republic.
8. Wrote and edited the bi-weekly newspaper of the Republic.
9. After the monarchy was restored, she was hanged.
10. One potential reason was that she wrote pamphlets denouncing the queen as a lesbian.

"See, don't fuck with the lesbians," says Yang.

"True," I laugh.

Christmas Alley, Naples, Italy: Tuesday, 4:50 p.m.

Hallmark Channel addicts beware. You will leave Christmas Alley with no money, if you leave at all. For the rest of us, twenty minutes of shop after shop with handcrafted ornaments, wooden mangers, wreaths, and creepy looking wise men is enough to make you want to barf candy canes.

"I have to get my mother an ornament. If I'm not out in ten minutes, come rescue me from the elves."

"Okay," says Yin, licking the *nocciola* gelato that's melting onto her hand.

"Get her one with the god Saturn, since Saturnalia is the Roman pagan holiday the Christians co-opted when they made up Christmas, DLT," smiles Yang.

"She'd love that." I give her a look.

"Marina, you should come with us to Positano, on the bus," suggests Yin.

"Thanks, but I've got an itinerary I should stick to. I'm going to stay a night here and then head south to Salerno. I'm researching Trotula of Salerno. She was a pioneer in gynecological medicine."

"Naples is full of crime," says Yin. "Thieves, sex workers—"

"As fun as that sounds, DLT, you should still come with us," interrupts Yang. "You can research your Twat-ula gyno online anywhere."

"I don't know guys. I usually make a plan and stick to it."

"Positano is south, on the way to Salerno," smiles Yin. "Just make an extra stop. You'll have fun."

"Well ... I did want to see Capri," I concede.

Bus from Naples to Positano, Italy: Tuesday, 6:00 p.m.

The bus is nice. The seats are comfortable and new (the old ones were sent to second-class train cars.) There's even Wi-Fi. A call to Rosalie is overdue.

VIDEO CALL

Call - ROSALIE TAYLOR - No Answer - 6:30 p.m.
Call - ROSALIE TAYLOR - 6:34 p.m.

"Hello? Marina?"
"Hi Mom!"
"I can hear you, sweetie. I can see myself, but not you."
"Press the video button."
"What's that?"
"The one that looks like a camera."
"Where is it?"
"Mom, hang up. I'll call you right back."

Call - ROSALIE TAYLOR - No Answer - 6:36 p.m.
Call - ROSALIE TAYLOR - No Answer - 6:41 p.m.
Call - ROSALIE TAYLOR - 6:55 p.m.

"Mom, I said I'd call you right back."
"Hello? Marina? Oh, there you are! Now I can see you, but I can't hear you."

"Because you hit the mute button or you chopped your ear off?" I ask, staring with alarm at her right ear, bandaged like Van Gogh.

"Now I can hear you. Sorry, sweetie, I had to go to the bathroom. I put Coffee-mate in my coffee and you know what happens."

"Mom, what happened to your ear?" I ask.

"I'm fine, it was just a hot curler accident. Donna went a bit overboard with the first aid bandages," she says. Yin and Yang pop their heads over the seat behind me and smile and wave at my mother.

"Hello mum!" they say in unison.

"Oh! Hello girls!"

"My new travel buddies. We met on the train from Rome," I explain.

"Praise Jesus! I've been worried about you alone. You girls stick together, okay?"

"We go everywhere together," says Yang. "Even the bathroom."

"How's the quilting going?" asks Yin.

"Marina told us all about you. Show us one of the manatees you made from repurposed sweat pants," begs Yang. I cringe.

"Oh! Well hold on and I'll go get all my craft samples . . ." Rosalie says, pleased.

"Mom, no. Just send us photos. I'm not sure how long the Wi-Fi will work. We're on a bus on our way to the *Costiera Amalfitana*," I say, hoping to change the subject. "Positano, Capri, Amalfi, Ravello."

"Oh how exciting! Okay, I'll send you photos of the stuffed flamingos I just made from a quincea-ñera tablecloth, and you send me photos of Capri.

I've always wanted to go there. Like in the Frank Sinatra song, 'Isle of Capri.'" She begins to sing it. Like me, Rosalie cannot carry a tune (okay, four things in common). Yin joins in with her, a lovely soprano.

"Check out this view." I put the tablet up to the window. The bus negotiates an L-shaped bend in the narrow road. A car coming the other direction is backing up to give us room. On one side of us is a sheer cliff face, on the other side, a steep drop hundreds of yards to the sea. Whitecaps roll in on turquoise waters.

"Just like the travel channel." Rosalie is thrilled. I feel a pang. She's spent her life stuck in the disillusioned paradise of Key West, Florida. My dad had all the adventures abroad and at sea.

"Too bad you're not here with us, mum!" says Yang.

"Yeah, that would be great," I say. Rosalie looks surprised. "We could have a glass of *vino rosso* together," I add with a smile. In this moment, I actually mean it.

"*Vi-no ross-o.* So exotic," she repeats. She looks away. "You girls have fun. I've got guests checking in and a ton of work to do." She's looking everywhere but the camera now.

"I'll send you a postcard from Capri, Rosalie."

"Don't call me that, and don't forget to email me everything you're doing."

"She will. She's keeping notes in a diary. Every single thing!" says Yang. I shoot her another glare and hang up the call.

End Call - ROSALIE TAYLOR - 7:06 p.m.

"Your mother really loves you," says Yin with a hint of envy.

"Well, I'm her only kid, so it's non-negotiable."

"Not true. Mine's a lawyer," says Yin. "She can negotiate her way out of anything." Yin falls quiet as the bus slows for another hairpin curve, and suddenly we see Positano sprawled below us.

"Come to dinner with us tonight, mate. So I have someone to talk to in English."

"*Oui*, you must come and meet my friends," Yin agrees. "One is an architect, one is a pilot for Alitalia, one is in business, and one is a well-known photographer. He's French-Italian. Oh! *Arrête, pas dans le bus!*" she cries. Yang has her hand up Yin's skirt. Perhaps this is why I miss that last, vital piece of information.

Chapter 12

How Not to "Find My iPhone"

Positano, Italy: Early Wednesday Morning

We do not need to relive what happened on this night, while Modesty lay passed out on the floor of my alcohol-soaked brain. So, here are the CliffsNotes, to remind you.

HERO: sauced American writer.

FATAL FLAWS: pride, lust, and thinking she can fake it.

PLOT: while negotiating for return of unflattering photos by engaging in lewd sexual activity outside bathroom, writer assaults French-Italian photographer and loses entire contents of purse while fleeing.

Pensione del Sole, Positano: Wednesday, 1:02 a.m.

I'm back in my room, but freaking out about my lost stuff. I can't find Yin and Yang, because the name of their hotel is in my phone, which I now do not have. That's two phones in ten days if you're counting. Despite the trek back down the six thousand stairs (in my torn dress with vomit on it) retracing my steps, *and* the empty-handed climb back, I'm still not exactly sober. Unwisely, I pull out my tablet.

VIDEO CALL
Call - Will Kittridge - 1:07 a.m.

"You lost your phone *and* your wallet?" he asks, sweaty, still in his softball jersey. I have a memory flash to the hard wooden bleachers, watching him play "copball" as I called it. He was the catcher of course, the glue that holds the team together.

"Extenuating circumstances," I say as I lean back on the bed.

"What happened to your dress, Marina? Did somebody do that to you?" He's calm but intensely protective. It makes me want to climb through the screen into his arms.

"No. I'm fine—"

"Tell me the truth, right now. I will get on a plane tonight." His voice is even but the emotion behind it makes my stomach flutter.

"Will, it was me. I tore it trying to climb in my window because I lost my room key along with everything else in my bag when it fell open, okay? Who gives someone a designer bag that flies open and launches your valuables out like a piñata? This is clearly all Sarah's fault."

"Clearly. Why didn't you call Sarah?"

"It's my wallet and phone. You're the police and there are police here. Aren't all of you on cop Facebook or something?"

"It's called Interpol, and they don't give a shit about your phone, Marina. Did you lose your passport?"

"No, they took it when I checked in and put it in the safe. It's a thing they do at the hotels."

"You have your tablet. Did you turn on 'find my phone'?"

"It has that?"

"Yes, but you have to switch it on. Go into the app, I'll stay online with you." I minimize the video window, so I can hear him but not see him anymore as I click around on the tablet. "It should be in your settings."

"Found it."

"Open it and tap 'find my phone.' A map should pop up, showing your location as one dot, and your phone as another."

"The blinking one?"

"Yes. That's it. Good work."

"Now what do I do?"

"Go find it, Marina. I've gotta jump in the shower."

I have an involuntary memory flash to the extremely hot showers we used to take together after his softball games. Will was the sort of guy with just enough chest hair, and not too much. He looked great naked, but he looked fucking amazing when he was wet and naked. He was six foot one, and I was five nine, so our bodies fit together perfectly standing up. The whole bathroom would fill with steam, water pouring over both our bodies, chasing soapsuds down his chest, across his perfect abs.

Long, hot, wet kisses, his body pressed against mine. He would wash my hair and I would arch my back, rubbing my soapy ass onto his big, gloriously firm—

"I've gotta go, I've got a date." The sexy shower flashback comes to a screeching halt. Date? I click back on the video chat window and suddenly he appears again. But I immediately wish I hadn't done this. His shirt is off and he can see my expression.

"Oh?" I say, trying for casual. "So, Cowboy's back in the saddle?" I fake smile.

"Just some girl my mom wants me to meet."

"That's great." There's a long, awkward silence. Then I notice something. "Hey, what's the yellow blinking bar on the bottom of the map? Nineteen percent?"

"That's . . . sub optimal. Your phone battery only has nineteen percent left."

"What happens after that?"

"You're out of luck, Mermaid." The sound of my pet name is like a knife in the heart. "You better get going. Good luck."

"You too." I reach for the button, but can't tap it off. He gives me a wink and then suddenly—

End Call - Will Kittridge - 1:15 a.m.

I stare at the screen. His handsome, bittersweet smile is frozen, and then gone. The whole time we were dating, he never hung up first. It was a thing. Not anymore, apparently. Moving on. Both of us. I've kissed two guys in the past few days. So why did I now feel like I wanted to throw up?

Suddenly the yellow blinking bar on the tablet turns red. The numbers beside it say thirteen percent. Thirteen doesn't come after nineteen!

HOW NOT TO "FIND MY iPHONE"

What the hell? I grab the pad of paper on the desk and frantically write down the name of the road where my little phone dot is. *Viale Santa Cristina*, borders that cute little park, next to a tiny church. I hope it's where my wallet fell out too. Wait. I zoom in. You've got be kidding me! The cute little park has the symbol of a cross on it. A cemetery.

Chiesa di Santa Maria delle Scogliere, Positano: Wednesday, 1:25 a.m.

I find my lip gloss halfway down the hill. Not far from this is my compact, the powder inside exploded. I hope the phone had a softer landing. I walk down one more flight and there is the little church. Well-worn stones, weathered but strong. It seems like it's been here forever, as much a part of the cliffside as the rocks it's built from. To my great relief, the little courtyard on the side of the church is not an actual cemetery. There's a little shrine and a couple of ancient headstones with the writing worn off, but the full-blown Halloween-style, pee your pants cemetery I'd been picturing is nowhere in sight. There is, however, a lot of high grass that hasn't been cut in . . . ever?

PROCEDURE FOR CANVASING CHURCHYARDS AFTER MIDNIGHT:

1. You cannot use the flashlight on your phone to find your phone.
2. Begin on one end and crawl on all fours in a zig-zag formation, sweeping the grass and gravel with your arms and hands.
3. If you find a bone, don't assume it's human. But don't touch it.
4. If you find any coins, put them on the shrine, not your pocket.
5. If a large stray dog suddenly appears, stand up quickly. Throw a small rock near it, but not at it, just to show it who's boss.
6. If the one-armed man who owns the dog you mistook for a stray sees you do this, apologize profusely.
7. Do not ask why he's out for a walk with his dog in the middle of the night.

8. Do not mention that he reminds you of Magwitch, the creepy ex-con from *Great Expectations*. He doesn't speak English anyway.

9. If he offers his phone for you to call yours, don't refuse because you don't want Magwitch the Night Walker to have your number. (It won't matter who has your number if you don't have your phone.)

10. When your phone rings in the corner of the yard and you run to it with the wild, euphoric joy of a mother reuniting with her lost child, tears in your eyes, don't then try to act casual and say, "Cool, *grazie*."

Chapter 13

How Not to See The Blue Grotto

Ferry to Capri, Mar Tirreno: Wednesday, 11:15 a.m.

When traveling, it's important not to let minor setbacks like losing all your cash, credit cards, and ID, or small inconveniences like spending three hours at the police station just to fill out two forms, ruin your good time. Credit cards can be cancelled online, but I opt for the twenty-four hour "good faith waiting period," believing my fellow man will not disappoint and the wallet will turn up. Ferry tickets purchased in advance online can be retrieved via email and are valid all day. Americans are taught to depend on our plastic and "not leave home without it." But Aeneas sailed the Mediterranean without a credit card. Surely I can spend the day on Capri.

So, here I am, free from the fetters of capitalism, wind whipping through my unwashed hair, swimsuit under my sundress, backpack with everything I need: my journal, half a bag of trail mix, one bottle of water, a rapidly melting chocolate bar, a hunk of cheese I've been carrying since Rome, and two squished croissants wrapped in napkins from the free continental breakfast this morning. As we plow through the blue-green waters, frothing and churning cappuccino-like foam around the sides of the ferry, I spot something fast and gray leaping from the water. A dolphin. Then another. I point, and the people around me begin to take photos. The dolphins race in front of us, dive underneath us, leaping and plunging. I laugh like a child. Yes, I've seen dolphins all my life. I'm from Florida. I've even swum with them. But these are *Mediterranean* dolphins. They've been to Sicily, Tunisia, Spain, Sardinia, and Gibraltar. Their ancestors saw Vesuvius erupt, their great-grandporpoises watched submarine battles. These dolphins are dope. The playful pod follows us for about fifteen minutes before disappearing as quickly as it came.

Yin and Yang have still not answered any of my texts this morning. Maybe accidentally sexually assaulting a dinner companion and losing your wallet is not a valid excuse for a dine and dash?

ME: hey girls, sorry again
ME: lunch on me when I get new plastic
ME: heading to Capri if you want to meet

Crickets. I put the phone away. That's fine. Better actually. What better way to truly appreciate the isolated beauty of a Mediterranean island than spending some time alone? This is exactly what I need. My phone chirps. I grab it quickly.

YANG: All good. Have fun DLT.

          ME: not mad?

YANG: busy

          ME: doing?

YANG: APAD

          ME: ?

A photo pops up. Holy shit! I turn it sideways, trying to figure out which girl is actually holding the phone and how, but then I quickly turn the phone off and put it away so nobody thinks I'm looking at porn. The girls are busy. *All pussy, all day*. Suddenly wondering what Frantonio is doing today, I take my lonely *figa* for a walk along the shore.

Viale of Tranquil Independence and Serenity, Capri: Wednesday, 1:00 p.m.

I slowly make my way along a little road that winds along Capri's coast. Why spend time poking around the crowded tourist shops in port, with no money to spend?

My brave plan had been to rent a scooter and tour the perimeter of the island, but now, without driver's license or credit card, I will have to do it on foot. I strike off, choosing the road less traveled. This one meanders lazily along the coast with wide bends and curves, a thin line of rocky shore on my left, cliffs and million euro villas on my right. The gravel along the side of the road crunches under my sandals. The warm sun is a nice break from the wind on the ferry. I look up at the stunning private homes: glass picture windows, gurgling fountains, bright flowers spilling out of window boxes, classical statues. Who *owns* houses like these?

HOUSE 1: must belong to a French fashion designer, who is currently sketching a haute sheer tank top with a row of tiny pockets, an espresso on one side of her easel and a glass of wine on the other.

HOUSE 2: must have been purchased by a Swiss banking company for company retreats, but right now the CFO is dodging objects his Japanese mistress is hurling at him because she's just found out his wife is pregnant.

HOUSE 3: a five-story monstrosity, which is surely owned by Tony Stark, who has been here a grand total of two times.

HOUSE 4: an elegant little shack with solar panels all over it must belong to Elon Musk, who bought it because he heard Tony had one.

HOUSE 5: with the blue shutters must be the haven of an elderly porn star who waited a bit too long to retire so she could afford an elevator in her hideaway.

Suddenly I hear a sharp whistle. A man has walked out onto the patio of one of the houses above me on the hill. Is he whistling at me? He turns around as he whistles again . . . it's Harvey Keitel. I'm one hundred percent certain of it. He's wearing blue bikini briefs and a furry rug of gray chest hair. Harvey Keitel is whistling at *me!* I look down and keep walking. I can't explain why, but I'm suddenly nervous. Am I trespassing? Harvey Keitel is one of those celebs who are hard to separate from their characters. It's him. Absolutely no doubt in my mind. I'm ninety percent sure. I wish Yang were here. Why do you always see cool things when you're alone? I glance back, but now he's gone back inside. It's him. I'm seventy-five percent sure.

It doesn't take long to leave civilization behind. This is what I want. I breathe in the fresh salt air, scented with fish, flowers, and exhaust from the occasional two-stroke engine that passes me by with a lawnmower-like hum. I'm enjoying the walk. I pass a little shrine built into the side of the hill, featuring a blinding white statue of Mary. Faded silk flowers in brass pots. Tall red candles in glass. I can just picture the old lady who walks out here every evening at sunset to light them. Her wooden cane and black orthopedic shoes, her black socks, long skirt, and the scarf on her head. She's seventy-nine but still has a cigarette hanging from her mouth. I wonder what she would say about Harvey's blue bikini briefs. I keep walking.

I'll just find a quaint little fishing village, take some photos for my mother, and have a swim. Who wants crowded beach clubs with rented umbrellas and lounge chairs? This way I'll find my own patch of paradise, have my little picnic on a secluded beach and, who knows, maybe take part in the local custom of topless sunbathing. I smile at this thought. *Perché no?* Why not? Probably the handsome son of a local fisherman will see me emerge from the crystal blue waters like a mermaid, my hair perfectly fanned out across my breasts. He'll offer me a towel (which I forgot) and ask if I've seen the famous Blue Grotto.

"No, I haven't seen anything," I'll reply.

"*Bene*, I want to show you everything," he will say, taking my hand and leading me to a wooden dinghy. "*La Grotta Azzura* is full of boats and tourists. There are caves all through these majestic cliffs, many even more beautiful." Then with his biceps straining against his white T-shirt, he'll row us through a bay peppered with rocks, over coral reefs and schools of fish, along a winding shoreline, until our little boat bumps against a giant rock shaped like a sandcastle. Here, the tiny boat will slip into a beautiful, cool cave of shadows, with light reflected off the water, dancing on the walls. Shining, backlit drops of cold spring water from the heart of the mountain will rain down on us from the cave ceiling, as our voices echo softly.

"This is my favorite cave," Sebastiano will say (that's his name). "I've never shared it with anyone." Here, he will tie up the boat and pull off his shirt and shorts. His body is lean and fit, an athlete's body. His muscular chest and legs are a deep tan. Wearing only his underpants, he'll dive gracefully into the dark water. I'll laugh as the boat rocks and then suddenly stop laughing as he climbs out of the water, onto a rock. His underpants are now *gone*. Standing on the edge of the rock, he will look sheepishly at me over one of his broad shoulders. "*Mi dispiace*," he will apologize, "I can only swim without clothes. It is how I grew up." Water dripping down his muscular back and off his perfectly shaped ass, he will remind me of a statue of a Greek god.

"Oh, I hadn't noticed," I'll say nonchalantly. Then he'll smile and jump into the air, splashing down into the water, rocking the boat wildly. He'll be under so long that I'll get worried and look over the edge, peering into the depths. Suddenly, he'll emerge with a triumphant grin, holding a large conch shell.

"I have a large conch," he will smile. "It is beautiful, no?"

"*Sì*. You do have a very nice *conch*."

"You like conch?"

"I do like *conch*."

"If you want my conch, you must come and get it," he will laugh. And I will slip out of the boat and glide through the shallow water toward him. Placing the shell on a nearby rock, Sebastiano will reach out, pulling me into his arms, wrapping my legs around his waist, and kissing me with gusto. Thrusting his salty tongue inside my mouth, he'll hold my body close to his, his strong hand gripping my ass. With his other hand, he'll pull my wet hair gently but firmly back as he bites my neck playfully. I will kiss him back, feeling my pulse race as the soft waves beat against our bodies. I'll reach down beneath the surface of the water between us and take his large, beautiful *conch* in my hands, gripping it gently as his fingers slip into my bikini—

HONK! A truck blasts its horn at me as it passes. I'm absentmindedly walking in the actual road, and seem to have a hand on my own breast. Oops. Best not to get arrested for public lewdness on my first trip to Italy. I pause for water. I've been walking for hours (actually about fifty-five minutes). My sandals have worn blisters on my feet. The sun is beating down on me and sweat is pouring down my face, arms, legs. I can't believe I haven't come upon a single village or anything. The bend in the road I'm approaching will be the fourth time I've said, "I'll just see what's around *that* bend and then turn around if it's nothing good." Each previous bend revealed only more winding shoreline, white sand, hazy blue waters . . . and another bend.

If I have one admirable characteristic, it's the fact that I don't give up easily. Once I've invested in an idea, I will see it pay off—if it kills me. Will calls it stubbornness. I call it tenacity. How was I going to find Sebastiano if I didn't find a little fishing village?

Finally, around bend number seven, I see a small wooden dock stretching into the water. It reminds me of one at my mother's bed and breakfast, old and falling apart. But there is a small motorboat tied up nearby, and two more dinghies further on. The hillside is dotted with a few tiny houses. Not a soul in sight. I guess this is as good as I'm going to get. In the distance I see larger fishing boats, but I simply cannot walk any further. I walk out to the end of the little dock. The water is clear and beautiful, deep enough for a swim, but not over my head. *Perfetto.* I smile, thinking of Ernesto. I spread out my sarong on the splintering wood, set down my backpack, pull off my sandals, and unpack my picnic. The cheese has sprouted a nice layer of mold. I wrap it back up. Instead, I smear the molten contents of the foil that previously held a chocolate bar onto one of the croissants and devour it. By the time I'm finished I have chocolate on my face, neck, fingers, and elbow (no idea).

I pull off my sundress. Remembering the locals go topless at many beaches in Italy, I work up the courage to actually try it myself. I look around. Nobody in sight. Two seagulls on the beach, arguing loudly over a piece of decaying crab, are my only companions. I slide into the cool water. Fuck it! But then, *"What if someone drives by?"* Modesty whispers inside me. I thought I'd ditched her in Rome. What a pain in the ass. She's always piping up just when things are about to get fun. I ignore her and untie my bikini top. My breasts float gently in the water. I submerge myself and peel off the rest of my suit—my *figa* is free! I toss my suit onto the dock.

In my natural mermaid state, I dive under the cool, clear water, swimming as far as I can in one breath. I resurface and realize I'm only about five yards away from the dock. I do the breaststroke. I swim with my feet together like a tail, and rapidly sink. I float on my back, aiming my breasts skyward, letting the sun kiss my entire naked body through the clear water. *Perfetto!* Pleased at how easily I float, I squint at the white puffy clouds above me. The Mediterranean Sea is much older than the Gulf of Mexico. It's saltier. *That's* why I'm floating more easily. (Not the nonstop pasta, pizza, and gelato.) I splash my feet with joy. My shoulder scrapes against something slimy.

Yelping, I turn, freaked out. It's only a little buoy, floating and bobbing on the surface of the water, covered with algae. I peer downward and see a crab trap at the other end of the tether. It's wedged against some rocks. Curious, I dive down to see if anything is inside. The water is clear but salty, so I only open my eyes a bit. Through the cracks in the wooden cage, I see . . . tentacles! WHAT? Surprise robs me of all the air in my lungs as bubbles rush upward. I resurface quickly. There's an octopus in there! A real, live, beautiful Mediterranean octopus! Something I'd never dreamed of seeing in the wild. How fantastic. And horrible! He's caught in that awful crab trap. With horror, I have a vision of that beautiful pink creature carved into pieces and dressed with lemon and olive oil on somebody's plate tomorrow. Maybe even tonight! I have no time to waste.

THINGS TO REMEMBER WHEN FREEING OCTOPUSES FROM TRAPS:

1. Don't.
2. It's stronger than you are, and apparently smarter.
3. It's not stuck. It's enjoying a meal.
4. It will exit the way it entered, through the cracks.
5. Crab traps come with locks.
6. Bashing something underwater is harder than it looks.
7. If some of the tentacles are out of the cage, do not gently pull on them trying to help the octopus escape. It's trying to escape from *you.*
8. A scared octopus will squirt ink.
9. Octopus ink contains Tyrosinase, which will badly irritate your eyes and make you lose your sense of smell for a while.

I burst through the surface of the water, yelling in pain, eyes burning like fire, arms flailing like a—well there's nothing that comes close really.

Wading blindly out of the water, I hear a voice and stop in my tracks. I pry one burning eye open with a grimace and find myself standing naked in front of a very angry man. This is not Sebastiano. But it may be his grandfather.

"*Cosa stai facendo alla mia trappola?*" There is no sympathy here. Not even a trace of appreciation or amusement at the fact that I'm standing naked in front of him. He's pointing at the trap, so it's obviously his.

"Do you have water?" I ask. "My eyes are on fire! I can hardly see." But what I do see is the woman on the porch of the small house on the hill who begins to yell at us both.

"*Sciattona Americana! Cosa stai facendo con mio marito?*" she yells angrily. "*Vattene, sciattona Americana!*" I don't need to know the words—her meaning is clear.

The husband yells back at her. I take this opportunity to limp quickly over rocks, using one eye like a pirate, and get back to my bag on the dock. I wrap my sarong around me, pour the rest of my bottle of water into my eyes (I will regret this later), slip my sandals on, and grab my swimsuit. With squinted eyes, I make it back to the road. As I go, I repeat the Italian phrase I've come to know best: "*Mi dispiace molto.*" (I'm very sorry.)

Chapter 14

How Not to Hitchhike

Viale of Bloody Blisters and Humiliation, Capri: Wednesday, 3:49 p.m.

The road is definitely much longer on the way back. My blisters are bleeding. My mouth is dry. I'm once again drenched with sweat. Also, the sun is definitely hotter than it was before, now bouncing off the asphalt and frying me from all directions like a convection oven. My eyes are still burning and my salty skin itches. But, on the bright side, I can't smell the fish and exhaust of passing motorists anymore.

In fact, I can't smell anything. This sensation is more than slightly disturbing, but I distract myself by brainstorming different scientific applications of this special quality of octopus ink. Just imagine if we could improve the lives of people who worked around terrible smells all day: garbage men, elephant trainers, daycare workers, or those ladies in the Macy's perfume department. One quick squirt of octopus ink up your nose before work, and you'd be invincible for hours. Granted, the application technique needed some work, but the idea was solid. The biggest challenge was going to be acquiring the ink humanely, since an octopus inking is basically the equivalent of a human shitting his pants.

Viale of Unending Torture, Capri: Wednesday, 4:17 p.m.

I'm still walking and I haven't even reached the little shrine yet. How does the old lady that lights the candles do this walk every day? No wonder she has orthopedic shoes. I decide to rest—there's a nice rock in the shade. I take off my sandals to examine my blisters. Won't be wearing my ridiculously uncomfortable stilettos anytime soon. My shoulders are burnt. My water bottle is empty. Crap. That's when I hear a rustling in the bushes behind me and jump up in alarm. Mountain lion? Goat? I take a few steps into the road, away from the sounds, and a black and white dog emerges.

"Oh, hi pup," I say. I love dogs and have a compulsion to pet every dog I see, despite the fact that I've been bitten twice. This one is a cute, mid-sized mutt with a collar. He's someone's pet. Harmless, I decide. He looks at me, his head cocked, tail stiff. Apparently the jury is still out on me. I rummage in my bag and pull out the moldy cheese. Dogs love cheese. Especially moldy cheese, right? He's already sniffing the air. "Come on boy, have some cheese."

His tail wags a bit. Realizing he's an Italian dog and probably speaks Italian, I try, "*Formaggio, mmmm.*" He takes a step toward me. I hold the cheese out and he creeps closer to me. "*Buono, mmmm.*" I sniff the cheese (I can't smell it, thank God), and hold it out to him again. He takes a final step, stretching his neck out, and gingerly takes the cheese from my hand. Yes! I now speak Dog Italian. I reach out to pet him and he growls and lunges. I jump back, terrified. The dog grabs the cheese and takes off toward the port. "Asshole! I gave you moldy cheese!" The dog disappears. I start walking again. Slowly.

A car passes me, and I see a toddler wave at me from the passenger seat. That was nice. I suddenly remember that people here are very nice (unless you're meddling with their crab traps—or their husbands). Why am I walking? I should just stick my thumb out and get a ride back to the port. Easy. Somebody will surely stop. A nice Belgian couple on vacation with their baby perhaps? A local grocer on his way to the post office? Harvey Keitel? A mentally unstable butcher's apprentice looking for a fresh piece of meat to practice carving? On second thought, maybe I'll keep walking. It can't be that much farther.

Aunt Catherine, my father's sister, would not be proud of me right now. She walked for eight weeks along the Camino de Santiago, a pilgrim's trail in Spain, for her sixtieth birthday. Next, she plans to do the Pacific Coast Trail. Having recently seen *Wild*, I'd stupidly promised to accompany her, and I'm now regretting that with every step. It's been half a day of walking, and I'm falling apart. What is wrong with me? I thought I was young and fit.

After another fifteen minutes, all my convictions collapse. I want a ride. I try to block out the *Unsolved Mysteries* episode I'd seen on TV as a child, where the girl is last seen getting into a 1986 brown Camaro with a hand-painted fender. I try not to remember how mad Will was when Laurel and I hitched from Miami to the Suwannee Music Festival in college. "You're lucky you weren't found in the trunk of some nutjob's car. This is why hitchhiking is illegal." Wait, is hitchhiking illegal in Italy? Surely not.

DO'S AND DON'T'S FOR HITCHHIKING IN ITALY:

1. Do: walk on the edge of the road.
2. Don't: stick your leg out a little.
3. Do: stick your arm and thumb out.
4. Don't: change your mind and retract both leg and thumb.
5. Don't: decide to wait until you can see who is in the car first.
6. Don't: see a woman and her kids and put your thumb out too late.
7. Don't: see a man driving alone and hide behind some rocks.

8. Don't: see a truck with old geezers and put your thumb out too late.
9. Do: throw caution to the wind, close your eyes, and stick your thumb out.

I hear a car pull over. I open my eyes. It's the police. *Shit.*

AT THIS POINT, IF: a police jeep is pulled over with its lights on . . .

YOU SHOULD: walk calmly up to the window and say, *"Buongiorno."*

DO NOT:
1. Try to run the other way. You won't get far on your bloody stumps.
2. Put your hands in the air. This is not American TV.
3. Ask if hitchhiking is illegal. It is. But they don't care.
4. Pretend you have injured yourself, limping up to the jeep. Later you'll forget which foot is supposed to be hurt.

My heart pounds as I limp (right foot) up to the window of the jeep. Inside are two port policemen. The driver looks younger than I am, his partner early thirties. I expect them to issue me another fine or at least tell me hitchhiking is dangerous.

"Ciao," smiles the driver.

"Ciao," I reply.

"Lei Americana?"

"Sì, I'm American."

"You are hurt?" he asks, looking down at my foot.

"I walked too far."

"Andiamo al porto," says his partner, "We go to port. *Prendiamo un caffè."* Then, to his partner, *"Come si dice?"*

"You want to go to take a coffee with us?" the driver asks. I process this. I'm not under arrest. I'm an attractive American girl in a swimsuit

98

and sundress. These are Italian men, who would like to practice their English. I'm fairly sure I smell terrible, drenched with sweat, but I still can't smell much so I hope they can't either.

"*Sì, grazie.*" I smile.

"Ok-ay," says the younger driver, just as his jeep stalls out. He looks embarrassed as he starts it up again.

"*Ti piace la musica* country?" asks the older one, but he doesn't wait for a reply. Of course all Americans like country music. "Gianni Cash!"

"*No, non di nuovo,*" protests the young driver. His partner ignores him, fiddling with an older model phone, rigged via life support cables to the stereo. Suddenly, "Cry! Cry! Cry!" blasts from the speakers. Today, I love country music.

Bar La Vela, Marina Grande, Capri: Wednesday, 5:02 p.m.

I've dubbed my new Italian police pals Tango and Cash. Enjoying a latte, I relate what happened this morning with the octopus, as well as how I lost my wallet the night before. I'm not sure if it's the stories they find highly entertaining or my broken Italian-English-charades routine. My sense of smell is starting to return when Cash, the older one, lights up a cigarette at the table. He's having espresso and cigarettes. Tango, the young one, is having *gelato con panna* (whipped cream). With hat and sunglasses off, I realize he's much more handsome than I'd realized. Maybe it's the uniform, or the fact that he rescued me from dehydration and death by vultures, but Tango's looking cuter by the minute.

He's also pretty nervous around me. When my foot accidentally brushes his under the table, he jumps a little, smearing whipped cream from his gelato onto the tip of his nose. He's got blue eyes and dark brown hair, cut short. There's a little scar on his left cheekbone, under his eye. Cash tells me that Tango's only recently completed his port police training. I wonder if there was a lesson on picking up stray girls, or if this is a skill Italian boys are born with. The tiny scar is intriguing.

99

"Were you in a fight with smugglers?" I ask Tango, gesturing to my own cheek to indicate his scar.

"*Come* smug-lers?" asks Cash.

"You know, criminals who take the drugs on the boats," I explain.

"Ah! *Miami Vice!*" Cash finds this hysterical.

"Yes," I say, pleased. Tango looks embarrassed.

"He was big fight—with surfing board," says Cash, laughing. "After looking Patrick Swayze *Point Break* movie."

"I try to do surfing," explains Tango, irritated at his partner. "Only one time." Now, I feel bad for bringing it up.

"Well, surfing is hard," I say. "It takes more than once." Tango puts his sunglasses back on, feeling self-conscious. "No, let me see." I reach up and take them off. This gets Cash's attention. "It's cool. It makes you look tough," I say. Tango likes this. I reach up and gently touch the scar. "Kinda sexy," I nod. He blushes.

Cash starts laughing again and says something in Italian. Tango shakes his head, shrugs. But Cash keeps goading him. Tango looks at me, uncertain. Cash puts his cigarette out—he means business.

"You stay at Capri tonight?" asks Cash.

"No, I'm taking the ferry back to Positano," I reply. "I have friends there."

"Boyfriend?" Cash asks.

"No, girlfriends," I answer. Cash grins, pokes his partner. Tango relents.

"My friend has a birthday party tonight. Would you like to come there with me?"

"That sounds fun, but my room where I'm sleeping tonight is in Positano," I say.

"You sleep here, with him," says Cash. I raise an eyebrow at him. Tango just gives me a nonchalant shrug and a nod, trying to look cool, but I notice beads of newly formed sweat on his brow. "*Perché no?*" asks Cash. Why not?

CONS:

1.   No ID or money.
2.   No idea who this guy is.
3.   New friends in Positano.

PROS:

1.   No ID or money. Can't go out anyway.
2.   He's cute.
3.   I can't resist a man in uniform.

It's a tie. Their radio squawks loudly on the table. A gritty voice on the other end says something about dogs? Tango stands, relieved. I stand up too.

"Smugglers?" I ask with a smile.

"We must go, the dog is in the hotel pool again," explains Tango.

"And they call you? Why?"

"He is throw-up-ing in pool."

"But, you're the police."

"*Sì, però*, it is . . . *come si dice, delicato* . . . ."

"Delicate?"

"*Sì*," Tango nods.

"Why, whose dog?" I ask. I'm just about to mention the dog I saw.

"A famous actor," he says, rolling his eyes.

"I saw him!" I say triumphantly. I'm sure it was Keitel now. But, then I realize he wasn't whistling at me, he was calling his dog. The same dog I called an asshole and fed moldy cheese. And now, he's "throw-up-ing" in the pool. Tango leans in and awkwardly kisses me goodbye on both cheeks.

"He is finish here, later, at six." Cash points to a small office on the other side of the marina, in case I change my mind about staying with Tango.

"That's my ferry," I say, pointing.

"Ok-ay. No problem. *Ciao, bella*," Tango says sweetly. Cash also kisses me goodbye and whispers into my ear.

"He virgin." Cash's face is über-serious as he nods toward Tango. He walks to the jeep. I stare in surprise. Why's Cash telling me this? Because I'm a *sciattona Americana*? Tango starts the engine and waves innocently, no idea his partner just ratted him out. I smile back. He gives me the surfer shaka hand sign, like he's in California. Adorable. He smiles and revs the engine. The jeep stalls out again. This kills me. I try not to laugh as they drive away. I look at the ferry, now docking. Must re-evaluate.

CONS:

1. No ID or money.
2. No idea who this guy is.
3. New friends in Positano.

PROS:

1. No ID or money. Can't go out anyway.
2. He's cute.
3. I can't resist a man in uniform.
4. Duty as independent, sexually confident American woman to help cute Italian boy-cop across the finish line to manhood?

I watch the ferry, now starting to board. Then I remember that I want to "date like a man." A man would not get on that ferry.

Chapter 15

How Not to Sleep With a Virgin

Rando Apartment, Capri: Wednesday, 8:37 p.m.

Tango has taken me for a pizza and beer after work. Now we're ready to party. Apparently a local's birthday party on a Wednesday in Capri consists of a bunch of young people sitting around an apartment, drinking, eating junk food, and smoking pot. Not so different from a college party back home, minus the frat boys doing keg stands. All of Tango's friends are nice. Few of them speak English as well as he does. Mostly I sit around and listen to word soup. Tango keeps asking if I'm okay, if I'm having fun. Yes, actually I am. They're a lively group, laughing and joking. He puts his arm around me as he introduces me to his friends. His palm sweats on my bare shoulder.

"Maybe something to drink?" I ask. He needs to relax.

"What do you like?" he says.

"Something cold," I smile.

"Prosecco?"

"*Perfetto.*"

Tango goes to the kitchen. There are so many cute, young girls here, and he seems fairly popular. I have to wonder if Cash was lying. He can't really be a virgin. I watch him in the kitchen, interacting with a short, well-endowed redhead as he unwraps the foil on a bottle of Prosecco. But when she pulls the neckline of her top down to show him a tattoo on one of her breasts, he's completely unprepared. The wet Prosecco bottle slips from his hands, lands on her foot, and rolls away as she hops up and down in pain.

Tango chases the bottle down, apologizes, and offers her ice. As she bends down to ice her foot, he opens the now shaken bottle of Prosecco, spraying the girl down like a victorious racecar driver. Okay, Cash wasn't lying. Tango is definitely a virgin. I look away. It's too painful. Bless his little heart. Fear not, adorable-yet-awkward-Italian-boy-cop. Your youthful-yet-experienced-American-sex-goddess (Italian translation: *sciattona Americana*) is here to liberate you from the torturous prison of your virginity. I congratulate myself for having made the right choice to stay.

Deciding to practice my Italian, I focus on the conversations around me. It's fun to try and figure out what they're saying. The three boys on the sofa discussing European politics impress me with their maturity, until I realize they're actually talking about *Game of Thrones*. The young girl next to me is very polite, trying to make conversation with the newcomer. When she tells me she's taking classes, "*Per essere un ambasciatore,*" I think she's learning about basket weaving.

"That's great," I smile. "My mother does quilting." I mime sewing, and she looks confused. Tango walks up with three glasses of Prosecco.

"Chiara is going to be ambassador one day," he says.

"Oh, wow," I say, impressed. "And how many ambassadors can also weave baskets?" Tango gives me a confused look, but nods, clearly proud of his friend. She smiles and looks kind of embarrassed. There is a moment between them. It's fleeting, but I catch it. Chiara takes the Prosecco, thanks him, and goes to sit by the boy with the guitar.

"This is, Paolo, the brother of Chiara," Tango tells me. "We grow up together." Paolo's been watching us, and if I'm reading him right, he's pleased to have Tango's attention now on me instead of his kid sister, Chiara.

HELPFUL TIPS FOR ITALIAN PARTIES

1. Sing the AS Roma football song you learned. The Roma fans will be charmed, the Roma haters will love that you're butchering it.
2. "Mambo Italiano" is not the Italian equivalent of "Shout."
3. *Fragolino* is NOT for shots. Didn't you learn this the first time?
4. Don't correct them when they sing the wrong words to "Hotel California."
5. When you realize the condoms you brought are back in Positano, don't rifle through the cabinet in the bathroom, knocking the pin out of the shelf and sending everything crashing into the sink and the toilet that you haven't flushed yet.

Tango's Aunt's House: Thursday, 12:26 a.m.

Paintings of cats, photos of cats, cat fridge magnets, cat pillows, cat curtains, and actual cats. Black ones, an orange one, two white ones? I can't be sure. I'm tipsy. There is tangled yarn strung from sofa to floor like a giant yellow spider web. Tango is staying here while his great Zia Claudia is away in Denmark. The cats are a pain, he says, picking up what's left of his aunt's knitting, but it's nice to get away from his house for a while. He has a ten-year-old brother who follows him everywhere.

A tiny toy bird with hot pink feathers dangles from the end of a stick wedged into the cushions of a floral chair. I've had way too much wine and am exhausted from a full day of rescuing octopuses and hitchhiking. Trying to focus my tired eyes, I pull the cat toy from between the chair's cushions, and cat hair billows up as I plop down. Tango goes to get us water. I swing the bird in tiny circles around the stick. Immediately there is a fat gray cat with two heads in my lap, batting at the toy bird. I put the toy down and stroke the cat. No wonder he's fat. He's got two mouths.

Just as I'm trying to decide which of the cat's two heads to scratch, Tango comes back with the water and shoos him away.

As I drink the water, Tango sits on the sofa, takes off his shoes. He's not as nervous around me as he was before. It's either the wine, or the fact that I overflowed his friend's toilet. I lean my head back against the chair and realize how much I just want to close my eyes and have a short nap. But I've got a job to do. I've got an Italian virgin to deflower. If not me, who? If not now, when?

Tango is intently trying to untangle a giant handful of yellow yarn. He is clearly not going to make the first move. I stand up, slowly take the yarn out of his hands, and place it in the knitting basket. I put a knee on the couch and gently straddle him, sitting on his lap.

"Is this seat taken?" I ask.

"No," he laughs awkwardly. I lightly touch the little scar on his cheek with the tip of my index finger.

"Can you feel that?" I ask.

"Little," he nods.

"What does it feel like?" I ask.

"Feather on my face."

"You like it?" He nods, smiling. I lean over and grab the cat toy with the hot pink feathers. I trail the bird's tail lightly over Tango's forehead, cheeks, chin, and then down his neck. He smiles. His young, luminous skin responds to the tickling with a rippling wave of goose bumps. Slowly I unbutton his shirt. Now he looks both aroused and worried. I lean in and kiss his lips gently to reassure him. Then I trail the pink feathers down over his smooth, nicely shaped pecks. I wiggle the feathers across his stomach. He laughs.

"You're ticklish?" Delighted, I wiggle them more, zigging and zagging the toy bird across his chest. He laughs harder. I spin the bird in a tight little circle around his navel and Tango—YELLS IN PAIN as the gray cat pounces out of nowhere, onto the toy, sinking his claws into Tango's stomach.

"Che cazzo!" Tango leaps up flinging us both off his lap. The cat lands on its feet. I do not. *"Testa di cazzo!"* Tango throws a pillow at the cat. I watch it bolt from the room from my position on the floor, and I wish I could follow it.

"Oh my God, I'm so sorry. That was a bad idea. Are you okay?" This seems like a sentence I should practice in Italian. Tango regains his composure, but he's got scarlet red scratches on his belly. "Let me see," I reach for him, but he steps back.

"I'm ok-ay."

"I'm sorry." I feel even worse now.

"It's ok-ay." He sits down in the chair. He needs some space. Ok-ay. Mood ruined. Fuck. I hand him his glass of water. Retrieving some ice from the kitchen, I wrap it in a cloth, but he seems to not want me touching him.

What now? I can't let his most promising evening end with disappointment. If I have one admirable characteristic, it's the ability to make a bad situation better. Getting an idea, I reach for my bag, pulling out my phone. There's a little battery left.

"Can I put on some music?" I ask.

"Ok-ay, no problem," Tango replies.

"No Johnny Cash, I promise," I say with a smile. He laughs, relaxing a little. Good. I click around on my phone and find Buena Vista Social Club: "Chan Chan." *Perfetto.* If sex was converted into music, this is what it would sound like. Cuban guitar notes drift through the air, punctuated by bongos and the sensual shushing of maracas.

"You relax. I'll just be over here, a safe distance away," I say, and I slowly begin to move my hips back and forth. I raise my arms gracefully into the air, holding my hair up off my neck, as I sway my head back and forth with the melody. I turn in a slow circle as I untie my sundress, letting it fall away from my chest, revealing my breasts in my black bikini. Tango's eyes are fixed to my breasts—my hands glide around them, squeezing them gently together. I smile and moisten my lips as I continue to dance, slipping my own fingers into my bikini top, teasing my nipples to attention, teasing him as he stares. I turn sideways so he gets the full silhouette of my breasts and ass as I wiggle my dress over my hips, bending to slide it down my legs, to my ankles, and off. I toss it at him with a wicked smile, and he catches it, smiling back.

His mood has completely changed. I can see his desire. Tango watches my fingers as I trace them up and down the strings of my bikini top. Pausing at the bow tied between my breasts, I give him a raised eyebrow. He swallows in anticipation. I blow him an air kiss and turn my back to him, shimmying my ass in time with the drums. I gyrate my hips in a figure eight, my fingers playing with the strings on the sides of my bikini bottom. Then, fingers spread, I drag my palms over my whole body, my ass, my hips. (Yes, I've done this striptease many times before. No, there was nobody actually in the room at the time.)

It's working. Tango is entranced. I move closer to him and he reaches out to grab me, but I glide away, teasing him. I smile. He squirms in his seat. Okay, time to throw him a bone. Turning my back to him once again, I slowly untie my bikini top, dropping it to the ground. I arch my back as I run my hands through my hair, flipping it sexily. I then twirl around to face Tango—and a very old Italian man wheeling an oxygen tank.

"Holy shit!" I yank a blanket from the back of a chair to cover myself, knocking a stack of records onto the floor in the process.

"*Merda! Zio Tomaso! Sei sveglio?*" Tango says, really loudly. The old man just stares at me, then smiles.

"*Non volevo perdere lo spettacolo.*" His throaty, wheezy laugh is lost in a fit of coughing. Tango helps his uncle put the oxygen mask back on and ushers him slowly down the hallway. I slip my sundress back on. Strike two. I pick up the records. One is broken. Due to unforeseen circumstances, we regret to announce that Signora Renata Tebaldi will not be singing the role of Madam Butterfly this evening. Tango soon returns.

"*Mi dispiace.* He is my uncle, Tomaso. I am helping to look him while my aunt is away. I did not know he was awake. He does not hear much."

Tango slips the broken record back into the cardboard sleeve and props it up by the record player. "I must try to buy a new one so my aunt will not know." He retrieves a bottle of grappa from the kitchen.

"Thanks, I definitely need that," I say.

"No, for my uncle. He is not allowed, because he might die. But if I don't give him—he will tell my aunt I brought a girl here."

"Of course," I say. "Clearly bringing me home is worse than killing your uncle. Anyway, I just remembered, I'm already drunk." Tango disappears down the hall. I sit back on the sofa, drink some water, yawn, and stretch out to wait. Renata Tebaldi in her geisha wig stares at me dramatically from her black and white album cover. We have a staring contest. She wins.

Tango's Aunt's House: Thursday, 2:18 a.m.

The cat pillow under my head is soaked with drool. It looks like the cat threw up. I hear my phone beep and realize what woke me. Fumbling around, I find the phone. It's barely alive at one percent battery.

YANG: okay DLT?

ME: stayed on Capri to deflower virgin

YANG: you wish

ME: serious

YANG: fuck yeah?
(emoji: big thumbs up)

I'm about to type a reply when the phone dies. My charger is back at the hotel. I flop back onto the sofa. Now I realize what I've just done. Shit. The lesbian sexperts are going to want to hear about it. How am I going to face them having failed? How do you spin cat attack and stripping for a ninety-year-old? I won't give up so easily. I will not fail.

I creep down the dark hall and peek into the even darker bedroom. Tango is snoring louder than a lumberjack from under the covers. I tiptoe

109

quietly into the room and slip off my dress. Wearing just my black bikini, I slide gently into the bed and then—Tomaso wraps his bony arm around me. I SCREAM, jumping out of his bed.

"Ritorna tentatrice sexy!" Tomaso wheezes, then laughs, then coughs, then suddenly falls out of bed, yanking his oxygen mask and pulling over the tank.

"Sorry! Are you having a heart attack? Fuck! Help!"

Everything turns to slow motion. Tango runs into the room. Tomaso is on the floor. I'm standing frozen in shock. Tango helps his uncle back up onto the bed, puts the mask on him. Then, Tango turns and scoops me up like I weigh nothing. He carries me out, down the hall, into another room, and tosses me onto a bed. He disappears again.

"No! Non la convideremo!" I hear him talking to his uncle. As I sit on the edge of his bed, the speed of the world returns to normal. I'm not a youthful-yet-experienced-American-sex-goddess. I'm a senior citizen molester. I'm a *sciattona Americana*. For real. By the time I get back to Positano, my face will be on the wall at all the nursing homes. I'm such an asshole! I cannot bear it—I start to cry. About ten minutes later, Tango reenters the room. I wait for him to yell at me, but he just puts the sheet around my shoulders and sits down next to me on the bed.

"Is he dying?"

"No."

"I thought it was you," I say.

"Sì, but I am bigger."

"He was snoring so loud!"

"Sì, he has *enfisema.*"

"I sexually assaulted a senior with emphysema?" I ask, tears running down my cheeks. Tango nods. My eyes well up again.

"No, it's okay. Don't cry *bella.* It is the best time of his week, trust me!" He laughs. My heart lifts. Tango isn't mad. He wraps his arms around me.

"He's not having a heart attack?" I ask.

"No, no. His heart is broken because he thought his dreams were coming true," Tango smiles, putting his arm around me. I laugh through my tears. "But, at least he now gets to tell all his old friends at the café."

"I just wanted you to have a sexy American girl for your first time," I sniff. Tango looks surprised and embarrassed. "Your partner told me."

"He is shit-head."

"And I'm a hot mess."

"Yes, very hot mess. Very sexy."

"I am?"

"*Sí!* Only just now you have the snots on your face." He reaches over, hands me his T-shirt lying on the bed. I start to put it on.

"No, is for your face," he says. He takes the T-shirt and wipes my face. "I like you without your clothes."

I blink wet eyelashes at him. What? Is this possible? Does he still want to have sex after everything that just happened? Tango smiles, leans in, and kisses me softly. Apparently he does. I kiss him back, a little less softly. His fingers slowly untie the straps of my bikini, and my top falls away, revealing my breasts. Tango cups one in each hand and stares at them appreciatively.

"Your breasts are perfect."

"Your uncle is right down the hall."

"It's ok-ay. He is almost deaf and I give him more grappa." Somehow, under the circumstances, this seems fine. Tango leans me back on the bed and kisses my nipples, sucking and tugging gently with his lips as he massages my breasts with his fingers. First one, and then the other. It feels amazing. My muscles instantly relax into the mattress. Wow. He certainly doesn't seem like a virgin. His shy awkwardness is gone. I run my fingers through his hair—then I sit up.

"You have a condom?"

"*Sí.*"

"Is the door locked?"

"*Sí.*"

"Are you sure?" Tango doesn't answer. He leans me back on the bed, puts one hand on my chest, another on my trembling stomach, and slips his head between my legs. I can feel his hot breath on my *figa* as my heart beats faster and my breathing quickens. But wait, aren't I supposed to be the one driving this car? "What about you?" I say, with less enthusiasm than I intend. "I want you to—"

"Ladies first," Tango says sweetly, as his fingers gently pry me apart, and all at once his warm, wonderful tongue slides inside me. I breathe in sharply. Okay, he can drive for now. I try not to grip his hair too hard as I stare at the ceiling. Warmth radiates through me. Every time his fantastically talented tongue slips in, out, and around my now throbbing, aching *figa*, I feel jolts of electricity. My head begins to spin. I close my eyes. His fingers dance around the edges of my *figa,* gently tickling me. Tango opens my legs further, his face pressing into me. I hear myself groan as his hands go to my hips, pulling me into his mouth. I climax and my back arches, my hands gripping the sheets under me, my breath stopped, my heart thumping madly.

But still, he doesn't stop. My knees begin to tremble as I feel his fingers slip back inside, and now a second unstoppable wave of intensity washes over me. My heart pounds in my ears. Holy shit. Just when I'm about to yell uncle (but stop myself because there's an actual uncle in the next room), Tango plants a final kiss and happily yields. I miss his proud expression because my eyes are still rolled back in my head. But I do hear his satisfied, sexy voice as he climbs on top of me. "Ok-ay. Now is my turn. *Sì?*"

"*Sì,*" I whisper. "Yes. *Sì.*" It's all I can manage.

*A note about good Catholic, Italian boys who grow up around good Catholic, Italian girls. They are masters of the art of foreplay and all imaginable forms of sex *without* penetration. This is thankfully true for virgins because once penetration actually happens, you've got about thirty seconds to enjoy it.

Chapter 16
How Not to Love and Leave

Marina Grande, Capri: Thursday, 7:45 a.m.

Tango and I enjoy our lattes and *cornetti con nutella* (croissants filled with hazelnut chocolate goo) while I wait for the first ferry to arrive. He has to work today, and I've got to check out of my room in Positano by eleven. We're both kind of bummed to say goodbye so soon after he took off the training wheels. He's a quick study and intent on improving performance. But I'm feeling good about training him up for the next lucky girl. I wonder if this will be Chiara.

"I wish you stay longer."

"My work here is done," I smile.

"No, I need more practice," Tango says as he wipes the Nutella from my cheek, and then kisses me.

"We practiced enough."

"*Non abbastanza*, not enough."

"*Abbastanza.* Enough. I like this word. *Si, abbastanza bello.* In bed this morning, the shower, the police office closet. It's enough." Tango takes my coffee, puts it down, pulls me close.

"Non è abbastanza. Tienimi stretto, bella."

"You said this last night. What does it mean? *Tienimi stretto?"*

"It mean, hold me tight." He leans in and kisses me, holding me tightly.

"I think you're good. You're ready for a girlfriend," I say.

"There are not girl-friends here for me. Capri is small."

"What about Chiara?" Tango looks surprised and then sheepish. He shrugs.

"Chiara is young and the sister of my friend," he says.

"She likes you a lot," I say.

"Sì," he admits.

"She's very pretty."

"Sì."

"And smart," I say.

"Sì," he admits. "Smarter than me."

"Then what's the problem?" I ask. He leans on the rail and looks out at the water, watching the distant ferry approaching.

"Chiara is too smart for Capri. My island is too small. She will not stay here," he says quietly. And there it is. The truth. He's afraid of getting his heart broken. And she will do it. Tango is right. She will leave. Like I did.

"So you wait for other girls to come love you and leave you?" I ask pointedly.

"It's better, no?"

"No."

"Perché no?"

"Perché . . . it's different, dude."

"How?"

"We just had sex. We didn't make love. Making love is being with someone who gives you chill bumps when she smiles," I say. "Who can make you laugh and cry at the same time; who thinks more highly of you than you do of yourself . . ." I trail off. There's a tightness in my chest. I've only been with one person like this.

"You had this?" asks Tango. I nod.

"What happened?"

"I left."

"Why?"

"My island was also too small," I smile. The ferry gets bigger and bigger as it gets closer. "You cannot hide from love because you're afraid," I say.

"I am not afraid," Tango objects.

"You are. And you're missing out. Enjoy her while you can. She needs it too." I dig out my journal. "You know that opera record, the one that broke?" He winces.

"*Sì*, Renata Tebaldi, famous soprano. She is my aunt's favorite."

"I looked her up on your phone while you were getting dressed. She was pretty awesome. This was my favorite quote: *I was in love many times. This is very good for a woman.*"

"What about a man?"

"A man too." The ferry sounds its horn as it docks. "I have to go."

"*Trie-nnei-mi straight-o*," I smile.

"*Tienimi stretto*," he corrects, and hugs me tightly. "*Grazie bella*," he whispers.

As the ferry pulls away, I take a deep breath of cool wind. I look back over to the dock, but he's gone. The ferry plows steadily forward. I look down, watching the waves. From time to time, I see fish hurling themselves out of the water, into the air, crashing back down, to swim like me, haphazardly in some new direction. With the twenty-four percent charge my phone got in Tango's jeep on the way to the marina, I decide to read up on Renata Tebaldi.

NOTES ON ITALIAN WOMAN OF INFLUENCE:
Renata Tebaldi

1. Born: 1922, Pesaro, to a mother who had wanted to be a singer and a WWI vet father who played the cello.
2. Tough chick: Polio survivor! (Battled Polio age three to eight.)

Sang during the war—while traveling during wartime, her train came under machine gun fire. Co-star killed by a bomb before a performance—she still sang!

3. A lirico-spinto soprano, of *verismo* ("true") roles. The "realism" movement of Italian opera was like naturalism in world literature, seeking to portray a realistic world. Composers wrote about the lives of average people, not gods or royalty.

4. Fiery rivalry through 1950s with Maria Callas began with a joint performance in Brazil: Tebaldi took two ovations after both women had agreed not to. Their rivalry was based in this: expression of emotion through sound (Callas) vs. beauty and quality of sound (Tebaldi); this rivalry fanned their fame, with verbal barbs about each other quoted in *Time*.

5. How much of this was a Bette Davis vs. Joan Crawford style rivalry, exaggerated by male agents and press? There are positive quotes from each, and when Callas quit La Scala, Tebaldi announced she would not sing without Callas.

6. Tebaldi performed at: La Scala, San Francisco Opera, and at the Met. Tebaldi was known as "Miss Sold Out." She only sang in Italian. Even Wagner.

7. She never married: "How could I have been a wife, a mother and a singer?" she famously said to *The Times* in 1995.

8. By the end of her career, she'd performed 1,048 operas including: *Aida*, *La Bohème*, *Madama Butterfly*, *Tosca* (forty-five times!), *Otello*, and *Falstaff*.

9. "Tebaldi's soprano was rich and creamy, totally secure in technique and breath control." —*London Times*. "Dimples of iron." —Rudolf Bing, Met manager. "Your memory and your voice will be etched on my heart forever." —Pavarotti.

10. Died 2004. Museums to visit: Villa Pallavicino in Busseto and Castello di Torrechiara, Langhirano.

She was quite unique and yet, anyone who heard her could feel her emotion. "I was in love many times. This is very good for a woman." My mind drifts back to Florida. Back to Will. When he fell for me, did he know my island was too small? That I was going to leave? To break his heart? Did he choose love anyway? How did his date go? Did he meet someone without ants in her pants? Did he get *into* her pants? Just the thought makes me feel nauseated.

What was he doing right now? It was just after lunch there. He was probably sitting in his squad car, finishing his turkey and cheese sandwich from Which Wich and tossing the sliced pickles out the window for the pigeons. Maybe I'll just send him a message. Just to say *ciao*. My phone is on airplane mode to save charge, but I switch it back to normal. Instantly several messages pop up. My heart leaps a little. But no, none are from Will. My heart sinks a little. That's fine. *È meglio.* It's better.

YIN: having fun?

> **MOM:** Hi Marina, it's Mom. Did you change the settings on the printer? It's only printing blue. Are you having fun? There's a tropical storm south of Cuba named Catherine, like your aunt, isn't that funny? I wonder if it will leave a wake of destruction too? LOL (see I know how to do phone talk). I saved you a newspaper clipping about a Christian women's book writing fellowship in Miami. Don't forget to send me more photos. Love, Mom.

YANG: party car to Amalfi, DLT!—noon

Party car to Amalfi? All thoughts of Will, my mother, and home fly out of my head. Amalfi wasn't on my itinerary. I planned to take a bus to Salerno to research Trotula of Salerno, a pioneer of women's healthcare. But . . . party car to Amalfi? How can I decline? My phone rings.

"Hello?" I answer.

> "*Pronto. Ci siamo incontrati l'altra sera.*"

"I don't speak Italian. This is Marina Taylor. *Non capisco.*"

> "*Sì, Nati-vity Marina Tay-lor. Ho trovato il tuo portafoglio.*"

"*Portafoglio?*" (My wallet!) "Are you from the hotel?" I ask.

> "*No hotel. Le tue carte di credito, e ID* . . . I found near *la chiesa* . . . church." My heart leaps. It was Magwitch The Night Walker. He'd found my wallet! YES! God was rewarding me for imparting life lessons to young men.

> "*Non c'erano soldi.* No cash," says Magwitch. Ok-ay. God was rewarding me, minus the virgin tax.

Private Car, Highway SS163, Amalfi Coast: Thursday, 1:04 p.m.

Lady Gaga belts from the stereo of the private car Yin has hired with her mother's credit card. The sunroof is open and Yang is standing up, pretending to fly. All the windows are down. We're in our bikinis. Mimosas are flowing. Cool wind. Warm sun. The driver is a hot Italian woman— also in a bikini. Apparently you can order a lot of things in Italy. I wonder what else she's been hired for, but I don't ask. Life is good. We are hanging out the windows. We are in our seats. We are singing at the top of our lungs. A winding coastal road with amazing views around each turn. A kaleidoscope of eye candy whisks by us. Deep blue sea. Brightly colored villages wedged into hillsides, with houses stacked up like gumballs in a machine. White, wispy clouds. Magenta flowers cascading down trees. Beautiful green grass.

Side of Highway SS163, Amalfi Coast: Thursday, 1:45 p.m.
We are vomiting in the beautiful green grass.

Side of Highway SS163, Amalfi Coast: Thursday, 2:05 p.m.
We are peeing in the beautiful green grass (again).

Private Car, Highway SS163, Amalfi Coast: Thursday, 2:13 p.m.
We are sleeping in a pile.

Private Car, SS163, Amalfi Coast: Thursday, 2:25 p.m.
I wake to a buzz on my phone. I wipe Yang's drool off my arm as I pull my phone out of my pocket and try to focus on the message:

She bewitches me,
she kisses me,
I need no one else.
She is everywoman.
She is.

Wow! A love poem. But from whom? I look at the number and see a +33 country code. France? Can it be Frantonio? Did Yin give him my number after the dinner debacle in Positano? But why did he wait so long to text me? Or maybe it's Ernesto? He kept running out of money on his phone and texting me from other numbers. He wants to be a writer . . . so the poem makes sense. I stare at the words. Do I answer? As I ponder this, Yang sits bolt upright and shouts:

"Pull over I'm gonna spew again!"

Chapter 17

How Not to
Go Unnoticed

Piscine di Paradiso, Amalfi Coast: Thursday, 3:01 p.m.

We are late for lunch at a private hilltop swim club where we are to meet Yin's mother's friend, Regina. Our dresses are wrinkled. Our faces are wrinkled. Our hair is tangled. Our makeup is running. We have all smelled better. Much better. We are looking for one thing, the bathroom. A concierge heads us off at the entrance. No doubt we've wandered in by mistake, looking for the youth hostel or local women's shelter. He's about to throw us out when an alto voice turns our heads.

"Allora, there you are, darlings!" There in front of me is the most beautiful older woman I've ever met. She could be fifty or even sixty, but it's hard to tell and doesn't really matter. Her white chiffon dress floats around her like a sparkling mist, kissing her legs and shoulders, hugging her waist, plunging into her cleavage. Her smile is incandescent. She has a natural looking tan and radiant glow—the magnetism of Sophia Loren. She is a goddess. I feel like a roach in her presence. She embraces Yin with gusto. *"Belle comme toujours, chérie."* Turning to Yang, she kisses Yang on both cheeks. "And you, still full of trouble,

yes?" Finally, she's looking at me. "And who is this?" My antennae droop under her gaze. My wings twitch nervously. I want to scurry under the carpet. I am vile.

"This is our new friend, Marina Taylor. She's a writer from America."

"A writer! You have brought me another artist. *Fantastico! Benvenuta*, Marina Taylor, I am Regina. Please join us for lunch by the pool." She's Italian, but speaks perfect English with a British accent. Unlike Yang's, her accent is like a newly made bed—fresh, clean, with ironed sheets.

"We'll just . . . powder our noses first," says Yin, feeling as scuzzy as I do.

"Of course, dear. I'll order you girls some mimosas," she smiles. Yin and I look at each other. Oh, God. Please no.

UNHELPFUL HINTS FOR SOBERING UP IN THE BATHROOM:

1. Cold water in the face.
2. Have your friends slap you.
3. Run in place to sweat as much as you can.
4. Vomit.
5. Take a multi-vitamin.
6. Massage your hands and feet to increase circulation.
7. Press your naked skin against the cold tile of the wall.
8. Deep breaths of fresh air until you feel light-headed.

NOTE: none of these actions lower your blood alcohol level. The only thing that will help you sober up is TIME.

Yang has apparently decided to try the emergency sobering tactic of taking a huge shit right before you plan to drink more, because she kicked us out of the bathroom about ten minutes ago. Yin and I are sipping coffee and sitting quietly waiting for her. I look back at the mysterious poem message on my phone.

"Would you know anything about a certain French-Italian photographer requesting my phone number?" I ask.

"Would that be a good thing? Or a bad thing?" She returns with a smile. That doesn't really answer the question. The bathroom door swings open.

"Let's get out of here before someone goes in there and faints," says Yang.

Poolside Bar, Piscine di Paradiso: Thursday, 4:27 p.m.

"Sex is used to sell anything, anywhere in the world," smiles Regina. She was the reigning *regina di lussuria nazionale* (queen of the nation's lust) for twenty-five years. "Italian ads are just more honest about it," smiles Regina. She should know. Remember that rigatoni commercial I mentioned earlier? Starring in that ad was only the beginning for Regina. Films, television, magazines. She was an actress, model, European sex symbol. Regina even had her own talk show for a while, *Segreti del Sesso,* or "Secrets of Sex." It was half celebrity romance gossip and half advice for your love life. She interviewed actors, models, marriage counselors, gynecologists, plastic surgeons, famous mistresses, strippers, porn stars, call girls, and orgasm coaches (yes, these exist). Oprah meets Masters and Johnson. Who wouldn't watch that show? Okay, my mother wouldn't. But I certainly would. My phone buzzes again, but I decide not to check it in front of the other girls. I still haven't answered the poem text and prefer to keep my delicious secret for now.

"Yeah, I get what you're saying," says Yang, "I'm just not sure a topless model is going to make me want to buy toothpaste. It makes me want to suck on titties, not brush my teeth." Yang and Regina are embroiled in a discussion of the economics of the "sexual gaze" brought on by a commercial Yang saw on Italian cable at her hotel last night. They're enjoying mojitos while reclining on fluffy poolside cabana beds. Yin and I soak nearby in the pool and sip fizzy water. We're both done drinking. I listen, fascinated, as does a nearby hotel employee behind the wet bar as he shucks fresh oysters and arranges them on plates of ice between wedges of lemon and orchid blossoms.

"*After* you suck the titties, *then* you brush your teeth?" I suggest.

"No, she doesn't," says Yin.

"You are still affected by the commercial. You see something you want, you equate that with the product. The sexual gaze is a non-negotiable force of nature," says Regina.

"What, like gravity or inertia?" I laugh.

"*Esattamente*, yes. But the difference is, you cannot control gravity."

"The object on which the force is acting need not be passive," explains Yin, "but instead, control the gaze, and in so doing, the gazer. It's simple."

"Innit?" Yang reaches down and yanks the string of Yin's bikini. "You cunning little siren." Fair skinned, small perky breasts and nipples get a glimpse of sun, exposed to the world as Yin giggles and reorganizes her top. I glance over at Oyster Man, expecting him to have slashed a hole in his hand with his oyster knife, but he's not even giving the blonde waif a second glance. He's fixated on Regina, a woman thirty years older. She comes here a lot, so it's not just the fact that she's famous. He's surely captivated by her grace, confidence, style. There's a gentle power to her poise, a fluid sensuality to her movements. I watch him watch her. The way she holds her shoulders back as she gently shakes out her hair, unfolding a long graceful arm to retrieve a vintage sunhat. Arching her back slightly, she positions her hair under her hat, exposing a swanlike, bare neck. He drops something behind the bar and we hear glass break.

Oyster Man bends to clean it up, and as he stands, his furtive glance back at her is met by a simple, reassuring smile. He blushes. Regina lifts her glass, places her lips around her straw, and delicately drains the last of her mojito. Within mere seconds Oyster Man is by her side with a new drink.

"*Signora, un altro?*" he asks.

"*Ce l'ho.*" Our waiter has appeared simultaneously, also holding a mojito.

"Yeah, I'll take that, mate." Yang's mojito glass has been empty for ten minutes. As the men return to their corners, I glance around the pools and realize there are others, and they're not just men. A woman reclining by the saltwater pool has draped her body in the exact same position as Regina's, unconsciously mirroring.

"So, what you're sayin' is, basically men are just penis puppets," Yang says.

"No. Not just men. And not just sex. It's bigger than that and not as crass, *mon amour*," objects Yin.

"*Absolument, chèrie.* Sex is just one intention. Beauty and strength create desire, admiration, love. There is an energy that draws others. It is simple but powerful," explains Regina.

"Raw but not savage," I say.

"Precisely, my dear." Regina looks at me and smiles. My heart does a tiny cricket leap. So, I am not immune. I desire her approval. I desire her knowledge. I want to remember everything she says.

"The gaze is there," she says. "You may reject or embrace it."

"I embrace the energy," says Yang, slipping into the pool, wrapping her arms around Yin's waist, biting her gently on the neck. I take her spot next to the oracle.

"This energy is a female power," I say, toweling off.

"And should be used with respect," adds Yin.

"Not only female, but often female. This is because recognizing it takes awareness," Regina explains. "To command it you must first surrender to it."

"And some don't surrender easily." I am thinking of myself.

"I do not mean give yourself always. You can share in many ways," Regina says.

"Regina's like the Jedi master of sex," Yang laughs.

"Not exactly. But it's an art I've been practicing my whole life. Even as a girl, I noticed boys and men staring. The butcher saved me the best cuts of meat to take home to my mother. The florist let me take any flower I wanted from his shop. My brother's friends kicked the football at me, and when they got older, fought over who would fix my bike or carry my books. It was terrifying and wonderful. I could not escape it, so I embraced it. But twenty-five years in the public eye does teach you a lot about yourself." I digest this, nodding. The music from the nearby speakers breaks through my thoughts. It's a French love song, sung in English. "*She is everywoman. She is.*"

"I love this song," Yin smiles. "It's better in French, though."

"Marina is writing a book about influential women," Yin says to Regina.

"And sex," says Yang. "I told her to put a lot of sex in there."

"*È fantastico,*" Regina says. Then, to me, "You are writing every word we say into your brain as we speak, are you not, *scrittore?*" Regina laughs. "My dear, come and stay at my little villa on the hill. There are some other artists you should meet."

"Wow, that's so generous," I say, thrown. I look over at the floating pretzel that is now Yin and Yang.

"We're staying at Regina's too," Yang says.

"You can enjoy yourself, relax and write," Regina says.

"Alright, thank you," I say, trying not to sound like I just won the lottery.

"*Elle m'ensorcelle, elle m'embrasse, et je n'ai besoin de personne d'autre,*" Yin sings along with the song, but in French instead of English.

"The other artists will inspire you. Painters, musicians, a poet," says Regina. "Always creating. In fact, tomorrow there is a photo shoot in the garden. My friend visiting from Florence is a talented photographer with exhibitions all over Europe and millions of followers on Instagram," she says. Photographer? My stomach twists.

"You met him at dinner," says Yang with an evil grin. She means Frantonio, but I already know this.

"*Elle est chaque femme. Elle est,*" sings Yin. Suddenly, the words to the song that Yin is singing snap my brain to attention.

She bewitches me,
she kisses me,
I need no one else.
She is everywoman.
She is.

Elle est. The mysterious message was a song, not a poem. *Elle est* is a French love song. I smile to myself. Frantonio had called French the most powerful language in the world. The message had to be from him.

Chapter 18

How Not to Command the Gaze

Casa di Pavone: Thursday, 6:35 p.m.

Perched on a regal hilltop between Amalfi and Ravello, Regina's "little villa" is more like a small resort, with garden, fountains, pool, sauna, spa, terraces and patios with tables, loungers, couches, and winding steps that lead to more terraces and patios. That's just the outside. There's even a peacock that wanders around.

"He just showed up one day." (Of course he did.) "That's how we named the house," she explains. The inside is just as beautiful as the outside, simply yet fashionably done with retro Italian furniture from the sixties. *Objets d'art* and archaeological artifacts from all over the world decorate shelves: Egyptian vase, Aztec death mask, samurai sword. A vintage poster from the film *Le Mans* is autographed to Regina's father from Steve McQueen. "The first film I ever did was with Steve McQueen. He and my father would talk about cars and motorcycles for hours." (Of course he did.)

But this poster is not what demands your attention in the main living room. It is the large, black and white, nude photo of Regina that hangs between two windows. I am one hundred percent certain that nobody is ever looking *out* of those windows. It's Caravaggio meets Mapplethorpe: dramatic lighting and contrast that dilate your eyes, sinewy curves that tighten your jaw. I'd taken one photography course with my minor in art history, and my attempted nude self-portraits all had me looking uncomfortably constipated.

"My French-Italian photographer friend took that." (Of course he did.) My stomach tightens at the mention of Frantonio. Every time we enter a new room, I wonder if he's going to be there. Regina introduces me to a few people who are reading in the library, one in the kitchen, two more on a terrace, but so far, no Frantonio. I can't stop thinking about the mysterious message. Did he send it? Was he thinking about me too? I would find out soon.

A gorgeous young man who is certainly a stripper or Olympic swimmer greets us and takes my bag. "This is Piero, one of my assistants. He will show you to your room."

"Maybe you want to have a nap before dinner?" he says. I try not to stare at his perfect ass following him up the stairs. Maybe I want to have a *lap dance* before dinner. We take a series of halls and staircases. I should be dropping breadcrumbs.

My Room, Casa di Pavone: Thursday, 7:23 p.m.

Despite my exhaustion, I do not nap. The prospect of seeing Frantonio fills me with excitement and dread. In Roma, I'd rejected the sexual gaze, as if I'd not publicly invited it. Then in Positano, I'd courted it back again, but lost control on the curve. Amateur. Regina would have crossed the finish line. I try to remember what she said. I have to surrender to the power of the gaze if I am to master the force. Ok-ay, but what did all that sexual *Star Wars* crap mean in real terms?

GUIDELINES FOR COMMANDING THE SEXUAL GAZE:

1. **Receive the Gaze:** Do not be afraid of your own allure. It's not always about sex. It is part of you, like your shadow, only the opposite. It's the fire inside you that attracts others. No matter what you look like, you have this. Find it. Light it.
2. **Interpret the Gaze:** Determine the gazer's intent: love, admiration, or desire? Some want merely to bask in the warmth of your fire. Some want to burn like you do. And, others want you to light their fires.
3. **Respect the Gaze:** Do not underestimate the power of the gaze. It can burn both ways. If someone wants something from you, the power lies with you. Do not abuse it. If your intents match, act. If not, extinguish flames immediately.
4. **Command the Gaze:** This does not always mean action. Sometimes a slow burning candle is better than a bonfire.

"Marina?" It's Yin at the door.

"Quit flicking your bean and get out here, DLT. Cocktails on the terrace." And Yang.

"I'm almost ready, I'll meet you there," I answer. Actually I'm in my underwear and haven't done my hair. I stare at my list of rules. Ridiculous. How is this going to help me? Frantonio is a professional gazer. He gets paid to record his gaze and share it with others. But he did photograph me dancing around a fountain in Rome. Okay. Accept the gaze: I'm gaze worthy. In Positano, he followed me to the bathroom and kissed me. Interpret the gaze: he wants me to light his fire. He's an attractive, talented, wealthy French-Italian artist, and a very good kisser. Yes, I want to light it. Respect the gaze: our intents match. Now, I just have to command the gaze. My attempt at a bonfire backfired, so I'm going for the slow burn. I got this. I dig out my ridiculously uncomfortable stilettos. They're now torturously uncomfortable thanks to my Capri blisters.

Dining Terrace, Casa di Pavone: Thursday, 8:16 p.m.

I make my entrance into the dining terrace with a slow glide that's meant to be graceful, the way Regina floats as if she had wheels instead of feet. I lead with my breasts, arms swinging, hips swaying. But, every two feet my heels stick between cobblestones on the terrace.

"You hurt yourself, DLT? Why you walkin' like a prossie with lead boots?" Yang hands me a glass of wine. How is she still drinking? The English and Irish have hollow legs. I'll just hold the glass so nobody offers me another. The large, open terrace is lit with beautiful hanging lights and candles. A waterfall gurgles. A man sitting on a bench plays guitar as a young woman next to him sings softly. I notice a camera set up on a tripod between the bar and the koi pond. Frantonio must be here somewhere.

"I like your dress," offers Yin. I'm wearing a backless plum-colored halter dress, made of silk. I hung it inside the shower stall during my shower to steam out the wrinkles. It fell. Now it has no wrinkles because it's wet. But nobody else knows that.

"Why are you wet, mate?" Yang asks.

"I'm not wet," I say.

"You sweatin'? You nervous or something?" Yang asks.

"No, I'm fine." I glance around. There are about eighteen people enjoying cocktails and wine, some standing, some seated at the table, or on couches and benches. "Are all these people staying here too?" I ask.

"No, some are local friends and others are models, in town for the photo shoot tomorrow," explains Yin. As she says this, my eyes fall on Frantonio.

"But he is," says Yang pointedly. Frantonio is wearing a light blue dress shirt with the top two buttons open, and a stylish sports coat. His hair a bit ruffled; he's got blue-rimmed glasses, elegant and manly at the same time. Leaning against a column, chatting with two gorgeous women, Frantonio doesn't even notice me. "Maybe you should check if his prick is still broken from the other night," laughs Yang. I watch Frantonio put his arm around one of the girls with a flowing red mane. "Scratch that," she says. "Looks like it's back in working order."

"Be nice." Yin elbows her. The second girl also drapes herself on Frantonio.

"I am. She doesn't need to be wastin' her time with that arsehole photographer anyway. He's got an ego the size of Russia." She leans in closer. "Look at all these gorgeous girls, mate, try something different." She raises an eyebrow at me.

I'm looking at the gorgeous girls—hanging on Frantonio. I position myself in his field of view and laugh loudly at Yang's suggestion, as if I'm having the time of my life. He doesn't look over. How am I supposed to command the sexual gaze of a man who's not even looking? The guitar player transitions into a faster piece by the Gypsy Kings. I'm suddenly filled with purpose.

"Let's dance," I say.

"There's not really a dance floor," Yin says.

"We'll make our own, near the bar," I say as I pull her by the hand, closer to the music . . . and Frantonio. But he still doesn't look at me.

"Nobody else is dancing," says Yin shyly. But I'm already moving around her, swaying my body to the sexy sounds of the guitar. Yin joins in, half-heartedly. I twirl slowly and sensually—but Frantonio isn't watching me, he's flirting with the redhead. Sliding up behind Yin, I pull her to me by her hips. Our bodies move together as one.

"Yeah baby." Yang is enjoying this heartily. Frantonio is oblivious. The music gets faster. I spin Yin out and dip her over the fishpond. She squeals as the tips of her hair skim the surface. I twirl her quickly, flinging droplets of water from her flying hair onto the small crowd of people now watching us. Frantonio is still not looking. I raise my arm for Yin to spin me, and she does. Around and around I go. I break free and keep twirling, faster, across the stones like a ballerina, knocking into the tripod, sending the camera crashing into the fishpond. *Now*, Frantonio is looking at me.

Chapter 19

How Not to Apologize

Dining Terrace, Casa di Pavone: Thursday, 8:38 p.m.

I cannot breathe. I cannot see straight. The party now looks like Picasso's Guernica mural: gasping faces, arms in the air, wailing heads floating toward me—how did that screaming horse get in here? The music has stopped. Everything has stopped. People are staring at me, and at the sunken camera with tripod legs sticking out of the water like a giant, upside-down, drowning insect.

IF YOU ever find yourself in this situation, DEFINITELY DO NOT:

1. ~~Cry.~~ Okay you can cry.
2. Yell, "It's fine, it's fine, these new ones are all waterproof! The underwater shots of the fish are going to be totally amazing!"
3. Laugh hysterically while you cry.
4. Tell everyone to stand back as you jump into the pond.
5. Climb out of the pond, clutching the camera to your breast like a rescued puppy, tripod legs sticking out behind you.

6. Run dripping and barefoot through the house with tripod legs knocking into antique furniture, slipping and sliding on the tile in the wrong hallway, and burst into the wrong room where an old lady is getting dressed.

My Room, Casa di Pavone: Thursday, 8:55 p.m.

Why am I such a walking disaster? My mother is a complete klutz, hurting herself all the time. Maybe it's genetic. Even as a girl, I was falling, crashing, bungling my way through one debacle after the next. Aunt Catherine used to say my mind was always three steps ahead of my body. I think she's right.

Now, sweat beads on my forehead as I hover over the bed, holding a hairdryer set on "low-cool" at a forty-five degree angle to the army of tiny camera pieces lined up in formation across the bed. Online emergency instructions to just "open it up and dry it out" seemed like a good idea when I started, but now I want to hunt down whatever nerd typed that and throttle him. There's no easy way to "open it up." The first piece led to the second, to the third, to the one hundred and sixtieth. The warranty is definitely void on this baby now. Of course, that was probably true when it flooded with fish poo water. As I wave the dryer in circles, I wonder how I'm going to get it back together, and if the elderly Italian woman I barged in on is now lying dead of a heart attack. Her door looked just like mine. Honest mistake.

"Open the door, DLT," demands Yang. "You've been hiding long enough. I've brought you something you need." I switch off the hairdryer and open the door. There stands Yang with the samurai sword from the living room. "I can hold it for you while you throw yourself onto it, see?" She demonstrates.

"Thanks." I do not laugh.

"I'm just fuckin' with ya. You're overreacting. Regina's rich as fuck, she can get another camera." It turns out the camera is Regina's. Somehow this makes me feel worse. Yang follows me into the room and sees the five million tiny camera pieces, laid in orderly rows of increasing size. "Holy shit, mate!" She loses it, laughing so hard she has to put the sword down.

"Don't touch!" I turn the hair dryer back on and resume my hopeless operation. "Who's the old woman? Did I kill her?"

"Regina's ex-mother-in-law? She lives here, used to all sorts, don't worry. It's a simple cock up. The whole thing was like hugely entertaining. Somebody called you Buster Keaton after you ran out."

"*Perfetto.*"

"Regina's not cross. The only one who got bent was that pretentious photographer, 'cause he'd taken some shots before you came outside. Fuck him."

"No. That will clearly not be happening now."

"Good. Come out and talk to that cracking hot singer, DLT. I think she likes you. She had people helping her write a funny song about you. It was like a game."

"What?" My heart sinks.

"Yeah." She sings, "Kooky American girl likes to twirl, but grace turns to dis-grace in a whirl—"

"Stop! *Basta!*" I turn the hairdryer on Yang. I love this new Italian word.

"That feels good. Do my pits. What was the second part of the song?"

"Get out, please. I don't want to hear the song."

"No it's really good, there's a bit where she rhymes mortification with slutty gyration and ruined vacation. Everyone's so fuckin' creative around here."

"GET OUT!" I throw a pillow. Yang ducks and moves for the door, laughing.

"Don't stay in here all night, DLT. You need to eat to keep your strength up for your next comical catastrophe." I throw another pillow and it hits the back of the door as she closes it. Great. I had been given a free stay at an impossibly amazing villa with fellow artists and writers . . .

who were now composing ballads about my blunders. Where do you go from here? I will just stay in my room until the morning and then slip out while everyone was still asleep. Feeling tears welling up in my eyes again, I turn the hairdryer on my face to fight them back. Eyes wide like a lizard, I try not to blink as my eyeballs dry out. Another knock.

"Go away, Yang! I'm not coming out." But she knocks again. Angrily I throw the hairdryer down, pick up the samurai sword, stomp over to the door, and throw it open. It's Frantonio. He sees the sword and takes a step back and holds up his hands. Sport coat off, his face a bit flushed from the wine, he's now looking more relaxed.

"I come in peace," he says. "You proved your Amazonian might in Positano."

"Sorry, I thought you were someone else," I say, putting the sword down.

"I came to help with the prognosis," he says.

"Come in, see for yourself," I say.

"Putain de merde!" he whispers in disbelief, staring at the bed. A smile spreads across his face as he looks back at me. "How is the surgery going, doctor?" He's teasing but not mocking. Maybe he's not angry. I muster some gumption.

"When I put it back together it's going to be an espresso machine," I say. He laughs. This is encouraging. "I'm very sorry about your photos," I say. "And, for kneeing you in the balls in Positano. And, for ripping your shirt. And, for thinking you were trying to abduct me and sell me into sex slavery back in Rome. Did I miss anything?"

"Don't think so. But we will start a list so you can make it up to me," he smiles.

"What?"

"Your *incroyables* fuck-ups? You are talented there."

"Well you must have a good view from such a high seat," I say. Arrogant bastard. He laughs and takes my chin with two fingers, winking at me.

"That's what I like about you Americans. You're proud even as you fall."

"Nobody's falling, anywhere," I stammer. Who does he think he is? "I take it back. I'm not sorry, for anything, you photo stealing jerk!" My hands are shaking. "Just because you get paid to take pretty, pervy photos, doesn't mean you can take them without asking!" I don't realize how loud my voice is.

"No, shh shh shh." He turns and half closes the door. His voice is soft. "*S'il vous plaît, ma chèrie.* You are right. I am sorry for taking those photos of you without your permission," he cedes. "But, I am not sorry I took them. They are fantastic. I have caught a fifth fountain nymph, turned from stone to precious flesh, sprung to life in a sublime moment of pure *joie de vivre.* Wet, wild, and alive. This is not 'pervy,' this is raw beauty. If I see this and do nothing, I cannot call myself an artist. I had no choice." I stare at him, wordless. He's an artist all right. A bullshit artist. But, though he is unapologetic, there is no trace of contempt. He seems utterly sincere. Raw beauty?

"Fine then," I take a deep breath. "Show me the photos."

"They are at my studio in Firenze."

"Convenient," I say, annoyed.

"I will show you, *ma chèrie,*" Frantonio says. "But please do not take them from me." His eyes blink, silently sincere. He reaches out and takes my hand gently. Without warning, the security blanket of my anger is whipped away, leaving me totally exposed. I squirm. Leaning over, I pluck the camera's memory card from my pillow and put it into his hand.

"Here. You can still save the group photos you took." I take micro-steps backward as I babble nervously. "Stellar Phoenix Photo Recovery can recover inaccessible photos from SD cards. Just preview all recover-able photos and hit the recover tab."

"A little online reading?" he smiles, slipping the card into his pocket.

"Not the first time I've dunked a card," I admit.

"Or yourself." His gaze is soft and steady. I shrug, trying not to look directly into his brown eyes. Instead I look at his perfectly rumpled hair. How is it always perfectly rumpled? He reaches out and touches my side. "You're still in your wet dress?"

"This one you're supposed to wear wet." I think he's going to take his hand away, but he doesn't. The warmth of it permeates the damp silk of my dress and sends a shiver through me. Does he still want me? *Did* he send that message?

"*Elle est,*" I whisper with a smile.

"One of my favorite songs," he smiles. *It was him!* I knew it. "*She is everywoman.*"

"*Oui* but much better in French." He sings, "*Faire danser mes doigts sur son dos.*" He slides his hand down my bare back. "To dance my fingers down her back."

"I don't slow dance," I whisper weakly as I take a step backward. We were making out like teenagers by the bathroom back in Positano, why am I nervous? He takes his glasses off, slips them into the breast pocket of his shirt. Is he going to kiss me? Am I going to let him? He moves closer. His face is inches from mine.

"*Elle m'ensorcelle, elle m'embrasse . . .*" He says this last with his warm lips on mine. He tastes like salty olives and oranges. I kiss him back. He kisses me harder. My hand is now in his perfectly rumpled hair. It's soft and fine between my fingers. My tongue is in his sweet, salty mouth. His left hand slides down my bare back into my dress, to my ass. The fingers on his other hand expertly unhook the halter strap behind my neck, and suddenly plum-colored silk is swiftly cascading down my chest to hang limply at my waist, revealing both my breasts. I come up for air. Is this happening? I step back again, and now my back is against the wall. "*The door is open!*" shouts Modesty, clawing her way into my consciousness.

"The door's open a little," I whisper.

"*Now* you are shy? After the fountain and the bathroom?" He pushes me gently up against the bedroom wall. "Don't worry, *chèrie.* Everyone is busy." He kisses me more deeply and hungrily, his teeth gently raking my tongue. I forget the door. I abandon Modesty on the high ground and dive headlong into Frantonio. I *am* falling. We kiss long and hard. We cannot get enough of each other. It's like our mouths are fucking. My chest heaves as my breathing grows faster. Frantonio pulls his chin back, also breathing heavily. Our foreheads pressed together, he looks down at my chest. As his left hand grips firmly onto my ass, his right begins to caress my breasts, my nipples, my belly, my navel. Goosebumps ripple across my skin. I can feel my *figa* tingling, getting wetter by the second. My heart thumps loudly. I'm sure he can hear it, feel it.

"That tickles," I laugh, shivering.

"You like being tickled? *Oui*?"

"*Oui*," is all I can manage. My body is shaking, not because I'm cold. "Your breasts and belly are exquisite. Like the Venus de Milo," he murmurs, entranced. He now holds a breast in each hand. He squeezes them gently, stroking, tickling as if he's sculpting my body. Wow. My breasts and belly are *exquisite*? I am the beautiful Venus de Milo. I smile to myself as he turns his attention to my neck, kissing my throat, my collarbone. His hands over my shoulders, down my back, to my ass. He leans into me, burying his face in my hair as his hands massage my ass cheeks. Wait. Isn't the Venus de Milo the one with no arms? How exactly am I supposed to grope him back with no—

"OH!" My wandering mind is yanked back like a dog on a leash. His left hand has slipped lower and the tips of his fingers are now exploring my *figa* from behind. I react, stepping forward, but this only pushes my bare breasts against his chest, enfolding me further into his embrace. His heart is now pounding too. Our chests are smashed together, mine sweating. There's sweat on his neck as it rubs against my cheek. The crown of his head presses against the wall as he leans over me. His fingers slide deeper inside me. Tickling and teasing. In and out.

"*Ç'bon*?" he asks, his breath quickened too.

"*Sì . . . oui . . .* whatever, yes!" My hips push involuntarily into his. I can feel his hard cock pressed against my now throbbing *figa*. A moan escapes my lips. He holds me tightly against him, plunging his fingers deeper. In and out. In and—Oh, my, G-ood. It's so fucking good.

My knees start to buckle, and now I'm whimpering softly, but he doesn't let me go. Frantonio's right hand holds my ass firmly in place as his left fingers fuck me faster and harder. Again and again. In and out. The blood rushes to my head. My back arches. My legs fold. I cry out, and he covers my lips with his mouth. Kissing me one last time as I gasp for air, Frantonio guides me gently down the wall, where I collapse onto my knees. I can't remember my name. Suddenly I remember to breathe, and I suck in sweet oxygen as I resurface from my deep orgasmic dive. I see him pull out a green cotton handkerchief with white stripes. He wipes his wet fingers. Who carries handkerchiefs anymore? Does he carry *that* for after he does *this*? Do I care? I don't care. I love those fingers. He crouches next to me.

"My dear, you have fallen," he says softly, as I sit helplessly before him on the floor. I am speechless. I have no clever come back. "You should come eat something. You look weak." He winks, adjusts his pants, and then he's gone. Bastard.

Chapter 20

How Not to
Admit Defeat

1. Take a cold shower. Twice.
2. Sit between your friends at dinner.
3. Don't make eye contact with him for more than five seconds.
4. Do not picture him naked in your head.
5. Pretend he's a dentist.
6. Do not visualize him on top of you in the dentist chair.
7. Pretend he's a telemarketer.
8. Do not wonder if he's good at phone sex.
9. Sit tall and proud, with your shoulders back and your tits up.
10. Forget that less than an hour ago you were reduced to a puddle of whimpering pleasure on the floor.

Dining Terrace, Casa di Pavone: Thursday, 10:01 p.m.

Frantonio's smugness is almost as unbearable as my body's unquenchable response every time he comes near me. When he sits opposite me at dinner, I wonder if I'm going to taste anything I eat. Over the pasta course there is a debate, in Italian, about Martina Stella's latest film, which I have not seen. Then Frantonio surprises me.

"Why don't we speak in English so everyone can understand."

"That's okay, I haven't seen it," I smile, embarrassed that I'm the only one at the table who doesn't speak Italian.

"Ms. Taylor, Regina tells me you're writing a book about influential Italian women," says Frantonio. "I do hope you're planning to include Virginia Oldoini?" I give him a blank look, start to feel stupid, but then decide to own it.

"I'd love to. Who is she?"

"Virginia, the Countess of Castiglione, was the selfie queen of 1800's Paris."

"—and Napoleon's mistress," Yang chimes in. "Don't leave out the sex."

"The sex is always there," says Frantonio. "You needn't go looking for it. It's the art that matters. The countess was quite influential in the early history of photography. But, that's all I will say. I won't rob you of the joy of chasing down the rest of her story on your own."

"Well I do love a good challenge," I smile.

"Good for you, Ms. Taylor. Most of us grab our phones anytime we have a question. We cannot resist instant gratification at the touch of our fingers." He waves his two fingers in the air and stares back at me with a smug smile. "It's refreshing to meet someone who can." *Touché.*

"Au contraire, I like a quick taste to whet my appetite just like anyone else, but that just makes me hungrier. You've got to plunge in deep if you want real satisfaction," I smile. "Don't you agree?"

"*Absolument,*" he agrees, raising an eyebrow. Checkmate. Others are now wondering if we're still talking about research. Yin knows we're not.

"You pair sound like a couple of swots!" snorts Yang. "Have your nerd fest in the library after dinner. Let's get back to movie goss. Is Billie Piper gonna get her gear off again in her new film, or what?" At this point, a very handsome cook enters and places a giant silver bowl in front of our hostess.

"*Allora,* here is the *cioppino,*" announces Regina, "I thought, in honor of our American friend, we'd do an Italian-American mash-up." She smiles at me, and I nod. Regina lifts the lid off of the bowl and a cloud of steam billows out like a piñata of smells, launching nose candy in every direction. People react—this is a special dish. Regina serves up bowls and passes them down the table. I realize with a lurch that *cioppino* is seafood stew. I don't eat fish. Maybe I can fake it and fill up on bread? All the guests are ooh-ing and ah-ing over their bowls of magical stew. Everyone except Frantonio, who is staring at me. I stare back. Is this a contest? Each of us refuses to look away.

Our bowls land in front of us. But still we stare. Decadent scents of rich tomato, fish, crab, shrimp, and garlic tickle our noses. I try not to inhale. Why did it have to be fish? I focus on him. Who is the gazer and who is controlling the gaze? The steam from Frantonio's soup fogs his glasses up. He chuckles as he looks down, removes his glasses, wipes them clean. Yes! I win. I control the gaze! He glances up, his light brown eyes blinking long, curly lashes at me, and smiles. The candlelight softly lights his beautiful face. He's gorgeous. I suddenly see that I have it backward. I am gazing at him. He's controlling my gaze.

"Way too hot to dive in," he warns with a wink. "Some things take patience." Later, when dessert is served, Frantonio bids us all *"Buona notte."* He has to get his rest before he shoots tomorrow. I pretend to be focused on my *torta al cioccolato*. But then he is behind my chair, leaning in. He whispers, *"Sogni d'oro, bella."* I hope it means: "Meet me in my room in ten minutes. I cannot bear to sleep without your beautiful, naked body next to mine." But, sadly, it does not. Damn.

"Dreams of gold," Yin translates for me. How sweet, I think. But, you have to sleep in order to dream.

My Room, Casa di Pavone: Friday, 1:12 a.m.

No rest for the wicked. Unable to restrain myself, I'd texted him back around midnight. I thought I was being clever picking a new song:

> *There's a star above, winking at me*
> *It's you, I know. It's you I see.*

But he must be asleep. No response. My mind keeps replaying the scene that transpired in this very room, only hours ago. I must find something creative to do. My eyes fall on the pile of camera pieces.

Hallway, Casa di Pavone: Friday, 1:20 a.m.

I walk through the now still house carrying a small bag. My goal is to find some tools or glue or something. I creep past an open balcony, and a cool breeze off the ocean carries in cigarette smoke and low voices from some unseen terrace above. Walking past a door, I hear people having sex. I walk more quickly. Descending the short stairwell at the end of the hall, I hear the faint sound of music. Is that ... Bob Dylan? Following the gravely tones, I venture down another set of stairs and then a third. Bob's voice grows slowly louder until I'm standing in a small, open studio.

It's filled with bits of junk, materials of all forms, and sculptures of all kinds. Clay. Metal. Organic materials. There's a giant dog made of watch parts. A watch dog? In the middle of the rubble, a very small, very old woman glues coins onto a cow skull. My first instinct is to turn around. Here, you'll remember my allergy to old people. South Florida is ruled by a blue-haired mafia with a high turnover rate. They keep rock concerts out of the park and vote against same sex marriage. But *this* oldie was singing Bob Dylan. I could tell she was different.

"'The Hiiigh-waaay siiixty-one.'" Rosalie would love this. She's a closet Dylan fan.

"Mi scusi, signora?" She does not hear me. I walk around a nearby table slowly, so as not to startle her. Her gray hair is piled high into a sculpture of its own atop of her head, like an inverted silver tornado struggling to escape a myriad of hair pins—wood, metal, jeweled. I'm now standing right in front of her. It's the same woman I startled when I burst into the wrong room earlier. She's obviously not deaf, but she doesn't look up. Her hands move confidently and rhythmically, sorting coins, selecting the right one, finding the perfect spot on the skull, and gluing it into place. She's blind, I realize. I reach over and turn the music off. She looks up immediately.

"Chi è?"

"Hi, sorry to interrupt," I reply. She turns to face me.

"Sei tornata?" Her Italian dialect sounds different from what I've heard so far on my trip.

"Do you speak English?"

"L'inglese? Sì. 'Blowin' in the Wind?'" she says. I smile, thinking of another song title.

"'Like a Rolling Stone'?" I reply. The sculptor smiles. "I love your work," I say.

"'Don't Think Twice, It's All Right,'" she replies.

"'It Ain't Me Babe,'" I counter. She slaps her hand on the table with vigor and laughs heartily, startling me. I can see from her grin she's missing a tooth. She reaches toward me, beckoning. I have passed her test. I let her squeeze my hand, feel my shoulders, my face.

"'Forever Young,'" she grins. Another one of Bob's songs. She pats my cheek. Her finger feels the chain around my neck and she lifts the tiny star made of gold wire. *"Una piccola stella?"*

"Little star, *sì*. I made it myself, but I'm not very artistic." I remember the bag I'm holding and turn to the workbench next to us. Carefully I empty out the contents. Hearing the tinkling and clicking of metal and plastic, her hands investigate the small pile of camera pieces. Her fingers expertly twist and turn each piece like a spider with an insect.

"Mi aiuti?" I ask for help. "It was a camera . . . *una fotocamera."*

"Un macchina fotographica?" She makes a disparaging noise with her mouth as she shakes her head, unimpressed with my request. *"Forse qualcosa di meglio?"* she counters.

"Something better?" I think about this. Yang was right, Regina would just buy another. What would be better? Then I smile. "Un *pavone?"*

"Un pavone?" She lays her hands flat on the pieces, closing her eyes to visualize. *"Un pavone. Sì. Perfetto."* She reaches under the bench and pulls out a stool for me. *"Riaccendi la mia musica,"* she says, motioning to the stereo. I walk over and switch the music back on. She smiles. Together

we sit. Together we sort the pieces according to size to make a peacock. Together we sing Dylan. *Perfetto.*

Library, Casa di Pavone: Friday, 8:42 a.m.

Everyone is still asleep. I have found Regina's library. The room is stunning. Walls covered with wooden shelves full of ancient tomes and new paperbacks. Marble floors and faint smells of incense and old paper. Pages of illustrated books, hand lettered by monks, hang in gilded frames on every wall. Warm light from Tiffany stained glass lamps completes the ethereal effect. As a writer, I'm awestruck.

Having taken Frantonio's bait, I'm reading about Virginia Oldoini. It will be fun to talk to him about her. Because I can find only one short entry about her in a book Regina has, most of my digging is online. I'm struck first by the unique photos I keep finding. She was stunning and mysterious.

NOTES ON ITALIAN WOMAN OF INFLUENCE: Virginia Oldoini

1. Known as the Countess of Castiglione, born 1837 in Florence.
2. The daughter of a Marquis, she was married to a count at seventeen.
3. Went to Paris in 1855 to discuss Italian unity with Napoleon, and ended up his lover.
4. Known for her flamboyant and exciting costumes at court (e.g. the Queen of Hearts), her exceptional beauty, and her eyes that apparently changed their color.
5. At court she met photographers Mayer and Pierson, and began to sit for portraits, wearing her elaborate costumes.
6. After the affair she returned to Italy, which was declared a kingdom not long after. Had she bewitched the mighty Napoleon on behalf of her homeland? Many think so.
7. She spent her fortune and forty years directing Pierson in

elaborate photo shoots, many of which tried to recreate moments of her life.

8. Some of the photos, showing her bare legs and feet, were considered hot and scandalous for the day. Her head was cropped out.

9. There were over seven hundred photos. Four hundred and thirty-three are at the Met.

10. Must find and read: *La Divine Comtesse* by Robert de Montesquiou.

I realize how much Regina and the countess have in common. Both the subject of hundreds of photos, representing both art and fashion. Each had power, arguably derived from beauty, and each parlayed that into control of the public gaze. But, while Regina spent years cultivating her image as a whole, the countess directed each individual image or photo. Complete control of how she was seen. I wonder if it took seven hundred photos for Virginia to find herself through photos. Or did it take these men seven hundred photos to finally capture how she saw herself? Both she and Regina are utterly self-aware. Am I?

So far, I've been at this house less than twenty-four hours and I'm already the subject of comedic ballads. I must somehow revise everyone's opinion. Until I come up with a good plan, I vow to keep my head down, lie low.

Chapter 21

How Not to
Lie Low

Garden, Casa di Pavone: Friday, 10:54 a.m.

In the still cool light of late morning, I sit at a table in the garden next to Regina, sipping my second cappuccino. We're talking about the Countess of Castiglione. Regina found one of Virginia Oldoini's original photos at an auction once. She purchased it, but in the end, donated it to a museum in Milan.

We both watch Frantonio. He's setting up already. Working around the fountain in her garden, which is now turned off. I had an answer to my midnight text waiting for me this morning when I awoke.

A flower blossoms under the sun,
Like I blossom in your arms,
I come alive with you.

It's a different lyric from the same song I picked. He's good. Regina leans in and whispers to me.

"I think our photographer has secretly found some of the Countess's photos and keeps them locked away at his studio in Firenze," she smiles. "You should ask him."

"You remind me of her," I say.

"Me?"

"Yes," I answer. "Beautiful camera candy with a strong sense of self." Regina laughs.

"It is a strange compliment that I will accept with honor. *Grazie.*" Here, another of Regina's impossibly handsome assistants brings me a second chocolate croissant and Regina an orange juice. I have no doubt it was freshly squeezed by his strong, young hands, moments ago.

"*Grazie*, Piero," says Regina. After he walks away, I look at her, puzzled.

"His name is also Piero?" I ask, remembering the gorgeous assistant who showed me to my room when I arrived yesterday.

"They're all called Piero actually," she laughs. "It's so hard to remember their names, they come and go every season practically. But number four's been with me a while."

"You rename them all?" I say, incredulous.

"No! That would be ridiculous," she says, sipping her juice. "I only hire boys named Piero." Oh. Right, I think. This is much less ridiculous.

"All your Pieros are very beautiful," I comment with a smile.

"*Sì*, but they're not just pretty. Piero #1 is an excellent chef. Piero #2 is a bartender, training to be a sommelier. Piero #3 works miracles with my roses, and Piero #4 helps me organize the guests, my travel, everything."

"Number four looks like an Olympic swimmer," I say.

"Retired Turkish football player," she explains.

"Named Piero?"

"That's what his CV said," she laughs. "I think he just wanted the job." An injury ended his career prematurely. Now he's doing some courses for sports medicine, including massage therapy. If there's anything you need his help with, just ask him. I'm sure he'd be eager to assist you." She gives me a coy look. I stare—is she saying what I think she's saying?

"Oh, I'm fine. But thank you." I feel myself blushing. "I'll keep that in mind." Then, as if summoned by my embarrassment, Piero #4 appears with some papers for Regina to sign. I try not to stare at the biceps peeking out of his polo shirt.

"Piero, did you meet Marina yesterday? She's a writer from Miami."

"Yes, we did meet yesterday. *Ciao*, Marina." He nods at me. Then, "I love Miami. It is hot, beautiful, and exciting all the time." He runs a hand through his wavy black hair.

"Just like Marina," Regina says.

"*Sì è vero*. It's true." He grins, and his eyes sparkle. "Sorry I missed your dancing last night."

"No. You didn't miss anything," I say, horrified.

"Perhaps you didn't have the right partner," he says. Is he flirting with me? "I am good with my feet, and other things . . . ." Yes, he is definitely flirting with me. I glance at Regina, but she's focused on the papers he brought her to sign.

"So I hear." Regina hands the papers back to #4.

"*Allora*. I have work to do, if you'll excuse me," he says. "But I am always around. I am easy to find. If you want me." With a wink, he's gone.

Thanks to the talents of "Bob" (my nocturnal artist friend), Regina's camera is now a stunning peacock mosaic glued to wood. She is delighted, and it currently holds a place of pride on a shelf over the bar. Apparently, Bob always sleeps during the day and works at night. "Some nights she turns herself into a bat to fly around the countryside, swooping into open windows. She sits on bedposts watching people's dreams, you know, for inspiration. She uses her radar," confides Regina.

"Sonar. Bats use sound waves to see," I correct her. Why this has caught me up, instead of "she turns into a bat and watches people's dreams," I have no idea.

"*Sì*, but she is Sicilian, so . . . ." I wait, but that's the end of her explanation. Yin and Yang have not emerged from their room, and I expect I won't see them until the photo shoot. They both plan to participate.

Frantonio's vision, as Regina explains it to me, is "to build a majestic fountain out of unclothed people, with water cascading across their bodies, frozen in postures of strength and beauty, as if they themselves are made of stone. Isn't he *fantastico*?"

"*Fantastico*," I agree, not referencing the same skills.

"He will position every model now. We will shoot in the final hour of daylight. *L'ora d'oro*. Golden hour. Then the fountain will flow." I watch Frantonio, linen pants and designer shirtsleeves rolled up. He belongs to the class of Italians who don't own T-shirts and make elegant dress clothes seem casual. Regina's class. I'm sitting here in my goofy sun hat, tank, and shorts. She's buttoned up to the bosom in a soft, lilac-colored cotton dress with ruffled skirt and thin lines of lace over each shoulder. The effect—with her golden tanned skin—is not unlike an upside-down cupcake with lavender frosting. I make a mental note to avoid seeing her closet, certain it will ruin me for life. "There he goes, into the water," she smiles.

Frantonio wades into the fountain to take focus measurements. He is meticulous and focused as he works. As I watch him, images of last night flash through my mind. In the fountain he adjusts his glasses. In my head I see those same glasses slip into his breast pocket as he smiles at me with a calm, hungry intention. In the fountain he runs his hand through his hair. In my mind I see my hand, grabbing his hair as he kisses my breasts. In the fountain he wiggles his fingers absently as he visualizes his upcoming creation. In my mind his hand is sliding down my ass, those same fingers slipping deeply—

"He'll begin placing people, designing and sculpting the shot he wants," Regina's voice snaps me out of my daydream. "Then we'll take a break before the shoot." Beautiful people, scantily clad, have trickled into the garden. Some couples are clearly in the afterglow of morning sex. Other people whisper quietly, watching. Frantonio walks over to his phone, which is sitting on a small speaker, and soon a French aria is floating through the garden. The breeze sends tiny fuchsia snowflakes drifting down from the crepe myrtle trees. A white cat watches from a bench. The peacock struts around. It's quite the scene. We're only a few goats and an ecstasy tablet shy of Bosch's *Garden of Earthly Delights*.

As Frantonio places the models one by one in the fountain, posing and adjusting them like live mannequins, I can see them each respond to his easy, affable manner. He is patient and respectful. His calm voice is confident and disarming. People outside the fountain wait with silent ardor.

"They crave his gaze," I remark.

"He is a master," Regina agrees. I realize I'm smiling just watching him. He continually checks his frame and returns to gently adjust an arm here or a leg there. As time passes, nobody seems to care that he or she has been standing in the same awkward position for nearly half an hour. They bask in his attention. As the Russian redheaded model balances on the "top tier" of his creation that is slowly growing, she teeters and slips, giving a high yelp. But Frantonio catches her. They're both laughing as he guides her gorgeous, bikini-clad body back into position, his hand on her perfect ass. I feel my stomach tighten into a knot. What's happening to me?

Slowly, the stone façade of the fountain is completely covered. In its place is a human mosaic in the shape of a regal fountain. It's totally and completely weird. But, I have to admit, bizarrely beautiful. One large spot in the middle remains open. "This is where I shall stand," Regina says. "In the very middle, with your friends on either side." She looks at me. "Would you like to join us?" Her question catches me off guard. "You may not get this opportunity again, to be part of such an interesting and exotic piece of art. Everyone who participates will get a large framed print to hang at home." I picture my mother welcoming guests to her cozy bed and breakfast: dried florals, paintings of pelicans in frames of weathered wood, and a print of Frantonio's fountain of naked bodies, her own daughter buck ass naked in the middle. "It's an opportunity for you to channel the countess. She would truly appreciate such artistic and unique staging for a photograph."

"She cropped her own head out of all the sexy ones she took," I reply.

"Regina, is the other case of lenses over there?" Frantonio calls from behind his camera. I turn and spot the case.

"I'll get it," I offer, hopping up quickly. Careful to ensure it's latched, I carry the case over to Frantonio as if it contained plutonium. As I put the case down, he smiles.

"Thank you, Ms. Taylor. F-Y-I, this is a no-dancing area," he announces. "*Una zona senza ballo.*" Now the entire sculpture of posed people is laughing at me. My face turns bright red. That wasn't nice. "We are only teasing, my dear. Come, I have saved you a special spot, in the middle, next to our hostess." He walks over to the fountain and holds out his hand to me.

"I'm just here to watch," I say.

"Nonsense. You are the one who inspired this fountain vision. It will not be complete without you. Come." His voice is commanding, relaxed, and easy. There's no doubt in his mind that I will do as he instructs. I stare at his outstretched hand. He waits. Everyone waits. Fuck.

Chapter 22

How Not to Create Art

My Room, Casa di Pavone: Friday, 5:49pm, Just Before the Shoot

HINTS FOR PREPPING TO POSE NAKED IN A FOUNTAIN WITH TOTAL STRANGERS, ALL OF WHOM ARE MORE ATTRACTIVE THAN YOU:

1. Don't waste all your prep time curling your hair. It's going to get wet.

2. Concealer on butt pimples just washes off.

3. Mascara is also a bad idea.

4. Do not try to shave your pubic hair into the perfectly symmetrical, upside-down teardrop shape you read about in *Maxim Magazine*, taking more and more off each side until you have an angry pink and white vagina that looks like the bald cat, Mr. Bigglesworth, from *Austin Powers*.

5. Don't try to use eyeliner pencil to draw your pubic hair back on, no matter how good an artist you think you are.

6. Don't do emergency pushups and crunches in a fruitless attempt to tone.
7. Do NOT drink two glasses of wine to get your nerve up.

Am I actually going to do this? Why? Because I want to channel the spirit of Virginia Oldoini? Because Frantonio asked me to? Because he saved me a special spot, right beside our hostess? Because he placed me there while everyone watched? Is there really going to be a naked photo of Marina Taylor, with twenty other also naked people, hanging on random walls of dining rooms, parlors, and bedrooms throughout Europe?

I've just got to reframe. I'll be glad I did it when I begin to receive calls from modeling agents and hip photographers asking what my fee is. And one day my teenaged son will stumble across the photo, buried in an attic, and say, "Wow, Mom used to be cool. Let's take it to space school for show and tell." And my daughter will say, "No, gross."

"DLT! It's time to go down." Yang is at the door.

"I have a silk robe for you." Yin is with her.

"I'll meet you down there," I lie and spring onto the bed like a panicked gazelle. Yang opens the door to find me jumping on the bed, tits bouncing, frantically trying to unlatch the window so I can make my escape.

"Are you trying to escape through the window, DLT?" she asks.

"No," I lie.

"You're naked. Where are you going to go naked?" she says.

"You look beautiful, *chèrie,* just take a deep breath," Yin says soothingly, approaching the bed as if she's talking to a spooked horse. "Here's your robe."

"What did you do to your snatch, mate? It looks like that cat in *Austin—*"

"She looks fine!" Yin puts the robe around me and motions at Yang's pocket. She pulls out a small pipe, already packed with pot and ready to go.

"Have a hit of this, DLT. You need to relax," says Yang.

"I don't really smoke," I say. I had tried pot twice in college and never really found the appeal.

"You want to pop an E tab instead? I got one in the room."

"No. I'm good."

"You're not good, mate. You want some coke? Luciano had some—"

"No, give me the damn pipe. I'll just have the pot, so when I commemorate my naked shame for generations to come, I won't care so much."

"Atta girl!" Yang hands me the pipe and the lighter.

Garden, Casa di Pavone: Friday, *L'ora D'oro* (Golden Hour)

I am standing in a fountain, just to the left of Regina, with twenty strangers, all of us wearing absolutely nothing. The pot must be working because I'm suddenly not worried about being tagged on social media. My butt is toward camera. I'm vaguely relieved that my *Austin Powers* cat pussy will not be on camera, and my sense of trepidation has melted into mellow acceptance. The guy next to me, Mario, is very attractive. I stare at his perfectly sculpted abs and decide I'm actually enjoying myself.

My arms are stretched upward, fingers fanned. Yin is next to me in similar formation. On Regina's right side, Yang and Frantonio's redhead are our mirror images, creating the other half of Venus's clamshell. I think to myself: I'm a part of something that nobody else in the world will ever be a part of. Well except for the twenty other naked people around me.

Regina, our Venus, stands front and center in all her aging starlet glory. The goddess of beauty with surgically boosted breasts, liposuctioned ass, and perfectly waxed, fifty-year-old *figa*. Unlike Venus, Regina's strong, slender arms and delicate fingers do not demurely cover her feminine assets, as seen in every painting of the deity. Instead they reach gracefully toward camera in a beckoning gesture. An open offer to a world that is clamoring to love her. It is perfect. How great is that, I ask myself. I want to be her. But not now—like in thirty years or something. Is that a frog sitting on the fountain spout? I love frogs. Maybe it's just a leaf shaped like a frog, or a very small alien. Come to think of it, maybe frogs *are* actually very small aliens sent here to—

"Stand up a bit please, Miss Taylor," Frantonio commands professionally. The upper left portion of Venus's clamshell is crumbling. I try to rectify the breech, but the twenty push-ups and hundred crunches I did earlier in a hopeless attempt to vanquish my paunch had only vanquished my strength. After ten minutes in position, my posture is turning to Jello. "Sorry," I say, correcting my position. My pruning feet are tingling and my bladder is faintly calling for help. Frantonio walks over and puts one hand on my stomach and one on my bare ass, firmly molding me back into shape.

"Tall, as if you're wearing an imaginary corset," he instructs. I suck everything in, remembering the time I squeezed myself into a vintage corset for Pirate Days in Key West—it was like a torture device. The more beer I drank the less I could feel my lower half. Why did women have to be little in the middle? That rhymes. Men need to be thick in the prick. I giggle to myself and suddenly feel dizzy. Without realizing it, I swoon. Mario, the guy next to me, puts an arm behind to steady me. "I know it's uncomfortable, Ms. Taylor, but we must all suffer for the art together." There are murmurs of agreement. "Although, Mario certainly seems to be enjoying himself."

I look over and realize that Mario now has an erection. Wow. That is a huge penis . . . right next to my knee. Almost touching it. His friends cheer and laugh. It seems like this should really bother me, but for some reason, I'm just staring at it. I don't think I've seen a fully erect penis in the light of day like this. Is it moving? I close my eyes. Too weird. It reminds me of one of those giant worms from the film *Tremors*.

Frantonio tweaks one or two other people and returns to the camera as a cloud passes in front of the sun. "*Merde.*" He pulls out his light meter, takes some quick readings. "One moment. *Tenete duro.* Almost ready." I can feel my body sagging again. I resist. "*Siete perfetti.* I'm only waiting on the sun." Fucking sun. Come on. I'm feeling sleepy. The faint call of my bladder has become a shouting, throbbing pulse. Shit. Why did I drink those two glasses of wine? I cross my legs tightly, hoping Frantonio won't notice. He snaps a few photos. "Why did you move, Miss Taylor? *Per favore*, uncross your legs, my dear."

"Do I have to?" The cold water tickling my shins is not helping my bladder.

"*Sì*, as you were," he says, now with urgency as the sun emerges from the clouds. He looks through his lens. "Quickly."

"I can't right now. Just trust me on this one."

"My dear, we have only moments of perfect light left!"

"I have to pee!" I blurt out, desperately. "Maybe I'll just run to the bathroom?"

"Are you joking?" he says.

"I'll go behind that tree," I say.

"No time!" Frantonio barks, losing his cool.

"You think you're the only one who has to pee?" yells Yang. "Clench up that snatch and uncross your fucking legs, mate!" People shout in agreement. I have no choice. I uncross my legs. My knees wobble. My bladder is now screaming.

"Thank you!" Frantonio begins to shoot madly. "*Paolo, testa indietro*. Beautiful Regina. Chin just a touch to the left, madam. Exquisite." My butt is clinched. My eyes are clinched. Everything is clinched. Why didn't I do more Kegles? Kegels are good for sex too. I did see this YouTube channel once with this girl, she was like a pelvic floor trainer. Like those guys in the gym that yell at you, only she talked to your vagina in a soothing, encouraging voice as you struggled to keep a jade egg on a string from falling out of it. My thighs are now shaking badly but I don't notice. I'm too busy staring at the small arcs of water shooting up from the base of the fountain, into the air, and then falling gracefully back down. What if water fell up instead of down? What if rain . . . as my mind wanders, the screaming of my bladder morphs into a triumphant opera aria and my body relaxes. Suddenly I feel fantastic. Oh God, no. No, no, no . . . I open my eyes to see: a golden arc of urine hitting Mario's leg.

"*Ma che cazzo!*" Mario yells. People around us react.

"Fuck it," I hear Yang say. "If she's pissing, so am I."

"*Anch'io,*" shouts someone from above us. "Me too." Yells of protest in multiple languages. People peel off.

"No, go back. *Non ho finito!*" Frantonio's desperate voice is lost in a chorus of pandemonium as the human fountain collapses. People pee, shove, slip, squeal, shout, laugh, scramble in all directions. I bite my lip and look up at Frantonio. "Fuck!" he yells, throwing up his arms in defeat. He glares at me. "You are a catastrophe." He throws his light meter into the bushes and stalks off, swearing in French. I feel like I've been punched in the stomach.

"Well done, DLT!" Yang grins, giving me the thumbs up.

Chapter 23

How Not to
Win An Argument

AT THIS POINT, IF: you have managed to sabotage a group artistic endeavor.

YOU SHOULD: keep your head down, stick close to your friends, and say little.

DO NOT: wait until the artist is drunk and follow him alone into the library.

Library, Casa di Pavone: Friday, 11:12 p.m.

I slip stealthily into the silent oasis, away from the noise of the after-dinner party. Frantonio has a half-finished bottle of Brunello in his hand, and he's perusing titles.

"That fountain mess was not my fault," I say with quiet indignation. At the sound of my voice, Frantonio turns and gives me a tired, bemused look.

"You? No. Go away. Out." He points to the door and turns back to the shelf.

"Excuse me? I am not a dog."

"No. Dogs piss on trees, not people," he says coolly, without looking at me. Wow. He'd avoided me throughout dinner and afterward. Was he really that mad? "You completely ruined my photo shoot." Yes. He was. "You're being melodramatic." He doesn't say anything, just ignores me and continues to search the shelf. "I read about Virginia Oldoini. She was considered influential because she directed these weird, fantastic photos. She was in charge. Not bullied into it because she was put on the spot."

"*She* had a disciplined respect for detail and patience for perfection. You could learn from her."

"You took a bunch of photos before it all fell apart. Why are you so bent out of shape? Because somebody's left butt cheek or kneecap was slightly in shadow?" He takes his glasses off and rubs his eyes, but still says nothing. "People had fun," I say. "Everyone left laughing and screaming. You got your pretentious porno photo, but you're still pouting." At this, he suddenly turns on me, his face flushed—from the wine or temper, or both.

"Pretentious?"

"Yeah. *Pretenzioso.* Pompous, overblown." His eyes narrow, but I'm on a roll.

"I'm an artist. I won't be judged by a naïve American girl whose idea of art is using digital stickers on her iPhone."

"You don't even know me! I'm an artist too. I'm a writer."

"Really? What have you published? My work has shown all over Europe."

"Yeah, Regina showed me the book from your Paris exhibition. It was lazy and uninspired."

"That's not what the critics said in the culture section of *Le Monde.*"

"I'm sure they didn't. You're so used to people blowing sunshine up your ass all the time, you couldn't see that your Spencer Tunick bird bath was about as profound as my mother's Noah's Ark quilt."

"You didn't seem so unimpressed with me last night on your knees," he snaps.

"I didn't know your head was harder than your cock!" I snap back. We're nose to nose, nostrils flaring. He stares. I stare. I can feel my heart beating, blood pumping. There is anger, but there is also incredible sexual tension in the fury. I know he feels it too. For a millisecond, I actually think he's going to grab me and kiss me. But this time, he does not. He simply shakes his head, gives a defeated chuckle, and retreats.

"I cannot win an argument with a writer. I give up. I just want to find my book, go to my room with my bottle of wine, and be pompously, pretentiously alone. May I do that?" I feel a pang of regret. The dogfight instinct in me was hard to leash—something I'd inherited from my father.

"I didn't ask to be in your photo," I say quietly.

"Yes, I know," he says. "But I needed you." This surprises and disarms me even further. His eyes aren't angry. They're disappointed. "Deep down, I knew you were going to somehow screw it up. But stupidly, still I wanted you." It's insulting and flattering at the same time.

"Why?"

"I don't know!" He throws his arms up. "I photograph supermodels all the time, you're nothing like them."

"Yeah, no shit. Thanks."

"But you have this thing. It makes me fucking crazy," he says. This is the first time I've heard his voice waver.

"Good crazy?" I ask.

"*Merde, no.*" He's not smiling. "You're like an exasperating, irritating mess." Now I'm not smiling either. "But you've got this heat, this light, you are ... *comment dit-on translucide* ... translucent. It's like I can see straight into your heart with my lens. And I see this raw, unbridled energy. You reflect this on everything around you." Wow. My head swims.

"Like a sunset?"

"No, like an atom bomb. But for a photographer, this is irresistible. One can search for this always, but find it rarely. It is hard to capture. But when you can, the photo comes alive. It is pure magic. This is what I wanted. This is why I needed you. But I guess that makes me pretentious."

I stare at him. My mouth is dry, silent. My heart races. My stomach is in a knot. No one has ever said anything quite so poetic to me. About me. This means much more than song lyrics. I can't believe I've insulted Frantonio so badly and this is what he actually thinks of me. I want to throw my arms around him and bury my face in his neck, cry mascara tears onto his expensive dress shirt and ask him to forgive me. I want him to kiss my forehead and tell me we'll laugh about it tomorrow, then take me back to his room. Instead he just puts his glasses back on. "The writer is out of words." He picks up his bottle of Brunello, with one last glance at the bookshelf. "And the reader is out of luck." He strides toward the door. I want to stop him, but my feet won't move.

"Wait..." I say. He turns around, but I don't know what to say. "What book were you looking for?" I ask, stalling. I just don't want him to leave.

"*The Alchemist*," he replies. "She doesn't have it." He continues to the door. This is the same book Will sent with me on my trip. My heart does a little leap.

"I do," I say eagerly. "I have it." Frantonio stops by the door and turns to look at me, surprised. "It's the only book I brought with me from home."

"Did you?" he smiles. The serendipity is not lost on him. I fail to mention it was my ex-boyfriend who gave it to me.

"It's in my room. If you want . . . to . . ." the words hang in the air between us as I hold my breath. He stares at me. I wait.

"You like this book?" he asks. Shit. Why did he have to ask that? I don't want to answer, but I have to.

"I haven't read it yet," I admit.

"Oh," he says. "You should," he smiles. "*Bonne nuit ma chèrie*." And with that, he's gone.

My Room, Casa di Pavone: Saturday, 12:03 a.m.

I'm calling home because I feel guilty for not "checking in often" as I promised Rosalie I would. Not because I currently feel completely deflated and miss the sound of my mother's voice.

Video Call - ROSALIE TAYLOR - 12:04 a.m.

"Hi Sweetie!" Rosalie chirps loudly over background music as she finally managers to answer. "Can you hear me? I'm at the Seven Seas Karaoke fundraiser," she says.

I recognize the setting of the local elementary school as a bad cover of "Beyond the Sea" is belted out by our mailman dressed as King Triton. My mother is wearing a crown of sea shells she's made herself. "I can hear you but I can't see you."

"That's because it's dark in my room."

"Oh, of course, it's very late over there! Are you okay?"

"Yeah, I just—wanted to check in," I say weakly.

"Oh, good! We're good. I can't dance because I twisted my ankle in a hole on the dock, but I'm helping with the bake sale. I'm selling those cookies shaped like sea horses that you love. Nora's here too. She's got peppermint porpoises. Do you want to say hi?"

"No, Mom, I'm good. Call me tomorrow or something."

"Okay honey! Chow!"

End Call - ROSALIE TAYLOR - 12:09 a.m.

I switch off the phone, roll over, and try to go back to sleep.

Casa di Pavone: Saturday, 12:43 a.m.

"Marina?" Yin's voice floats softly up the stairs after me. I'm standing in the hallway, in the robe she loaned me, with my copy of *The Alchemist* in my hand.

"Hey," I smile. With her white slip dress, alabaster skin, and long blonde hair freed of its ponytail, she looks like a lovely specter.

"I thought that was you, *mon ami*. We're just reading some of Carlo's poems in the kitchen and sipping scotch. Would you like to join us?"

"I'm tired. Maybe tomorrow?" Carlo's poetry stinks, but I don't mention that.

"Where are you going?"

"Just to . . . loan this book," I say. It's the truth. What else am I going to say? She knows my room is the other direction. Yin looks sideways at the book in my hand.

"That's a very good one. Maybe keep it for yourself. Some people don't appreciate unique things they're offered," Yin says quietly. She knows where I'm going. "We are all going hiking tomorrow afternoon. You too!" she smiles. "Rest up, *chérie*." She blows me a kiss and walks back to the kitchen. Hiking? I look at the book in my hands, the note. Maybe she's right. But then I remember Frantonio's words in the library. The light thingy. He said he needed me. I keep walking up the steps.

Frantonio's room was on the second floor. I'd seen him on his balcony yesterday and counted windows until I figured out which was his. (No, that's not stalkery, it's Sherlocky.) Feet from his door, I pause, open the book, and read the note I've written for the hundredth time.

Dear friend,
Without ego there can be no sense of self. Without self, there can be no individual expression. Please excuse the hot-tempered, ill-considered words of an inexperienced fellow artist. You make me crazy too.

Marina

I slip the note into the book and bend down to lean it against his door, stopping in surprise. There is music playing inside. A strange Italian jazz. A man of eclectic tastes. Clearly he's still awake. I knock softly. No answer. I knock a bit louder. The door opens.

"*Da?*" Standing in front of me is the Russian redhead—wearing nothing.

"I'm sorry, I have the wrong—" I sputter. I must have miscounted windows.

"Is that Ms. Taylor?" Frantonio's words are slurred. I stiffen. She sees the book.

"*Eto bibliotekar,*" laughs the redhead. I flush with embarrassment and jealousy.

"Tell her to join us," he calls. At this I bristle, shocked. What? Fat chance! Averting my eyes from the perfectly erect, rose-colored nipples on her size C breasts, I thrust the book out. Red takes it, surprised.

"I don't need it back." I make a hasty retreat, whispering angrily as I go. I'm so stupid, stupid!

Casa di Pavone: Saturday, 1:06 a.m.

I surprise myself when I seek out Bob in my state of distress. Have I actually made my first geriatric friend? Exactly as she was the other night, she is singing and sculpting. When I sit next to her, I'm grateful she can't see my eyes, red and puffy from crying. But the truth is, she knows without seeing. I've said less than three words to her since I entered the room, but I'm sure she can hear it in my voice. She says nothing, just sings along with Joni Mitchell as she whacks a large mound of clay onto the table in front of me, smashes my hands into it, pats my head, and returns to her work. I don't know Joni's "A Case of You," but her sad words seem to melt through me and settle into my soul. I just give myself over to it, crying again, smashing the clay through my fingers. Why did I care so much about a man I hardly knew? Was it because I thought he knew me? He saw something in me I wanted to see. He made me feel special and then not.

When Bob returns to check my progress at the end of the album, I've managed to create a clay bust of Frantonio (although it doesn't look much like him—especially now that it's been stabbed multiple times with the end of a paintbrush). "*È buono,*" she says. Bob scoops it up. Her warm, wrinkled palms and strong, knobby fingers fold Frantonio back into a ball. She smacks the clay onto the table again. "*Riprova.*" Taking my hand, she puts it on my heart and then back onto the clay. "*Più profondo.*" Deeper. She's right. We are strong women artists working side by side, listening to another strong artistic woman sing from her heart. I should dig deep into my artist's soul and sculpt something meaningful. I'll sculpt a donkey and name it Frantonio.

Chapter 24

How Not to See the Italian Countryside

My Room, Casa di Pavone: Saturday, 11:36 a.m.

I don't want to see anyone. Sociable is the last thing I'm feeling. Instead, I work on my book and eat an entire bag of *Abbracci* cookies. I read on my tablet about Catherine of Siena, one of the two patron saints of Italy. Making notes in my journal, I find myself distracted by the adventures in Rome I'd read to Yin and Yang. I begin to write up my embarrassing fountain episode. By the time I'm done, I'm laughing at my own expense. Maybe the girls are right. But this material is more like a blog. Suddenly, an idea. I can do both!

I click over and discover that my dear friend Michael (Mike's boyfriend) is currently online. I'll just do a quick video chat. As the tablet is ringing, I suddenly realize it's 3:15 a.m. in Florida. Shit! I try to disconnect, but then—

"Florida Woman Mugs Senior Citizen Over Last Airplane Seat!" Michael announces in his musical accent from the video chat window on my tablet. This is a running gag. Apparently most of the nation's ridiculous news headlines originate in my state:

Florida Man Shoots at Hurricane.

Florida Man, High on Meth, Tries to Rob Liquor Store With Dead Stingray.

Florida Woman Steals Gambling Fees Because Husband Spends Too Much at Lowes.

Florida Man Points Slingshot at Parents in School Parking Lot, Throws Armadillo at Car.

Michael, eating a taco, is still wearing his very loud turquoise and yellow silk shirt from whatever club they've been dancing at all night. Originally from Barbados, he's always been the most colorful dresser I know. With his good looks, confidence, and charm, he pulls it off.

"C'mon, you can do better than that!" I tease.

"Florida Woman Rides to Italy in Cargo Hold, Crammed into Dog Crate by Airline Employee?" Mike snarks, appearing behind Michael in frame. He is perky and fresh out of the shower, towel around his waist, waxed pecks gleaming, coffee in hand.

"Florida Woman, Blacklisted by Airline, Travels to Italy in Cruise Ship Pantry, Gains Fifty Pounds," suggests Michael.

"That's the one," I laugh. "What are you doing up?"

"I've got a flight to LHR at the ass crack of dawn, so we decided not to go to bed," answers Mike. Ever since he had to memorize the three-letter code for every major airport in the world, he's refused to say the actual names. We have to guess where he's going. Suddenly he notices Michael's taco bag. "Oh my God! You're disgusting!" He seizes Michael's taco. "I was in the shower for ten minutes. How did you get to Taco Shark and back?"

"I had it from yesterday, and you've never taken a ten-minute shower in your life!" returns Michael. A struggle for the bag ensues.

"You've been sneaking behind my back AND you're eating day-old Taco Shark?"

"It's just one taco, Mommie Dearest!" Michael says.

"There are two in the bag and you have one in your hand. That's three."

"They're small tacos!" Michael complains.

"That's not even a taco. It's dog food in a GMO corn shell!" Mike yells.

"This fucking vegan diet was your idea. I grew up on fish for every meal! I'm not watching any more documentaries with you," Michael yells back.

"Hello! I'm still here," I say. Michael grabs the end of Mike's towel.

"Give it back or I'm going to show all of Italy your penis."

"Go ahead, baby! I'm flying to Rome next week. Maybe you'll get me a date!"

"Guys, please! I saw quite enough penises yesterday," I plead. Suddenly I have their attention again.

"Really?"

"Do tell." They both stare into the camera.

"Florida Woman Makes Golden Shower at Golden Hour Posing Naked with Super Models in a Fountain." I shrug. They release the taco bag in unison.

"Whaaaaattt!!!!" and, "Holy shit!" and, "Caw!"

"You're making that up," says Mike. But Michael can't stop laughing.

"No, Marina doesn't make this shit up. It just happens to her. Remember the senior center and the stripper wearing balloons?" Michael and I had met back in college, working for the same party company. Michael was in the country as a student and shooting and editing party videos was putting him through film school.

"The senior center stripper debacle was an honest mistake," I object. "And the birthday man was fine. It wasn't a real heart attack."

"Back to the fountain! I want details," says Mike, "and I have to leave for MIA in fifteen minutes."

"Don't worry. I'm going to write the whole thing up. That's what I wanted to talk to you about, Michael. I want to start a blog. A travel-adventure one."

"Misadventure," Michael corrects.

"Okay, yes, misadventure. With . . . well, sex and stuff," I add.

"Oh good, you ditched the boring sexist book about historic females," says Michael.

"Nope. Still doing it."

"Well at least put a transgender person in there. Like Vladimir Luxuria, the first openly transgender member of parliament in Europe," Mike suggests.

"Good idea, I'm writing this down," I say.

"No you're not. We can see you Marina. This isn't a phone call," says Michael.

"Michael can set up the blog for you!" Mike suggests.

"Absolutely," Michael smirks, "I adore doing work for people who can't pay."

"Great! Thank you," I say.

"Do they not have irony in Italy?" asks Michael.

"Marina, I gotta get dressed for work." Mike waves at me.

"Mike—wait. Sorry about the airport. And thank you . . . I love Italy."

"Good food, great wine, and gorgeous men—what's not to love?" He winks and disappears into the bathroom.

"Email me some notes about what you want on the site, and your first post." Michael, glancing over his shoulder, pulls another taco out of the bag. "Keep it simple." Unwrapping the taco, he reveals a mushy, crunched shell mess.

"Simple, got it. Thanks!" I say. "I'm going to hang up now, so I don't have to watch you eat that."

"Okay, *ciao!* Don't do anything Mike wouldn't do," Michael says.

"Don't do anything Michael wouldn't do!" Mike calls from the bathroom.

"Ciao! Love you guys!" I click off, smiling to myself. Suddenly I'm craving a taco, something I've not seen my entire time here. I wonder how Rosalie's night went, but it's too early to call. It's 3:30 there. She's just fallen back asleep after her nightly ice cream fix. She had tried to hide this habit for a long time, but I would find ice cream cartons in the fridge instead of the freezer, with a fork still inside. Sugar addict! I laugh to myself, missing her just a bit more. My hand fumbles around in the bag of cookies and I realize I'm holding the last one. (Okay, five things in common.)

I wonder if Will is awake. Probably not. Bad idea anyway. I have a small pang of guilt as I remember him standing in front of me, in the rain, the night before I left. I've just given away the book he'd brought me. Reclaiming it from Frantonio would mean swallowing my pride and I'm not ready to do that. My stomach rumbles. Right now, I'd rather swallow some lunch. *The Alchemist* is a popular book. It will be easy to find another copy.

Path of the Gods, Italy: Saturday, 3:36 p.m.

HELPFUL HINTS FOR HIKING IN ITALY:

1. Don't eat a huge lunch right before, even if you skipped breakfast.
2. Sunscreen. Bring it.
3. Charge your phone battery before you leave.
4. Don't load your backpack up with snacks from the kitchen, including a bottle of rosé that will be "fabulous to share with friends overlooking the sea."
5. Sunscreen. Put it on.
6. Don't drink all your water in the first half hour.
7. Not everyone can fully appreciate the nuanced humor and complicated symbolism of gibberish camp songs sung loudly.
8. Sunscreen. Put it on. Again. You've sweated it off.
9. If someone offers you a hat that ties under the chin, take it.
10. Don't take any shortcuts.

My vote was for the *Atrani* to *Ravello* hike. (DURATION: medium, LEVEL: medium.) But Yang didn't want to miss *Il Sentiero degli Dei*, "Path of the Gods." (DURATION: long, LEVEL: brutal.) Regina had Piero #6 drive us to the trailhead. He's also cute, but #4 is still my favorite. Number six will pick us up at the other end of the hike. There are seven hikers: Yin, Yang, and myself, Carlo, Mario (the new friend I peed on in the fountain), and two Spanish girls. I didn't know I was signing up for a three-hour hike. But at least I got out of Regina's without having to see Frantonio.

The trail winds through the slopes of *Monte Peruso* with stunningly beautiful, heavenly views, worthy of God. But, after two hours, I feel like I'm in hell. Every muscle in my body aches and my blistered, swollen feet have morphed into flippers of dead meat that I'm wearing on the end of my ankles, slapping clumsily one in front of the other with numb determination. The downhill route is from *Agerola* to *Nocelle*. We, however, are walking from *Nocelle* to *Agerola*. Of course. As we crest a hill, I see the path before us winding into the distance as far as the eye can see. It has no end. Not with short, steep sections, but with one long, punishing slant. Gradually upward and onward forever we walk. Once again I think of my aunt Catherine. At least I can tell her I did this. She probably did it when she was six. I can feel my intestines now revolting against the huge bowl of pasta I had right before we left. Ill-advised, but I was "carbing up" like a marathon runner.

"I'm just going to dash off the trail and take a quick . . . pee. I'll catch up," I call. Carlo is pretty far ahead with the other two girls. Mario is with us.

"We'll wait," says Yin.

"It's fine, go," I say, not wanting them timing my nature poo.

"*Andiamo*, I don't need to see her pee again," Mario grumbles.

"Go on, I'm right behind you," I say. "I need to rest for a minute anyway." Mario walks on and Yin and Yang follow. I scramble off the path and climb uphill through scrub until I find a clump of trees. The nature poo takes longer than I expect. Maybe because it feels so good not to be moving. I stand back up and look out. Ahead to my left, I can see the group winding its way along. Directly in front of me, the path, a gentle slope, and then a sharp cliff drop to the ancient Mediterranean. From here it looks peaceful, stirring gently in a lazy afternoon slumber. As I enjoy the rest and the view, I notice something else to my left. A different path. This smaller path cuts more sharply uphill, through denser clumps of trees, but intersecting with the main path further ahead. A shortcut! My heart leaps for joy because my feet cannot. Without a second thought, I move in the direction of the smaller path. If I keep on this trajectory, I should meet up with the main path in the next few minutes. This sort of thing never backfires. What could go wrong?

Path of the Demons, Italy: Saturday, 4:14 p.m.

I've renamed the hike. The smaller path was either one of those disappearing paths, designed to lure tourists to untimely deaths, or an oasis hallucination. The logical thing at that point would have been to immediately turn back and retrace my steps until I found the main path. However, I'm not the backtracking sort. This involves admitting a mistake. I pivot, push on, and persevere. It's not until more bad choices have snowballed my original mistake into a hopeless, terminal mess, that I question my actions. This sort of bullheaded tenacity is great for winning political arguments at Thanksgiving dinners or playing Monopoly, but not so useful when hiking.

Currently, there is no signal on my phone. Most of the battery has been used up shooting videos of myself singing cheesy camp songs and trying in vain to email them home to my old sailing camp friends, Teresa and Frannie Fish Sticks. I realize that with each passing minute, my new friends are either moving farther away, or getting madder as they wait, hotly debating leaving me. Yin is certainly the only one in my corner. And frankly, I don't like her chances against the others. I will soon be alone in the wilderness. Fortunately, I was the only Girl Scout in the troop whose father said, "You sold sixty-two boxes of cookies? Big deal. A vending machine can do that without moving. Now take these two rocks and learn how to start a goddamn fire."

AT THIS POINT, IF: you are alone in a wild land . . .

YOU SHOULD: use the sun to navigate, or sit down and calmly wait for help.

DO NOT:
1. Eat all of the snacks in your bag.
2. Run blindly through the woods as if the Blair Witch has an Italian cousin.
3. Take your shoes off and climb to the top of the tallest tree you can find attempting to get a signal with your phone.
4. Mistake a vine for a snake, freak out, and drop your phone as you try to scramble back down the tree, scraping your arms and legs, losing your sunhat on a branch, breaking the last small branch, and cutting your foot as you land on a rock below.
5. Pour wine over your open wound because that's what they do in the movies to disinfect things.
6. Attempt to reclaim your sunhat by throwing rocks straight up at it, which will miss the hat completely and rain back down on your head.
7. Drink the rest of the wine, because, WTF, the bottle is already open.
8. Decide to close your eyes, just for a few minutes.

Lying back into the crunchy dry grass, I feel certain someone will come find me. Better to just wait in one place. I decide to focus on: Nap of Exhausted Discouragement (DURATION: long, LEVEL: pro).

Path of the Demons, Italy: Saturday, 6:17 p.m.

The sun is beginning to set when I wake up. Why does it feel like I'm wearing a beauty mask that's hardened? I touch my face and realize the mask is actually my red, sunburned skin. Fucking great. I'm going to die, alone in the Italian wilderness, looking like that imitation Barbie I'd left for a week in a bucket of sea water with my new red swimsuit when I was seven. The entire doll turned a shade of Pepto-Bismol, and my tears failed to move my mother. "Well, you wanted a 'Pink and Pretty Barbie,' now you got one. Next time, hang your suit up."

Remembering that afternoon, I now notice the sky in front of me is turning a similar shade of pale pink. It deepens with every passing minute. So pretty, so peaceful. I stop worrying that I am lost without help of rescue. This place is so beautiful. I can stay here forever. Yes, maybe I will. The soft pink clouds are breaking apart and forming shapes out of fluffy cotton candy. A baby elephant. A gondola. A giant dildo. I haven't had cotton candy in so long. Suddenly my mouth begins to water. The bushes beside me rustle.

"Hello." Ryan Gosling emerges, shirtless, with hiking shorts and a backpack. The sweat glistening on his beautiful pecs.

"Do you have any cotton candy?" I ask.

"I just finished it," he says apologetically. "What happened to your foot?"

"There was an anaconda in the tree," I say, pointing behind me. When I look back, Ryan is now dressed as Indiana Jones: hat, whip, complete.

"That's incredible!" he says. "They're water snakes. But don't worry," he unsheathes his machete. "I'll chop the head off, and make you a purse and boots."

"Boots?" I ask, confused. "But my foot hurts."

"Don't worry. I'm with Doctors Without Borders." Suddenly he's at my side, now wearing doctor scrubs and cradling my foot in his hands. "It's bad. Your bravery is very impressive."

"I need to check the rest of me?" I ask. "Make sure there are no other injuries."

"Good thinking," he replies as I unbutton my shirt, exposing my red lacey bra (not the sweaty jogging bra I wore on the hike). His hands massage each of my breasts. He's very thorough. "Your breasts are in superb condition. In fact, they're the best breasts I've ever seen. I'll need you to take off your pants now please."

"You first," I say.

"That's fair," he replies. He stands in front of me, pulls his shirt off, revealing (again) his gorgeously toned chest and abs. He then bends and pulls his—HONNNNK!!!! I'm yanked mercilessly from my mountaintop version of the bends. What the fuck was that? One thing is certain. It was not an animal noise. It was a human noise. A flood of relief washes through me. I put my shoes on quickly. Again I hear: HONNNNK!!!!

"Here! I'm here!" I yell weakly as I stand up, my knees nearly buckling under me. HONNNNK!!!! It sounds like a boat horn. Am I close to the water? I stumble toward it. My feet move independently of my body as I limp through the scrub, past trees, branches slapping me. "Here, I'm here, please help!" HONNNNK!!!!! The horn is louder. I push forward. "Help!" HONNNNK!!! Like an angry goose on a PA system, it beckons me. At last I burst through the brush and back out onto the path. And, there, standing in the middle of the path with an airhorn in her hand and a scowl on her face, is Yang. I rejoice. "Oh, thank God!" I say, leaning over on my knees to catch my breath, certain that my right shoe is full of blood. "I'm so glad to see you. My foot, I'm wounded . . . ." Yang walks right up to me, scowl still in place. She aims the horn at my head and: HONNNNK!!!!

Chapter 25

How Not to Dream

Casa di Pavone, Italy: Sunday, 6:27 a.m.

I am awake early, watching the sunrise from my window. Last night I fell asleep at nine, fully and completely relaxed. I slept like a baby. I only had one dream, which is unusual for me, as my mind is generally hard to turn off, even when I sleep. This dream was early in the morning, right before I woke up, so I still remember it well. I am lying in a hammock on the beach with Will, reading him a poem I wrote. The words of the poem are unclear, but the intense feeling of frustration and disappointment I feel is vivid. Will is smiling in appreciation but he just doesn't *get* it. Now, I'm angry and it's raining. There is lightning. A summer thunderstorm as I stomp angrily down the beach. I look back, expecting him to be there, coming after me, the way he always does. But he's not. My heart sinks rapidly and my whole body feels heavy. I sink to my knees in the white sand. I am now naked. *Lightning flashes.* I put my head in my hands and cry. *Flash.*

"Beautiful, now just tilt your head up a little, *bella*." It's Frantonio's voice. I look up. The lightning flashes have become camera flashes. I am still wet and naked, but now in a white marble tub, surrounded by bubbles. Frantonio peers through his camera into my soul. "Tears?" He puts his camera down. He takes my chin in his hand, wiping my cheek. "It takes an artist to see true beauty inside another artist." I gaze into his brown eyes. His voice is tender. "Others cannot truly know your intelligence, your potential, your soul. They see you as a mysterious, beautiful creature to be devoured, like this octopus here." I suddenly notice a bright red octopus floating next to me, clinging to the side of the tub, bubbles on its head. I scream. I wake up.

Even now, I shudder as I think of its tentacles curling toward my naked body underwater. The dream was pretty transparent until it devolved into tentacle porn. Why had finding Frantonio with another woman upset me so much? Hadn't I been doing strip teases with cat toys and fornicating in public parks with other boys just days earlier? I'd never even been on a date with Frantonio. It's not like he was my boyfriend. That's not what I wanted. Was it? I think about my dream. That's what I wanted. To be seen the way he sees me. To feel the way I felt in the library.

I hear a car pull up outside. As the cool purple-pink of the sky grows warmer and the sun stretches its radiant arms through the clouds, gradually brightening the world, I shake off my jealousy and just admit the truth. I still wanted him. I will find him this morning and ask to speak to him alone.

Tiptoeing through the front hall, I see Piero #4 enter through the front door. He is radiant and fit, as if he's just come from a work out. "*Buongiorno, signorina*. Would you like some breakfast?"

"You're up early, Piero."

"I was jogging and then helping to load *il maestro's* camera equipment into the car. Our photographer friend has an early flight today," he replies.

"He's—gone?" I ask, shocked.

"*Sì*, he left a few moments ago." Piero's voice is gentle. I can't believe it. Frantonio is gone? He left? Just like that? I feel as if I'm back in the tub and the plug has been yanked out. "He asked me to give you this." Piero hands me a book. *La Divine Comtesse.* On the cover is a black and white photograph of a glamorous Italian woman in an elegant costume, looking mysterious. It's Virginia Oldoini. In the book I find a note. The water in my tub drains from around my body, inch by inch, moment by moment. I see Frantonio's elegant, sweeping script. This is his goodbye. I feel the weight of my body, heavier and heavier, as I read.

My Dear,

Merci beaucoup for *The Alchemist.* I shall think of your irrepress-ible spark and keep it next to my bed. Enjoy the countess, you are as strong willed as she. May your adventures be romantic and your romances be adventurous.

With admiration,
Your pompous pal

As I stare at his words, my eyes sting. The last of the tub water vanishes down the drain with a gurgling echo and I am left lying naked and alone on the cold, white marble, heavier than ever before. I feel a hand on my shoulder. It is Piero, with a sweet expression on his face. Not sympathy, but understanding.

"I'm sorry you didn't get to say goodbye," Piero says softly.

"Thank you," I say, trying to hide the immense disappointment in my voice. "I'll just put this in my room."

Casa di Pavone, Italy: Sunday, 12:30 p.m.

I am not pouting. I am working. And, also hiding from everyone, because I'm hurt, annoyed, and sexually . . . disappointed. Yin and Yang are enjoy-ing each other in their rooms, and everyone else is enjoying a post-lunch snooze or a walk somewhere. Not far from the pool, I'm lounging in one of the garden cabanas with the curtains drawn. The luxurious cabana bed is covered with silk pillows and the "door" of the cabana is a long, gauzy, white curtain that billows softly, allowing a cool breeze into my hideaway. Romantic guitar music playing on my phone, I have the book from Frantonio open, but I'm mostly just looking at the photos. They're beautiful, odd, and provocative. No wonder he thought I would like it. I drain the last of my sparkling water and lean back on the lounger with my knees up. The breeze slips under my long skirt, and I suddenly remember I came out with no panties or bra. I took a shower after lunch and just threw on a tank and long, hippy skirt, intent on reading alone.

My head and shoulders now sink into the giant, down pillow behind me. I close my eyes and think of . . . yes, Frantonio. I wonder how it would have been to actually have spent the night with him. He was one of the best kissers I'd ever met. His confidence was bold and sexy. I remembered his tongue on mine, slipping in and out of my mouth. As I remember his hand on my breasts, my own hand slips into my tank top and I squeeze and caress my own breasts. My breath gets a little faster, and I smile. I remember his body pushing into mine against the wall in my room. I recall the feel of his fingers slipping up inside my wet *figa*. I wanted him so bad. I remember his hard cock pressing against my leg through his pants. I wonder what it would feel like pushing inside me now. But, I'll never know.

Here on the lounger, this realization throbs through me, and I want him even more. My eyes closed, I slip my own hand up under my skirt, widening my knees. As I remember the smell of his hair, and the sweat on his neck, I tickle my *figa*. My heart beats faster. I imagine him reaching down, pulling my silk dress off my hips and dropping it around my ankles. As my fingers rub harder against my now throbbing *figa*, I imagine myself unbuckling his pants and pulling out his—

"*Ciao, Marina.*" I hear a voice. My eyes fly open and I see Piero #4 standing just inside the gauzy curtain. He is wearing linen shorts and a white Cuban shirt.

"Oh! Piero! Hi," I sputter, embarrassed, yanking my hand out of my skirt.

"I would have knocked but there is no door," he says. "I am sorry to interrupt."

"*Non c'è un problema,*" I smile, trying to play it cool. So what if he just caught me with my one hand squeezing my own breast and the other up my own skirt? It's no problem. Fuck. In truth I'm mortified.

"I only came to see if you needed anything," says Piero. He steps closer and says a little more quietly, "I wanted to check on you."

"Oh really?" I say. Still too embarrassed to meet his eye, I find myself gazing at the button on his shorts. Now I realize it looks like I'm staring at his—

"You seemed *un po* unhappy this morning," Piero says as he sits down on the edge of the lounger next to me. He looks me right in the eyes.

"Thank you. I'm totally fine," I lie.

"*Bene.* I am glad," he says. "Then, I will leave you alone?" It sounds more like a question than a statement.

"*Sì?*" So does mine.

"Unless, you need help with . . . anything?" he asks with a little shrug. I stare more deeply into his beautiful dark brown eyes. They're almost black. "Sometimes, when I am sad or frustrated, a little sexercise makes me feel better," he winks.

"Sexercise?" I laugh.

"*Sì.* I am studying sports medicine and therapy," he grins.

"And you think some sexercise would help me?"

"*Sì,*" he nods. "*Cento per cento.* One hundred percent." He nods and gently puts his hand on my leg. Somehow, right now, this is all I need. As I launch myself toward him, his athletic arms are ready. I'm kissing him madly, my hands in his hair, on his shoulders, his back. I don't even waste time with his shirt, pushing him back onto the lounger as he laughs and kicks his shoes off. "Okay, let's play!" I'm kissing him again and then, quickly, hungrily unfastening the button on his shorts. I reach in to find his cock, stroke it a few times, and then plunge my head down, sliding his cock inside my waiting mouth, sucking and massaging him with gusto.

I moan with anticipation as he gets hard inside my mouth. His hand reaches under my skirt, tickling my already wet and ready *figa*. I can't do this long before I must have him fully inside me.

When he pulls a condom from his shorts pocket (he came prepared), I quickly open it and put it on him. Panting, I slide myself down onto him, rocking my hips back and forth. Piero sits up, pulling up my tank so he can grab my breasts. He moves his pelvis upward. I ride him up and down, as he grips my hips and pulls me onto him harder, thrusting his cock up inside me again and again. I finally throw my head back, gasping for air as I climax. He pushes into me a few more times, prolonging my pleasure, and then finishes also. He falls back onto the silken pillows as I collapse onto him in a heap of blissful satisfaction.

"You were right," I say, my face muffled in the pillows. "*Grazie mille.*"

"*Il piacere è tutto mio,*" he laughs. "Feel better?"

"*Cento per cento,*" I laugh.

Casa di Pavone, Italy: Tuesday, 9:32 a.m.

"The actual fall happens so fast you can't process what's happening. Your reptile brain is switched on, watching things flash by." Yang is telling Regina about a bungee jump she did in South Africa called Face Adrenaline: six hundred feet down from a bridge, over a river with about two feet of water in it. It's been a couple days, and the sting of Frantonio's abrupt departure has subsided, but I still find myself wondering if there's any chance we'll meet again.

"So what is this euphoria people speak of? The rush?" Regina asks.

"When it catches you. Then you're like, floating, flying back up, the world around you suddenly comes into the sharpest focus you've ever known. It's fucking glorious," says Yang as she rips a doughnut in half and dunks it into her cappuccino.

"It sounds like when you fall in love," I say.

"Yes," Yin smiles.

"Any moron can fall in love, mate. To make a jump like that you've got to override every self-preservation instinct you've got and just hurl yourself into the unknown."

"That still sounds like love," laughs Regina. "And the thrill doesn't last forever. It was like that with my third husband. He was a chef. A lot of passion, and heat."

"A lot of heartburn," quips Yang. We groan at her horrible pun.

"You were married three times?" I ask Regina.

"Four actually," she replies. "Marriage is great. Everyone should try it at least once." The girls laugh. "Speaking of ex-husbands, my second husband is due for a visit from his mother. I was thinking maybe you could take her?" The table goes quiet and then I realize she's looking at me. "Would you like that, Marina?"

"Me?" I ask, surprised.

"She likes you quite a lot. She showed me a dog you sculpted out of clay," Regina smiles. She's talking about Bob, my nocturnal artist friend.

"That was a donkey," I admit. Yang laughs.

"I would take her myself, but she refuses to fly and the boat to Palermo is ten hours from Naples," Regina explains. "Do you like boats? I'll pay for everything of course. You'll have a first-class cabin. If you haven't been, I think you'll love Sicily."

"What about you guys?" I ask Yin and Yang.

"We're returning to Rome tomorrow," says Yin.

"Oh," I say, suddenly feeling glum. "Well I was thinking I should try and get back onto my original itinerary."

"Fuck your itinerary!" says Yang. "When will you get another chance to escort an elderly blind woman who doesn't speak English to the birthplace of the mafia?" I consider her words and then look at Regina. She's been so kind and generous to me. How can I say no?

"I guess I'm going to Palermo," I say, still trying to wrap my head around it.

"Thank you! She'll be so pleased," Regina smiles broadly.

Villa Rufolo, Ravello: Tuesday, 3:55 p.m.

Ying, Yang, and I are spending our last day together exploring. After stuffing ourselves at a local trattoria with a three-course lunch, I suggest an espresso by the pool at the exquisite Villa Rufolo. Yin and Yang stretch out together and I find my own Belgian linen-covered lounge chair in the shade. I have tried not to check my phone every hour, to see if there are any more song lyrics from Frantonio, but I failed. There have been none. He's gone. He said his goodbye in a note. This is fine. For the best, really. So why do I keep thinking about him? To put my mind on something more constructive, I pull out my tablet and continue my research on an Italian poet, Alda Merini. Yin notices.

"Let us read some of your writing, Marina," begs Yin.

"The juicy parts, not the research," says Yang.

"I've decided to write an adventure travel blog—separate from my book."

"Brilliant," says Yang. "Put the good stuff online for free." She shakes her head.

"Okay, you've got a point. But some of these women may surprise you. You'd like Alda Merini, for example. Her poetry is pithy and sexy. Like an Italian Dorothy Parker. But Alda's tone is darker. Reading about her life, you understand why." I read the girls some of my notes.

NOTES ON ITALIAN WOMAN OF INFLUENCE: Alda Merini

1. Born 1931, Milan, to an insurance salesman and a housewife.
2. Her writing talent was discovered at age of fifteen, but by sixteen she was interned for a month at a clinic for mental health.
3. When she was nineteen, two of her poems were published. She married a bakery owner at twenty-two.
4. Committed by her husband to a psychiatric hospital, this time for seven years.
5. *La Terra Santa* (which she calls her masterpiece) are intense

poems inspired by her stay at this hospital. She fought long to get this published.

6. After her husband died, she remarried to a much older doctor, Michele Pierri; she then wrote twenty poems, *La Gazza Ladra* (The Thieving Magpie).

7. From 1986 to 2006, able to live outside the hospital, she published at least one book of poems or prose every year.

8. Wore fire-red lipstick; some of her work was collected into a book called *I Am A Furious Little Bee*, in which she describes herself as such.

9. In 2004, an album of her poetry sung to music was released by Milva.

10. Find and read: *Love Lessons*, and *Sogno e Poesia* (Dream and Poetry). Find and watch: *The Crazy Woman Next Door* by Antonietta de Lillo.

"That's fucking depressing," Yang says.

"No," objects Yin. "She's fascinating."

"Her writing is fierce, witty, rhythmic," I say. As I peruse my notes, I realize the woman completely baffles me. She's been through all of this shit in her life, and somehow still manages to wear her red lipstick and write about love. To me love is an anchor. To her it's a life raft.

Gardens, Villa Cimbrone, Ravello: Tuesday, Sunset

As the overripe sun smears itself across the sky like a soft, runny peach, we wander through the incredible gardens at Villa Cimbrone. Pale purple Wisteria flowers, like little bunches of floral grapes, drip from every wall and brush our heads as we walk under wooden trellis walkways. Roses of every variety explode in yellow, orange, red, various pinks, fuchsia, white, and cream. Blues and purples blush from every hydrangea bush.

"This garden is a wonderland. All we're missing is the fairies," I say.

"Wrong," smiles Yang, as she points her camera at Yin.

Yin has found a swing. Her ballet flats lie abandoned in the grass. She's floating in billowy arcs through the air. The ruffles of her pale yellow taffeta sundress flutter and flap around her like the wings of a hundred butterflies. Her bare toes point at the sun as she leans back in the swing. Blonde hair blowing freely around her face, she smiles puckishly at the camera each time she passes us. The dainty pearls she wears shiver on her earlobes and dance at her throat as she laughs. She is resplendent.

"Wow," I say.

"Yeah," agrees Yang.

"You've captured yourself a fairy princess."

"No mate, I captured nothing," Yang says softly. I've never heard her voice sound small like this. "She's just decided to fly next to me for a while, like one of those seagulls when you're on a sailboat. It drifts along, riding the same wind you're using. Then, when the wind shifts, it flies away."

"Maybe," I agree. "Alda Merini wrote about this idea: that we can never predict how long the tongues of our lovers are going to linger on us."

"Fucking true," she grins.

"And, she believed that we know we're in love with someone when our bodies are perpetually evolving."

"Okay. You can put her in your book. Alda's got it. That evolution is the painful gift our lovers bring to us as we cry like children outgrowing our toys."

"Wow," I say, impressed. "You may keep your fairy princess after all."

"No," Yang shrugs. "But it's okay. I'm still jammy as fuck right now." She's smiling but her eyes are sad. "Some people are sent into your life for a beautiful minute mate, and you can't waste any time worrying about next. Just enjoy now." She walks over to Yin, pushing her higher on the swing. I watch, knowing Yang's right. Was my minute with Frantonio already over? Had I wasted it?

Casa di Pavone, Amalfi: Wednesday, 1:00 p.m.

Piero #4 helps me bring my luggage out to the car. We haven't seen much of each other since the cabana. He gives me a sweet goodbye kiss.

"Thank you, Piero."

"You are a pleasure to know, *bella*," he says. "*Buon viaggio.*"

"Okay pretty boy, our turn," says Yang as she walks up, taking my bag from him. Yin is with her. Piero #4 gives me a wink and disappears back into the house. I don't do big goodbyes. I always think I'm going to see that person again. It's clear that Yang shares my MO, since she unceremoniously tosses my bag into Regina's car alongside Bob's luggage.

"See ya, mate. Don't have too many dick sandwiches," she says as she slaps my back.

"Good luck with the book. We can't wait to read it." Yin kisses my cheeks.

"Thank you both, for trashing my itinerary," I smile. "Really."

Chapter 26

How Not to Disco

Dining Room, *SNAV Mega Salacia*:
Wednesday, 8:36 p.m.

Bob and I enjoy a mediocre dinner in the dining room. Aside from needing help navigating new spaces, she's remarkably self-sufficient. There was a bit of effort involved helping her squeeze into the granny spanks she insisted on wearing to dinner. It was like squeezing a bony, old cat with loose skin into a scuba wetsuit. But her upside-down beehive hairdo she did on her own. I'm feeling good about my choice to come. Another adventure will keep my mind from dwelling on people it should be forgetting. Despite the excellent and well-timed sympathy fuck from Piero, I'm still thinking of Frantonio. Damn him!

Now, as I sip my mediocre wine and pick at my mediocre *verdure fritte* (fried vegetables), I notice a handsome young guy at another table. Tall, blond hair, well built. The handsome guy is with an elderly man wearing a dapper hat. We exchange knowing smiles. We must be thinking the same thing. We're both traveling with oldies. We're both do-gooders. We both deserve a drink together after our oldies have gone to bed.

I'm picking mushrooms out of my *risotto con funghi* (risotto with mushrooms) when I suddenly remember the Trusty Translator app on my phone. Why aren't I using that more? I pull it out and speak English into the microphone.

"Tell me about your son." With a tap of my finger, Trusty translates this into a computerized voice that asks Bob the same question in Italian (I hope). *"Dimmi di tuo figlio."* Bob laughs at the computerized voice. Apparently this is the funniest thing she's ever heard. She takes the phone from me. I show her where to tap, and then I hold it up to her mouth. She starts speaking.

"My- son- is- Alfredo, an asshole," Trusty Translator chirps. Someone at another table looks over. My eyes go wide and I turn the volume down. I didn't know Trusty was programmed with swear words. But Bob is laughing. Then she presses the button again and launches into a rant, during which she continues to eat, and Trusty struggles to keep up. Pieces of lasagna fly in different directions each time the roller coaster of Bob's rant reaches a pinnacle. Tears threaten to fall each time it crashes back down the other side. She gulps her wine. By the end, Trusty has crashed, and Bob's so upset I'm afraid she'll have a stroke. But I have learned the following:

1. Alfredo is either a heart surgeon or works at a quarry, driving a big machine.

2. His current wife, Gen, is a *strega manipolatrice* (controlling witch).

3. They have a son called Luigi. Or a dog? Luigi eats too much.

4. The also have a son called Akio. Or a cat? He doesn't eat enough.

5. There was a fight between these two sons. Or dog and cat?

6. Gen kicked Bob out of the house at Christmas. Or Bob kicked Gen out. Or maybe it was Luigi? Someone was kicked out at Christmas.

7. Two things are certain: Alfredo drinks too much and Gen is a bitch.

8. One thing is unclear: Why is Bob going to visit them?

At various times throughout the meal I've glanced over at Do-Gooder. Each time I do, he's talking to his companion, but looking at me. Clearly, this guy is totally into me. I'm commanding the gaze now and not even trying. I'm a sexy-siren do-gooder. What a great way to get Frantonio out of my head. I'll just tease him a bit. I shovel tiramisu onto my fork and then lift it gracefully to my mouth, sensually opening my lips and mouth, sliding the sweet, creamy, messy—shit he's coming over! I now have a mouthful of mush, which I'm still chewing as he arrives at our table.

"Good evening." His accent is German, but his English is perfect.

"Hello," I wave with my mouth full.

"There is a bit of—" he says. I realize I've got whipped cream on my lip and try to lick it off sexily with my tongue, but just smear it. I grab my napkin.

"Enjoying your dinner?" I ask politely.

"Yes, thank you. My friend, Mr. Gutzewarner, wants me to introduce us. I am Fritz. He is Mr. Gutzewarner."

"Oh, *he* wanted you to come talk to me?" I give Fritz a smile, playing along with his thinly veiled ploy to hit on me. "Well, nice to meet you both. I'm Marina." I introduce Bob, but she's more interested in disassembling her *cannolo*. I look over at Mr. Gutzewarner, who is now squinting in our direction, napkin tucked into his collar.

"Mr. Gutzewarner wanted me to inquire if you ladies have separate cabins for the crossing?"

"Wow, that's direct." I laugh. "Mr. Goosewarmer is interested in where I'm sleeping? Please tell him we're sharing a cabin."

"I see. Mr. Gutzewarner wanted me to let you know that he and I have separate cabins." Fritz smiles, all dimples and blue eyes.

"He did? That's promising," I smile. "Shall we make an appointment for later?"

"Yes! In fact, this is exactly what Mr. Gutzewarner would like." Fritz's accent is adorable, and so is this ridiculous pick up scheme.

"Oh yeah? He's pretty liberal for an old man," I continue the joke.

"Yes, indeed, he is," Fritz laughs, glad that I'm amused. What a cutie.

"Impressive," I say.

"Yes, quite. Mr. Gutzewarner has two different medications to ensure erectile performance. But he finds it difficult to sleep unless he has ejaculated more than once," explains Fritz. I stare. Suddenly his accent is not cute at all. WHAT?

"Mr. Goosewarmer wants me to sleep with *him*?" I'm appalled.

"Oh! Sorry. No. We have some confusion." Fritz is alarmed.

"You bet we do, Umlaut. You can tell Mr. Goosewarmer, I don't sleep with men who take their teeth out first. Sorry."

"Yes. Mr. Goosewarm—" He's flustered. "I mean, Mr. Gutzewarner would like to invite your *companion* to sleep in his cabin," Fritz explains. Bob? Seriously? The old lady is getting propositioned, not the sexy-siren do-gooder.

"Wait a minute. This whole dinner you're looking over making googly eyes at me, you're just trying to get your old man laid?"

"Googly? I am Mr. Gutzewarner's traveling assistant."

"You mean grandpa pimp. Look, my friend here is Sicilian Catholic and she doesn't speak English. I can't exactly proposition her for you. For him. Whatever."

"Oh. Okay, I understand," he says. "I can ask her." He turns to Bob and speaks fluent Italian. Shit! Bob looks up at the sound of his voice, listening intently. I wait for Bob to explode. Will she throw her *cannolo* at him? No she likes her *cannolo*. Her plate maybe? Fritz finishes and points at Mr. Goosewarmer, but Bob doesn't look around. In fact, she doesn't react at all.

"Wait, you told her the part about the sex?" I ask, confused.

"Yes. But, does she see him?"

"No, she doesn't see him. She's blind, you idiot grandpa pimp."

"Blind? Oh, I see," he says, startled. "Excuse me for a moment." Fritz returns to Mr. Goosewarmer for a consult. I'm fairly certain Bob missed his question, but suddenly she takes my phone and speaks into Trusty. "*È bello?*" ("Is he handsome?" recites Trusty Translator.) I am floored.

Bob's considering the proposition? Holy shit. I take the phone and speak into it. Our conversation via Trusty goes something like this:

"Not terrible."—"*Non è terribile.*"

"*Quanti anni ha?*"—"How old is he?"

"Eighty?"—"*Ottanta?*" I have no idea.

"*Preferisco più giovane*"—"I prefer younger," Bob says. I giggle, and suddenly realize the fifty-something, geeky Italian man I saw coming out of Bob's room the other day may not have actually been a doctor.

"*Ha i capelli?*"—"Does he have hair?" she wants to know.

"He has a hat."—"*Ha un cappello,*" I answer via Trusty.

"*Calvo.*"—"Bald," Bob decides.

"So?"—"*Allora?*" I ask.

"*Nessuna fiducia in se stesso, amante cattivo.*"—"No confidence, bad lover," she asserts. I giggle again. Okay, this oldie rocks.

"He's confident."—"*È fiducioso,*" I confide. "He has drugs."—"*Ha droghe.*"

"*Non facio più droghe.*"—"I don't do drugs anymore." Bob shakes her head.

"Drugs for him."—"*Farmaci per lui,*" I clarify. Her eyebrows go up.

"*Farmaci del pene?*"—"Penis drugs?" Trusty chirps.

"*Sì,*" I answer.

"*Perchè no?*" Bob smiles.

"Yes, *perchè no?*" I laugh. Theme of this trip. Why the fuck not? "Life is short"—"*La vita è breve.*" I say via Trusty.

"*La mia è più corta ogni giorno,*"—"Mine is shorter by the day." This hits me right in my soft spot. Now I want this for her. Holy crap. I'm about to arrange a sexual liaison for Regina's blind ex-mother-in-law with a stranger on a ferryboat! But then I see Fritz and Mr. Goosewarmer leaving their table. Wait, where are they going?

"Mr. Gutzewarner is feeling tired," Fritz calls to me. "We must bid you ladies good night." What? They're leaving after all of that? That rat bastard!

"That's bullshit!" I yell. "Your boss just doesn't want to screw a blind woman. He's no peach himself. In fact, he should be relieved she's blind!" People in the dining room stare at us. Bob looks confused.

"*Che cosa è successo?*"—"What happened?" Bob asks. But I'm standing up now, giving both men the middle finger as they hobble out.

"You tell Mr. Goosewarmer my friend doesn't fuck wrinkly, drooling, hairless, horny, drugged up bags of bones!" They don't look back. The dining room is now completely silent. Except . . . Bob. She's laughing. No, she's cackling. About to split her granny spanks right open. She pats my hand.

Private Cabin, *SNAV Mega Salacia:* Wednesday, 10:34 p.m.

Bob and I return to our little cabin. It's pretty small, with narrow single beds on either side of the room, and a tiny bathroom in the middle. It's not long before she's scrolled through the four television channels and clicked it back off. I offer to help her get undressed, and she looks confused. "*Perché?*" She asks. It dawns on me—Bob is nocturnal, she'll be up all night. *Perfetto.* Another long, sleepless night, trying not to think about Frantonio. Fine. I'm relieved not to have to try and pull her back out of those granny spanks right now. I sit on my bed and Bob sits down next to me. She reaches for my phone.

"*Grazie per essere venuta.*"—"Thank you for coming." She smiles. A small golden bee hairpin dangles from her hive of hair. I reach up and shove it back in.

"Of course. We're friends."—"*Ma certo, siamo amiche,*" Trusty chirps for me. Bob smiles, squeezes my hand.

"*Se siamo amiche, devo fare qualcosa.*"—"If we are friends, I must do something," chirps Trusty. Bob takes a small knife out of her pocket. My eyes widen. What the hell is she going to do with that? Cut our palms and mix our blood in some ancient Sicilian friendship ritual? I quickly reclaim my hand. But then Bob reaches over, digs in her bag, and pulls out a small chunk of wood. "*Fare qualcosa per te.*"—"Make something for you." Oh. Okay. That's nice.

I realize that Bob is going to camp out on my bed for her whittling project, so I lean back, get comfy, and pull out my tablet to work on my book. I scroll through music choices until Bob is happy. Tonight we shall be working to Leonard Cohen. Moody and mellow. That seems appropriate. Bob's whittling away, creating something wonderful for me out of wood, so I read about another inspirational Italian artist: Artemisia Gentileschi, the first woman to be accepted to the Accademia in Florence.

Things are going well until the playlist hits Leonard Cohen's "A Thousand Kisses Deep." The first few chords of the song drag my heart into my stomach. By the end of the first verse, my throat is aching. Will used to play this, one of his favorite old songs, trying to get me to dance with him. I don't slow dance. It's a rule I made on my sixteenth birthday. I've never broken it. There were other songs, lots of them, but Will always came back to this one. Now it cuts me to the core. I should have danced with Will. It's too late. Suddenly, I'm crying. And all at once, Bob's arm is around me. My head is on her shoulder. She fumbles with the tablet and manages to stop the music. But now I'm weeping openly. What is wrong with me? Am I crying because I left Will? Or because I lost Frantonio? Or am I just lost?

"*Shhhh, basta, bella. Basta.*" Bob wipes my face. "*Colpa mia. Leonard Cohen è troppo.*" She's right. Leonard Cohen is too much. She squeezes my shoulders. "*La discoteca è aperta!*"

"Disco?"

All-Night Disco, *SNAV Mega Salacia*: Wednesday, 11:24 p.m.

The twenty-four-hour Mega Disco is like a dive casino in Reno at four a.m., complete with slot machines, electronic poker, and a janitor vacuuming up puke from the carpet by the bathrooms. A flashing video DJ blasts Euro Techno music from a speaker that looks like it's going to vibrate itself right out of the wall. Badly shot music videos play on a screen. A deckhand is passed out on the bar in a puddle of drool. The female bartender swipes right unenthusiastically on her phone, unlit cigarette hanging limply in her mouth. Two teens make out in a dark corner. A baby stroller is parked right in the middle of the dance floor. WTF? Surely there's no baby inside. I walk closer and see a child, staring directly up at the slowly rotating, blue mirrored disco ball. Uhhh . . . I look around for the mother and see her slumped in a nearby chair, dark circles under her eyes, a colic zombie. I watch her, watching the baby, watching the ball turn. Anything to keep him from crying another six hours.

An elderly couple slow dances in place. Or they could be just leaning up against each other, swaying in their sleep? But the song is not slow. It's fast and loud, pressure washing the inside of my head. Bob loves it. She laughs and starts to dance. Her arms wave, her hips wiggle. Her black, orthopedic shoes slide along the tile as she inches like a Rhumba vacuum around the dance floor.

"*Stai ballando?*" she yells to me.

"*Sì!*" I yell back. "*Ballando.*" But I just stand there, watching her. I cannot dance to this crap.

"*Stai ballando?*" Bob yells again.

"She want you dance," Zombie Mom tells me. Yes, I gathered that. Reluctantly I move closer to Bob and move my hips a little.

"I'm dancing," I yell over the music.

"*Tutto bene!*" Bob grabs my hand and dances with me. She cackles with delight. She breaks free, spinning slowly like the disco ball above that showers us with blue spots. My arms float overhead, pulsing to the beat. I close my eyes, lose myself.

Private Cabin, SNAV *Mega Salacia*: Thursday, 12:54 a.m.

We're both sweating profusely and exhausted. I have managed to dance out my frustration, sorrow, and doubt. No thought of Will or Frantonio. Until I see the message, waiting on my phone.

Chapter 27

How Not to Refuse An Offer You Can't

Palermo, Sicily: Thursday, 8:55 a.m.

Sicily is a beautiful, old island. She has been had by many. The Phoenicians, Arabs, Byzantines, Swabians, Normans, Spanish, Moors, Neapolitan and Austrian royalty, and of course the pirates. Palermo, once richer than Rome or Milan, is still vibrant, if somewhat confused by her colorful past. I like Palermo immediately. She sits in a basin, surrounded by mountains. Her discordant style and character suggest one too many cultural makeovers. She doesn't quite know who she is anymore, with her baroque churches, Arab bazaars, and Spanish gardens. Her old and new bits are mashed together; ancient, crumbling beauty with urban seediness. A church, once Greek Orthodox, now bedazzled baroque, tries to ignore the bold, new vape shop next door, even as a hot pink neon sign bathes its stone cherubs with cold, rosy light. It's all a bit strange. But somehow it works: like Bob and I do. We are strange, young and old, mismatched together perfectly.

In the Borgo Vecchio, at the port, we're collected by Bob's grandsons, Luigi and Akio. Both are in their twenties, and apparently "Italian-

Japanese" translates to dark hair, perfect skin, and sexy eyes. So Luigi is not a dog, and Akio is not a cat. However, I see why there was confusion. Bob must have been describing them to me. Luigi, muscular and clumsy, is boisterously loud and overly happy about everything. He doesn't make eye contact for long, but he's very affectionate, lots of greeting kisses and touching. His brother, Akio, is lean and graceful. He stares at you until you're uncomfortable. He's moody and quiet. They're both fantastically patient and wonderful with their *nonna*, Bob. The boys strap our luggage to the top of their little blue Cinquecento, and we all squish inside. On the way, Bob snoozes and the brothers clue me in on some customs and house rules.

CUSTOMS IN A SICILIAN-JAPANESE HOME, ACCORDING TO LUIGI AND AKIO:

1. **NEVER:** wear your shoes in the house. Your host will provide you with rubber booties to be worn indoors. (Japanese)
2. **ALWAYS:** pause to knock on each side of the doorframe when walking through any doorway; this is for luck against earthquakes. (Sicilian)
3. **NEVER:** show your teeth when you smile. It's considered rude and aggressive. (Japanese)
4. **ALWAYS:** bow when greeting someone. (Japanese)
5. **NEVER:** blink when answering a question, it means you're lying. (Sicilian)
6. **ALWAYS:** keep your head lower than the man of the house, if you're a woman. (Japanese)
7. **ALWAYS:** burp during a meal to show true appreciation. (Japanese)
8. **NEVER:** touch another woman's husband without her permission. (Sicilian)
9. **ALWAYS:** say *"Bugitaimu!"* loudly, with conviction, when someone sneezes. (Japanese)
10. **NEVER:** refuse an offer from a host. (Sicilian)

Mondello, Palermo: Thursday, 12:04 p.m.

I'm happy to have some alone time in my room before lunch. Alfredo is at a hospital meeting (apparently he's a surgeon and not a driver of heavy machinery) and his wife Gen is shopping, so I haven't met either yet, but will at lunch. I'm told that Akio has been experimenting in the kitchen, so the family (and guests) are his guinea pigs. Luigi slipped me a bag of chips and an apple with a warning look. I'm guessing the experiments have not gone well in the past.

Lying on the bed, I stare at the new message I got last night. I'm still not sure what it means, but the very fact that I'm getting lyrics again has put a bounce back in my step. Frantonio is still thinking of me.

She flees like the wind
Hides like the sun in winter
But her warmth endures.

I can't answer him until I know the rest of the song. This is a fantastic game. I search the lyrics online. It takes a little digging and I soon realize why: the original lyrics are in Icelandic. The song is by a rock band. I play the song and listen as I lie on my bed. Ethereal tones, mystically romantic. It's beautiful. In the library, Frantonio had said I had a light inside me. So, he thinks I'm like the sun. I decide to answer with lyrics from the same song, so he knows I found it.

To the smallest whisper
I am listening. She is mine.

Alfredo's house, Palermo: Thursday, 1:16 p.m.

In the kitchen, Akio is tossing a strange-looking mush and Luigi is seated with a beer. They exchange a smile as I pause to tap the doorframe twice (#2: preventing earthquakes).

"Good, you remember," Luigi says.

"Don't forget the rest also," says Akio. "Very important." I nod. After the embarrassments at Regina's, I'm determined not to offend anyone here. Bob is going to sleep through to dinner, so I'm on my own with her family. Just then, Gen walks in, carrying shopping bags. She's tiny but fit: Japanese Kickboxer Barbie. High-waisted pants emphasize perfectly shaped hips, a silk tank shows off her biceps and her "just buff enough" shoulders. Her ebony hair is pulled into a ponytail. I walk up eagerly.

"Hello! I'm Marina," I bow politely (#4) and smile with my lips closed (#3, no teeth). She looks startled.

"*Oh! Piacere.* I am Alfredo's wife. My name is Gen. Welcome to our—" She stops, staring at my feet.

"Are those my scuba diving booties?"

"Uh . . . Akio gave me these to wear inside," (#1, no shoes) I say. Gen gives her son a look.

"She's from Florida, Mama. I thought she would like them!" he says.

"Don't wear those," Gen says to me. "Go barefoot, as you like."

"Oh, whew! Thanks. My feet are sweating so much I'm sliding around in these booties like a greased pig," I laugh. Gen doesn't laugh. She looks kind of disgusted.

"Put them in the laundry machine—through there." She points. I walk through, pausing to tap the doorframe twice (#2), and smile back at Gen with lips closed (#3). "No earthquakes today!" I exit, proud that I remembered.

When I return, Alfredo has arrived. He's a bit shorter than I am, so I'm careful to keep my knees bent as I approach so that my head stays lower than his (#6). Frankly, this custom seems completely sexist to me, but I'm not about to offend the son of my first and only geriatric friend. I bow and smile with lips closed (#3). "You must be Alfredo. I'm Marina." He also looks surprised when I bow. Ha! I think to myself. I'm not a clueless American. Alfredo sticks his hand out.

"*Piacere.* Alfredo." I shake his hand. He rolls up his sleeves. "You are my mother's friend, the American writer? *Bienvenuta.*" He washes his hands. "You must be special. Mama doesn't make many friends—that are women." Alfredo bends to dry his hands on a low hanging towel. Instantly, I hunch over too, keeping my head level lower than his.

"Well, we're both artists and both unique," I say, from my hunchback position.

"Are you okay?" he asks as he takes out a beer.

"Yes. I'm great!" I answer, without blinking (#5, so he won't think I'm lying). "Just hungry," I smile with my lips closed (#3).

"Food's ready!" announces Akio, as he places a giant bowl onto the center of the kitchen table. Alfredo opens a beer and drinks half of it down.

"*Allora*, what the hell is it this time?" asks his father as he sits. Luigi pulls out a chair for me, between himself and his father. As I sit, I have to slump in my seat a bit to keep my head lower than Alfredo's (#6). Luigi sees this and gives me a subtle nod. I smile, realize my teeth are showing, and slam my lips closed (#3). He smiles back, trying not to laugh.

"We are having kitfo," says Akio proudly. "An Ethiopian dish from my new cookbook, *Around the World in Eighty Recipes*. It's minced, raw beef, marinated in chili powder and butter with herbs. And those are jalepeños so watch out."

"Raw beef?" complains Alfredo. He finishes his beer.

"So Mama can eat with us. She's on her raw diet," Akio says.

"She got on that diet so she *didn't* have to eat your food experiments," laughs Luigi.

"*Non è vero! Grazie,* Akio," Gen says, scooping a mound onto her plate. She stares at it. "We need forks." She points to a drawer.

"Actually, Mama, the Ethiopian dishes are eaten with our hands." The rest of the family looks at him like he's nuts.

"He's right," I say supportively. "My friend went to Ethiopia." I smile with my lips closed (#3).

"May I serve you some?" asks Akio. I don't even like sushi, much less raw beef, but this is an offer from my host. I cannot refuse (#10).

"Yes please," I say. He scoops a large amount onto my plate and, to show how excited I am, I immediately take a too large clump of meat with my hands and try to fit it into my mouth. They all watch as meat sticks to my fingers and falls into my lap, onto the table, and onto my plate. "Mmmm!" The chili powder is hotter than I expected but I continue to chew.

"Actually, you're supposed to use this bread." Akio opens a flat, lidded bowl sitting on the table. "You scoop with it." As he hands me a piece, I bite into a chunk of jalepeño. My mouth is suddenly on fire. "How is it?" Akio asks as I force myself to swallow. Alfredo watches me. Akio's desperation to impress his father is palpable.

"It is so good." I'm trying desperately not to blink but my eyes are watering. "I've never had anything like it." I blink as I grab my water, downing half the glass.

"She blinked," says Luigi. "She's lying. I'm not eating this."

"No, it's good!" I say trying to keep from blinking again, but I do. Then I remember #7. I drink more water and: BURP! I belch loudly. "See, I love it!" I smile with lips closed (#3). Alfredo is staring. Gen is staring. Luigi and Akio are stifling laughter. I begin to realize something's afoot, but right now I'm too interested in refilling my water glass. Alfredo finishes his beer.

"Where did you buy this beef?" Alfredo asks Akio. "I'm not getting *mucca pazza* so you can get into fucking cooking school."

"What's *mucca pazza*?" I ask.

"Mad cow disease," answers Gen.

"That's not still a problem, is it?" I'm starting to sweat. Maybe it's the jalapeño.

"No. Only in places where the mafia bought all the sick cows for one-fifth the price and kept selling the meat to turn a huge profit," says Luigi. The blood drains from my face.

"Mafia? But isn't Sicily the birthplace of the—"

"No, don't believe everything in your American movies," says Luigi.

"Dumb movies," I laugh with nervous relief.

"The mafia's everywhere in Italy, not just Sicily. Since Ancient Rome."

I put my bread down. I'm sweating even more now. Fucking *Perfetto*. I'm going to have mad cow disease.

"I'll just have another beer," says Alfredo. The boys both try to get their father a beer at the same time, but Luigi makes it to the fridge first.

"There's fresh fish I can cook up. I got it this morning," Luigi offers.

"*No! Sta zitto!*" Akio stares daggers at his brother. "The beef is fine! Aren't you going to even try it, Papa?" Akio pleads. Gen gives her husband a look. Slowly Alfredo picks up a piece of bread and scoops up a bit of the meat. We all watch as he puts it into his mouth and chews. It's clear that Akio wants to please his dad, and his competitive brother is trying to sabotage his meal. We all wait for the judge's verdict. Finally, Alfredo shrugs.

"Not bad," their father says, as he scoops up more. Akio is ecstatic, victory. Luigi rolls his eyes in defeat. Gen picks up a piece of bread, scoops a bit of meat, but pauses to smell it first. The chili powder makes her sneeze.

"*Bugitaimu!*" I shout with conviction (#9). She stares at me in shock. "That's all the Japanese I know," I say, apologetically.

"So, you're not married, I guess?" asks Alfredo as he drinks his beer and leans back in his chair. The question takes me by surprise. I look at him and realize I'm sitting taller. I slump down in my chair even further (#6).

"No," I say.

"Neither are these two mama's boys. No houses. No jobs. No wives." Gen scolds her husband quietly in Italian but he ignores her. "Why don't you let them show you around Sicily? Maybe you'll take one home as a souvenir," he winks at his boys. Awkward! I decide not to answer. Wait, was that an offer from my host (#10)?

"Thank you for the offer, I accept," I say, embarrassed.

"Make sure you try them each out before you decide. You can't give them back," laughs Alfredo, and he swigs his beer. Gen angrily knocks

Alfredo's elbow and the beer bottle falls into his lap, then hits the floor. He swears angrily in Italian, leaning down with his napkin. I move quickly to the floor, trying to keep my head lower.

"I got it!" I say. I want to hide under the table anyway.

"No, it's fine." Alfredo goes onto one knee to mop up the mess. This forces me to practically lie on the floor next to him.

"I don't mind!" I say, hoping he'll stand up.

"Are you feeling okay?" He reaches over to feel my forehead and I freak out and roll out of his reach, like a wrestler on the mat (#8, never touch another woman's husband). Alfredo stands, bewildered. The brothers are laughing.

"Come up off the floor, dear!" Gen leans forward, reaching her hand out, but the chili pepper gets her again. She sneezes.

"*Bugitaimu!*" I shout (#9) as I pop up. The brothers are now laughing hysterically. Looking at them, I finally understand what they've done. Sandbagged me with a list of phony customs. I look at Gen, and even she is trying not to laugh. "What does that mean, in Japanese?"

"Booger time," she smiles, with lots of teeth.

Chapter 28

How Not to Choose

WHEN TWO BROTHERS COMPETE FOR YOUR AFFECTIONS:

1. Avoid touching either brother.
2. Avoid being alone with either brother.
3. Always laugh at both brothers' jokes equally.
4. Decline one brother's offer to fly his remote control drone to get cool video for your phone, which will require hours of close contact alone time.
5. Decline the other brother's offer to teach you to bake *cannoli* and impress your mother, which will require hours of close contact alone time.
6. Do not let one brother give you a foot massage, realize your mistake, and end up with one brother massaging each foot. (Didn't you read #1?)
7. Always refrain when asked to judge arm wrestling matches, or erotic origami contests (no matter how interesting that sounds).
8. Do NOT, under any circumstances, get into a hot tub with both brothers and a drink with a little umbrella. (Didn't you read #1?)

Around Palermo: Friday Morning

I should: insist we take the car on our whirlwind tour of the city.

Instead I: let them talk me into a tour on scooter, which requires me to choose which brother to ride behind, lean against, and grip tightly. Luigi explains proudly that his bike is faster, highly modified, which actually makes me choose Akio's safer, slower-looking Vespa. This puts Luigi into a sulk and forces me into a pattern of switching bikes at every sight we stop to see throughout the day. Each time I mount up, that brother seems to drive even faster, as if to lose the other brother and impress me with his skills of darting and weaving through traffic. Soon I'm ready to hurl. When we pause briefly to see the Fontana Pretoria, in Piazza Pretoria, I am only too happy to sit on the stable, unmoving stone steps, admiring the tiers of elaborately carved nude statues stacked atop each other like an ancient, bachelor party cake. The cool mist feels good on my face. "This is called the Fountain of Shame," explains Akio. "Because there are over forty naked statues."

"It is the most famous fountain in Palermo," adds Luigi.

"Of course it is." I chuckle at the irony, thinking of Frantonio's fountain of shame. A series of images involuntarily flash through my head: Mario's too close erection as I stand in shin deep, cold water; Frantonio's warm hand on my naked breast, as I find myself pressed against the wall; Franonio's angry, passionate, hurt brown eyes as he stares into mine in the library. My stomach twists, and this time it's not from my wild scooter rides. I pull out my phone. Nothing. Why hasn't he answered me yet? I answered his last message yesterday. I start to text again but stop. The next message needs to be from him. I've got two handsome Sicilian brothers vying for my attention. I'll have enough distraction.

Cathedral of Palermo, aka Cattedrale Metropolitana della Santa Vergine Maria Assunta, Palermo: Friday, 12:15 p.m.

I should: admire the Norman-Arab-Byzantine-Swabian-Romanesque-Baroque-Gothic architecture in the world's most multicultural church, without trying to participate.

Instead I: light a candle in honor of my mother in the chapel of St. Rosalia, Palermo's patron saint. My mother is not a Catholic, but her name is Rosalie, and I think it's especially fitting that St. Rosalia rejected a worldly life to live in the caves of Mt. Pellegrino. My mother seldom leaves the inn, much less Florida. Akio sees me light the candle and shows up ten minutes later with a nine-inch St. Rosalia figurine he's purchased for me. She's wearing a crown of roses and a tortured, mournful expression. "Wow, thank you. It's . . . precious," I fumble, resorting to that painfully polite southern expression invented for ugly babies, bad haircuts, and very old cats.

"For your mother," Akio explains proudly.

"Yes, fantastic. She loves figurines."

"Also this," says Luigi holding out *his* gift.

"And . . . a glass shoebox of plastic bones and silk roses!" I say. "You can never have enough of those."

"To keep your mother healthy," Luigi explains. "When St. Rosalia's remains were found in the cave, they were taken around Palermo in a parade and three days later the plague ended."

"*Perfetto!*" I smile. "She can stop taking those fistfuls of vitamins now." As we leave the cathedral I check my phone. Nothing.

At the Museo Internazionale delle Marionette, Palermo: Friday, 2:30 p.m.

I should: take a selfie with the smiling Pakistani man operating the Spanish Conquistador puppet.

Instead I: make the mistake of asking Akio to take my photo. Luigi, of course, pops into the photo with me, the Pakistani puppeteer, and the Spanish Conquistador. So then I have to take another photo with Akio, the Pakistani puppeteer, and the Spanish Conquistador. Luigi then wants a photo with me and the wizard marionette. Akio wants a photo with me and the French chef puppet. On it goes, for the rest of the day. A competition to see who can be in more photos with me. I finally resort to asking random passersby to take photos of the three of us each time. Posting these on social media immediately earns me comments from Mike and Michael asking who my two delicious boyfriends are.

At the Valley of the Temples, Agrigento: Friday, 4:45 p.m.

I should have: been content with the myriad floral and woody fragrances of the botanical garden of Kolymbetra, located between the Temple of Castor and Pollux and the Temple of Vulcan.

Instead I: pick a small white flower from an almond tree to put behind my ear; this causes Akio to make me a scented crown of blooming rosemary; which causes Luigi to fashion me a garland of bright yellow mustard flowers to wear around my neck; which causes me to look like Ophelia; which causes a very angry lady with bright magenta hair who works for the Italian National Trust in charge of the garden to kick us all out because we're not respecting the Kolymbetra ways. Didn't we read the sign? (No, we were too busy looking up pictures of edible mushrooms on our phones.) As we leave the gardens, I check my phone. Nothing.

Giardino Pacini, Catania: Saturday, 11:20 a.m.

Today's adventure started with Catania, an old port city. We're taking a bathroom stop after touring a beautiful little garden. When I come outside, I find Luigi with his eyes on the sky. Akio is gone. "My brother checks to see if our favorite pasticceria is open," explains Luigi.

"What are you looking at?" I ask.

"I heard the planes, before. Maybe they will return."

"What planes?"

"Greyhounds, or P-3 Orion or clippers maybe. They do drills some-times. But more likely PC-3 patrol squadron. We are near Sigonella, the naval air station." He points off in the distance.

"Italian Air Force?"

"Well, it is our base, and we have Breguet Atlantics, but most of the best planes are yours. It is a US hub. The C-5 Galaxy airlifts are *impossibilimente enorme, e stupefacente*. Lockheed Martin makes these." His eyes light up as he tells me about the massive US transporter planes. "*Però*, in the beginning they found cracks in the wings of many and they had to make modifications. The new Super Galaxy is even better and will fly until 2040."

"Too bad you know nothing about planes!" I joke.

"I know everything about planes," he says, confused.

"I was kidding. I thought you just liked flying model planes."

"No! I'm saving money even now for my flying classes. I want to join the air force but my mother, she . . . *come si dice*? Freak out." Suddenly he jumps up on the bench and shades his eyes with his hands. He's heard it before I have, but soon there is a distinctive engine purr that gets louder and louder. "Look!" he says, excited. I stand and see the plane coming toward us. To me, it just looks like a military cargo plane. But to Luigi, it looks like Christmas morning. "Super Hercules."

"Sounds like it could kick some ass."

"No, is for transport, four-engine turboprop, but original Hercules C-130 has the record, they make this one the longest, over sixty years."

"What's it got hanging off it?"

"Maybe jeep . . ." In fact, he's right. As the plane grows closer, I can make out not one, but two military jeeps suspended from cables. Luigi nearly poops his pants. He jumps up and down, grabbing me with excite-ment as the plane passes over us.

"Beautiful and functional. *Fantastico!*" he yells—wind ruffled hair, twinkling eyes, smile from ear to ear. His excitement is contagious, and in this moment I realize just how sexy he is. The muscles under his tight T-shirt, his strong arm around me. He's a total catch.

"You are *fantastico*, Luigi," I laugh. He looks at me, under his arm, and suddenly bends his head, kissing me sweetly on the lips. My eyes widen in surprise. He blushes, embarrassed.

"*Mi dispiace,*" he says. "I thought you . . ."

"No, it's okay." I put my hand on his cheek to reassure him, but this gives him the green light. He pulls me back into his arms, wrapping those gorgeous muscles around me, kissing me with even more gusto. I cannot help but kiss him back, leaning into him...

"*È aperto!*" calls Akio from across the small square. I don't know if he's seen us, but Luigi blushes, jumps off the bench, and holds his hand out to help me down. I give him a look and jump down on my own. The last thing I want to do is come between two brothers.

Chapter 29

How Not to
Be a Prize

Caffé Del Duomo, Catania: Saturday, 12:05 p.m.

I should: enjoy sitting in the cute little outdoor café on the square, drink my caffè latte, and eat my traditional Sicilian pastry without asking any questions.

Instead I: wonder aloud why every pastry shop on every street corner in Catania is selling this same pastry, which I saw nowhere in mainland Italy.

"*Minnuzzi di sant'Àjita* are traditional pastries of Sicily," says Akio. Luigi points to a plate on the bar counter that has two *minnuzzi* sitting next to each other.

"What do they look like?" he asks me. It seems painfully clear. Two white, perfectly shaped mounds with bright red cherries in the center of each.

"Breasts," I say reluctantly.

"*Sì, esatto.* Little breasts!" says Akio.

"I'm eating a little breast?" I ask with a smile, as I take another bite of mine. "Feels kind of dirty," I joke. "Why breasts? Where are the pastry penises?" Both of the brothers laugh as I lick the cherry off.

"St. Agata is the patron saint of Catania," explains Luigi. "When she refused the affections of a rich and powerful man, her breasts were cut off." Suddenly, I stop smiling. The sanguine cherry in my mouth now tastes vile, the seed of misogyny. I spit it into the potted bush next to us. Both brothers stare at me, wide-eyed.

"Are you kidding me? Every pastry shop in Sicily has breast-shaped pastries because some rich asshole got his ego bruised and hacked off some poor girl's tits? That's awful. It's not a joke."

"Yes. Is awful," Akio agrees. They're both looking quite sheepish.

"But is in *honor* of her. The city loves St. Agata," says Luigi.

"Okay, well let's cut off your dick then and we can honor you by making pastry penises and selling them in all the shops," I suggest. He winces at the suggestion.

"No, is not the same," says Akio.

"It's exactly the same," I protest.

"No. Nobody want to eat a penis . . . is ugly, not beautiful and delicious."

"Mine is," says Luigi. He raises his eyebrows with a smile.

"Actually, mine also," says Akio.

"But mine is more beautiful," says Luigi.

"Mine is more delicious," says Akio. I look at both of them, trying to keep my mad face on. I fail, cracking up.

Since I've no "Woman of Influence" for Sicily yet, I decide Agatha's story needs more investigation and ask the boys to take me to the library. As we leave the café, I forget to check my phone. I'm now a woman on a mission.

Biblioteche Riunite Civica e A. Ursino Recupero, Catania: Saturday, 1:31 p.m.

Every now and then, the very lucky traveler, not afraid to stray from the worn and beaten paths of tourists, will stumble upon a magical, breathtaking place the locals keep to themselves. The United Libraries of Civica and A Ursino in Catania is stunning both inside and out. As we walk into the Sala Vaccarini, we enter what feels like a two-story ballroom with an ornate domed and frescoed ceiling. Walls are lined with towering antique, dark wooden bookshelves, and row upon row of antique books ensconced safely behind glass. High, round windows let in natural light, and there is currently an exhibit of paintings on display. To my delight, they're all various artists' portraits of St. Agatha. This is a sign. Some are more modern interpretations. In one she seems to be wearing a Madonna-like bra. And I don't mean the mother of Jesus. I need to find out who this woman was.

Because most of the books are locked away, we must get a *bibliotecario* (librarian) to help us find a few books with information on Agatha. And because these books are very old, we must use white linen gloves when handling them. I can't type any notes on my tablet's touch screen while wearing these gloves, so I decide to let the boys handle the books. The books are all in Italian, so the brothers read them to me. Like everything else between them, this quickly becomes a contest. Each brother tries to find the best picture, the juiciest facts or bits of story.

NOTES ON ITALIAN WOMAN OF INFLUENCE:
Saint Agatha

1. Believed to have been born in 231 to a rich and noble Sicilian family.
2. Notable for her beauty, she became a consecrated virgin, choosing to remain celibate and dedicating her life to Jesus, the Church, and prayer.
3. Many men still made unwanted advances, and Quintianus, a high-ranking diplomat, continually made proposals trying to force her to marry him.
4. During the persecution of Christians by the Roman Emperor Decius, many Christians were imprisoned. Quintianus had Agatha arrested and brought before a judge.
5. Quintianus thought she'd renounce her beliefs, but she only reaffirmed her commitment to God and prayed for courage.

6. She was sent to Aphrodisia, the madam of a brothel. Here she suffered assaults to force her to drop her vows (saint of rape victims). She did not.
7. To intimidate her, Quintianus imprisoned Agatha and tortured her: stretched on a rack, burned, whipped, sliced with hooks.
8. Finally her breasts were cut off, and she was imprisoned with no food or medical care (saint of breast cancer patients). It is believed Agatha had a vision of St. Peter, who healed her wounds.
9. Quintianus then had her rolled naked over burning coals (saint of fire victims) and ordered her burned at the stake. It is believed an earthquake saved her from this fate (saint of earthquake victims).
10. Although she's a well-respected martyr and official Catholic saint, there are no reliable specifics about her death. She's thought to have died in prison around age twenty.

Rifugio Sapienza, 10,000 feet up: Saturday, 4:25 p.m.

I've had the entire drive up Mt. Etna to mull over the gruesome story of Agatha. Men still do such horrible things to women who reject them, and they get away with it. It's only now that some of the richest, strongest, and most famous sexual abusers have begun to fall that women are finding the courage to speak out. Will it take another thousand years to stop it completely? I realize with a mixture of guilt and gratitude how new, precious, and hard-won my own sexual freedom actually is. I have the freedom to travel alone. The freedom to choose (more than once, if I like). I have the sexual freedom of a man. Almost. I will not take this for granted.

From my vantage point at the outdoor picnic table, I look through the open doorway at the brothers, buying a late lunch for us inside. Neither of them has backed me into any dimly lit corners or become aggressive in any way. They're good boys, who probably don't even fancy me that much. It's just a game. A competition to please their father, like everything else.

Right now, they're arguing over which wine to order for our little lunch at this rustic restaurant and lodge where we stopped to hike. It is more like an alpine ski hostel. But thankfully there's no snow. I look out and take a deep breath. There are huge swatches of wooded areas with beautiful trees that make marvelous shushing noises as the wind blows. A pristine haven on an active volcano that has erupted many times, killing over 35,000 people. Good place for a picnic. A faint buzz brings me back from my mental flight. A message!

Estou bem sem você,
Como uma rosa sem espinho.
Como uma festa sem vinho.
Eu estou bem.

Spanish? I see Akio coming out with the food so I quickly cut and paste it into my translation app. Apparently it's Portuguese.

I am fine without you,
Like a rose without a thorn.
Like a party without wine.
I am fine.

Another song? I quickly search this online but don't get far.

"Hungry?" asks Akio. "The kitchen is closed. I make us a picnic from the shop. Luigi is picking some wine for us. He takes forever always."

"You balance those trays like a professional," I say, slipping my phone back into my bag. He places items around the table: fruit, cheeses, meat, bread, olives, etc.

"Since I was eleven I worked as a waiter. My *zia* has a restaurant."

"That why you want to become a chef?"

"No. She only serves traditional Italian, boring things."

"Where I come from 'traditional Italian' comes from a jar, gets dumped into a pot, and warmed up." I laugh. He looks bewildered as he peels an orange.

"But this is sad. Cooking is choosing fresh gifts from the earth, from God, and combining them together in perfect portions and in wonderful ways to create something new and delicious." He lights up as he speaks.

"Sounds like alchemy."

"*Sì*, I am an alchemist," he grins proudly. I feel a pang in my stomach, remembering I've given away the book Will gave me. "Cooking is a combination of science, imagination, and art," Akio continues earnestly. "Creating with food is the truest and most intimate form of art because it is always temporary. The act of appreciating it consumes it." I watch him slice a small melon. "It will not hang on the wall of a cold museum to be stared at by strangers for years. It is an act of artistic expression to be created and enjoyed together." His enthusiasm is catching. I watch him gift wrap a small chunk of melon with a paper-thin piece of prosciutto. Like a sculptor he carefully inserts a toothpick through an olive, then an orange wedge, and finally into the prosciutto-wrapped melon. His eyes sparkle as he proudly holds his *en plein air* mini masterpiece toward me. I reach for it. "You must take it all at once."

"That's a huge bite!" I laugh.

"Trust me," he smiles. I put the whole thing in my mouth. As I bite through the salty ham, the sweetness of the melon explodes across my tongue. The crisp, sweet acid of the orange cuts through the tangy vinegar of the meaty, green olive. It's wonderful.

"*È buono, sì*? The flavors, they dance together, like a tango in your mouth. It is wonderful."

"Akio, you are wonderful," I smile. He blinks his long, beautiful eyelashes at me, flashes his dimples, and then suddenly leans in and kisses me gently on the lips. It's not a greedy kiss, but he lingers long enough to taste the olives and oranges. He sits back.

"Sorry," he says, a bit shyly. I smile but say nothing.

"*Non è niente*," I say, blushing a bit. I have now been kissed by two brothers. "Actually, it's not nothing. It was very nice but . . . ." This could get dicey. I like them both. I'm not going to come between them. I notice, across the yard, Luigi emerging with a bottle of wine and three glasses.

"Here comes your brother," I say. Akio is suddenly very busy with the food as Luigi approaches.

"Here is the wine," Luigi says. "They had to go to the cellar to find the one I wanted." He shows me the label.

"*Petite rouge*—it's French?"

"French name, only for the sexiness. The soul is Italian." I immediately think of Frantonio.

"From *Valle d'Aosta* in North Italy . . . ." He goes on, but my brain is drifting. What song is this new one, and what does it mean?

On the way down the mountain, I make the mistake of trying to search the song lyrics again. The winding road, wine, lunch, looking down at my phone . . . soon I'm on my hands and knees vomiting in the grass by the side of the road. Wasn't I just doing this a week ago? I flashback to the party mobile with Yin and Yang. Maybe I should get a punch card. After your tenth roadside vomit, you get free breath mints and a smack in the head.

"How long is the ride home?" I ask from my hands and knees.

"Home?" Akio asks, surprised.

"Not home, Taormina," says Luigi.

"You cannot miss Taormina. The most beautiful beaches in the world."

"I'm from the Florida Keys," I remind them.

"You don't have beaches with ruins."

"You'd be surprised," I say. "It's after five, how far is *Tasca D'Almerita?*"

"Around an hour," Luigi says.

"You say that for every destination," I complain.

"From here, one hour and twenty minutes," Akio says, using his phone. "I want to take you to dinner at my friend's restaurant. He is the chef for one of the most exclusive spots in Sicily. This vineyard is amazing."

"Well, I can't say no to that," I say, wiping the vomit from my chin."
"Maybe he can get us rooms," suggests Luigi."
"Spend the night?" I ask.
"Si. If we are lucky. The hotel is very beautiful and the view *è mozzafi-ato e romantico,*" assures Luigi.
"Romantic? That's not the point. I'm not on a date," I say.
"Yes, you are on a . . . *come si dice in America?* A double date," smiles Akio. Luigi laughs and winks at me. God help me.
"We're not going to spend the night," I say.

Tasca D'Almerita, Regaleali Estate: Saturday, 9:15 p.m.

I should have: stuck to my guns and insisted we drive home so I could get some much-needed rest and work on my book.

Instead: I'm wowed by an amazing dinner on the terrace of an exclusive vineyard hotel, *Tasca D'Almerita.* Normally you must book ages in advance for a table or room here, but Akio knows the chef so we are special guests. I'm impressed not only by the food, and the fantastic wine, but also by *Tasca D'Almerita*'s sustainable mission. Stunning photos of their breathtaking vineyard landscapes are embellished with quotes reflecting the ideals of caretaking, respect and the building of a better environmental future. The vibe is both traditional and progressive. I love it.

Three glasses of wine and a complimentary *grappa* later, we have checked into rooms (separate ones) and are enjoying cocktails in the hot tub on the terrace at sunset. I fleetingly wonder if this was what Akio had in mind all along when he told me to pack my bathing suit and a change of clothes for "the beach." But as I sink into the blissful hot water and sip my drink with a little umbrella, I decide not to care.

Yes, more alcohol. But, this cocktail has ginger in it and is actually helping my stomach. The ancient hills blanketed with flourishing green vineyards and laced with roses of every color are now a soft shade of lavender under a majestic sky of dark purple clouds and the waning light of a magenta sun. How do people who live and work here see this living painting every day and not just stop what they're doing and stare? How do you function in an ordinary life surrounded by extraordinary beauty? Then I remember where I grew up. I'm surrounded by beauty every day at home. How quickly it becomes the unnoticed wallpaper of your life. I vow to stop and stare at my next Key West sunset.

"Is not the water too hot?" Akio asks me from his seat on the edge of the tub. Only his legs are in. Luigi sits on the other side of me in similar fashion. They also have cocktails with umbrellas, and they keep scooping handfuls of water onto their bare chests to make sure I'm getting the full effect of their glistening pecks and abs. I'm not a prize, I remind myself. Sip. Akio smiles and slides down into the water next to me. I feel his foot touching mine. Sip.

"Or are we too hot for you?" Luigi laughs as he slides down into the water on my other side. Sip. His muscular thigh touches my leg under the water. His gorgeously broad shoulder touches mine. Sip. Sip.

"Is this why you cannot choose?" asks Akio, sliding closer to me. Sip. His long, curly eyelashes blink at me. Sip, sip. This is not working.

"We can flip a coin," Luigi suggests as my eyes follow a drop of water from his sandy blonde hair, down his neck, across his collarbone, and down his chest. Sip. I'm rapidly losing conviction. I Date like a Man. Right? If a man were sitting here with two sisters, there would be no debate. He would fuck them both. Probably together. Sip, sip. So why did I care? Maybe I don't date like a man. Maybe not all men are mansluts. Then I remember; it's a game to them.

"This competition is ridiculous. I'm not a prize to be won! Surely you see what this fruitless, endless quest to please your father is doing to you both? He's never going to be happy. Trust me. I know fathers like him. You've got to stop caring so much what he thinks and just be who you are. Live your own lives!" The heat and alcohol are making me light-headed and the sexual tension is making me crazy. Both brothers stare at me, stupefied. They look at each other and then back to me.

"You are right," Akio says. "We care too much what father thinks."

"It's always been like this," admits Luigi.

"Aren't you tired of it?" I ask. They both nod. "You need to get the hell out of that house. Akio, you need to go to some fancy cooking school in France, and Luigi, you need to join the air force. Work with each other, not against. You're brothers! You're supposed to be best friends."

"You have a brother?" asks Luigi.

"Or sister?" asks Akio.

"No," I admit. "But I wish I did. I had a best friend, she was like a sister."

"What happened?" asks Luigi. I think about Laurel, everything we shared surviving Catholic high school together, college, and then how it all came to a screeching halt. Now we only text occasionally. But, for now I have escaped Laurel, Rosalie, Will, and all my tricky old relationships, and I don't want to think about any of that now. I give a quick, bogus answer.

"Competition," I shrug. "What you have is too valuable. Don't risk it."

Akio stares at me, transfixed. "You are wise and beautiful, Marina Taylor," he says, taking my hand.

"I know," I say.

"You are smart and sexy," says Luigi, taking my other hand.

"This too is true," I say. My jokes are my last line of defense.

"*Allora*, I have *una buona idea*," says Akio. "Each of us, we kiss you and then you will be able to choose one."

"No. I think you're missing the point here," I say as I stand abruptly. All the blood rushes to my head. Dizzy, I lose my balance and start to slip. Both brothers catch me. My heart pounds. They help me out of the tub. I peel myself out of their arms and grab a towel, wrapping myself up like a burrito.

"Where are you going?"

"I need coffee."

"We will come," they say in unison.

"You will stay!" I order. They look like sad puppies, but obey.

I lean on the bar as I order a double espresso. How did I get myself into this? Why am I not just hanging out with Bob and making weird art? Oh right, I actually sleep at night. But I didn't come for a *frères à trois* either. As the bartender serves me my espresso, I notice two attractive girls on a couch nearby, one with her head on the other's shoulder as they share a guidebook. Tourists. They're also in matching bathing suits and towels. Must be waiting their turn in the tub. They remind me of Yin and Yang. Suddenly I miss my friends. I walk over and ask if I can sit.

"Sure, honey! We're not havin' any luck with the boys anyways," says the one on the left. "You seem to be doing okay over there though!"

"Oh! You aren't together?" I ask.

"Gawd no!" they laugh. "We're from Houston, not Austin!"

"Sisters?" I ask. They nod. Of course. They look just alike. *Perfetto.* "You ladies see those two guys? They're Sicilian brothers—sweet, handsome, smart, and great tour guides. But in a few minutes, they're going to be very lonely, because I'm going to my room to take a shower and work on my book. Maybe you could help entertain them so I can get some work done?"

"You had us at Sicilian brothers!" laughs the one on the left.

As I watch the girls walk over, peel off their towels, and climb into the hot tub, the shocked look on the brothers' faces makes me smile. I pick up my bag from the chair and fumble for my room key, feeling my phone vibrate. I pull it out. Another message.

Chapter 30

How Not to
Have Phone Sex

Pensione Vista Celeste, Taormina: Saturday, 9:46 p.m.
More Portuguese. I'm beginning to feel more like a researcher than a flirt.

> *Estou bem sem você,*
> *Como um pássaro sem asas.*
> *Eu caio sem você, eu falho sem você.*

This translates to:

> *I am fine without you*
> *Like a bird without wings.*
> *I fall without you, I fail without you.*

I fall without you? I shake with excitement. Or maybe it's the fact that I'm standing here in my wet bathing suit? I strip off and jump into a nice warm shower, where I think about his message over and over. I fail without you? He still wants me. It's definitely the same song. I quickly towel off and jump straight into bed naked. Burrowing down in the duvet, I grab my tablet and pull it inside my cocoon to start my search for the song. I've got more lyrics now, should be easy. Wrong. I've got two stanzas and still can't put it together. I wouldn't have lasted ten minutes in *The Da Vinci Code*. But then, I realize I'm searching in English and the original song is Portuguese. I try a search with the Portuguese lyrics. BINGO. "I Am Without You." It's a song from a Brazilian singer in the 1980s. Wow. This guy knows his music. I catch myself smiling, staring at this tanned, Brazilian heartthrob with David Hasselhoff hair, in a banana yellow shirt. I play the song on YouTube. It is totally 80s, cheesy, sweet, and *perfetto*. There's even sax, or as I call it, the classic 80s sex-ophone. Grinning, I text back a sexier lyric from the song.

Sem o seu beijo, eu estou nua.

Without your kiss, I am naked.

I lie in bed, thinking of Frantonio's kisses that first night in the back of the restaurant by the bathroom. Those beautiful brown eyes behind his designer glasses—which I probably broke as I kneed him in the groin and ripped open his shirt. I think of his face, red with anger and unwanted desire as he stood in front of me in the library—after I had literally pissed on his artistic endeavor and stomped on his ego. And he still wants me.

Have I finally mastered Regina's lessons? Have I harnessed the sexual gaze? Or have I just fallen into the right man's arms at all the wrong times? Whichever it is, I'm still thrilled. I turn out the light and slide lower under the duvet. My hands caress my breasts and I imagine Frantonio's lips on them. My fingertips tease my nipples as his tongue did. My other hand slides around my bare ass, and my fingers find their way between my legs, the way Frantonio's did as he held me up against the wall—BUZZ!

My hands instantly go into the air like I'm being robbed. NOTHING!

NOT DOING ANYTHING! But it's only my phone vibrating loudly on the bedside table. It stops. Okay, just another message. I'm thankful it's not a call from Rosalie. She has always had the uncanny ability to interrupt my moments of solo pleasure, even when I was in college, living with my roommate Laurel. It's like she's got sexually repressed Protestant guilt radar.

I grab the phone in the dark and pull it toward me, but it's yanked out of my hands onto the floor by its cable. Right, I plugged it in. I slide half out of the bed, still naked, grope for the phone on the floor, and open the message, hanging off the bed, tits dangling. YES! It's from him.

Sem você a vida não tem aventura.

More lyrics? Come on dude. I sit back into bed and translate these with Trusty:

Without you life has no adventure.

Okay, so let's have some adventure. Stop playing games. Feeling brave, I text back.

Serenades are lovely,
but the words of others.
I wait for your voice,
under the covers.

Overly proud of my ability to rhyme, I smugly snuggle down and wait. How could he not call now? Then I realize what I've done. It's after ten, I'm in bed. I've just sent an invitation for phone or video chat sex. My whole body cringes at the thought. I'm really not good at this. I tried once with a Canadian firefighter I'd met on vacation, but had botched it badly and awkwardly rushed through it as if one of us was paying per minute.

HELPFUL HINTS FROM MY PAST FAILED EXPERIENCE IN VIDEO CHAT SEX:

1. Don't start the conversation in a vocal register you can't sustain because you're trying to sound like Scarlett Johansson or Kathleen Turner.
2. Don't try to channel your inner phone sex operator.
3. Don't forget that photos can be taken during the video chat.
4. When you remember this, don't *then* try to take a photo of your ass so you can see what it looks like on camera.
5. Don't try to watch *yourself* while you talk to him.
6. Don't say more than he does.
7. Don't show more than he does.
8. Don't forget to charge your device, the battery will die before you—

I'm desperate not to make the same mistakes tonight. I jump out of bed and check the mirror: the corpse of a drowned clown with half dried hair and smeared makeup stares back at me. Oh my God! I quickly clean my face and tousle my hair, going for a sexy bedtime look. It just looks messy. I tousle it more and rub some product in. Now I look like Cyndi Lauper. I grab my makeup bag to start fresh. Wait. Makeup in bed looks high maintenance. I go with naturally sexy Cyndi Lauper, ditching the makeup and jumping back in bed. I check the tablet to make sure I'm signed in. Phone on the left, tablet on the right. I position the sheet perfectly over my breasts to show just a hint of cleavage. Actually, there isn't much cleavage. Pulling a pillow under the duvet I bolster my breasts, arch my back just enough to look sexy and be uncomfortable, and reposition the sheet. Now I'm ready for my *Playboy* cover.

I wait. Why is it so hot in here? I realize I'm sweating. Will he be able to see that? What will I say on the phone? I can't talk dirty in French or Italian. I can barely talk dirty in English. I grab the tablet and quickly Google "phone sex for dummies." This is a really bad idea. Do not EVER do this. Trust me. Your laptop or computer will be imme-diately deluged with advertisements for escort services and photos of naked women rubbing phones on their breasts and vaginas. Gross. I wouldn't even want to use *my own* phone after I rubbed it on *my own* vagina.

RING! A video call! Oh my God it's him. No, wait—it's not him. Why is Will calling me in the middle of the—oh, it's the middle of the day for him. Do I answer? What if Frantonio calls? Will can see I'm online. I can't *not* answer. I reach over to turn on the lamp, pull the sheet up to my neck, and answer.

"Hello?" I try to sound groggy. Maybe he'll call back tomorrow.

"Marina?" Will is sitting on his back deck at home. I'm not prepared for the feeling his deep, soft voice produces in me. I had no idea I missed him so much until this exact moment. However, I quickly stuff this down deep and ignore it.

VIDEO CALL
Call—Will Kittridge—10:47 p.m.

"Hey. This is a surprise," I say.

"Yeah?" He seems a little confused.

"But it's nice to hear from you."

"Oh." He looks down. I can't really see his eyes. "You sure?"

"Totally. What's up? How are you? Everything good?"

"Marina, are you okay?" he asks. Am I acting strange? I glance down at my phone. Nothing yet. Keep it together. Will looks back at the camera. "You seem . . . weird."

"I'm fine. It's just . . . I was expecting a call . . . from someone."

"Oh." His expression completely changes. He stares at me. "You were."

"Yeah."

"You were expecting a call from someone, naked in bed." His soulful, hazel eyes blink away something I don't quite get.

"Uh . . . yeah." I look away. Everything inside me feels sick.

"Well, I better not keep you."

"It's fine—I can talk—"

"All good. Just checking in. You're keeping busy, so that's—yeah. I gotta go."

"Will, I—"

"I'm actually late to pick up Mom for lunch so—"

"Will, we're not together anymore. I don't have to feel guilty."

"Nobody's making you feel anything."

"You're still doing boyfriend stuff, like driving from Miami to give me books—"

"And FedExing tablets. You're right," he says roughly. *Touché.* Now he's looking at me again. "That book I gave you was a loan. I need it back."

"You do? Why?"

"Seriously? If you're asking me that, you haven't even opened it."

"Yes I have. I read the first four pages!"

"And you missed the inscription from Hailey?" His eyes are hard now, the way they used to get after we had a fight. A lurch of guilt washes through me. Shit.

"I guess so. I'm sorry, Will."

"I gave it to you because it was her favorite

book. I thought you needed it for a while. Take care of it please."

"Yes. Of course I will."

"I gotta go, Marina, have a good night."

"You too. I mean, lunch," I say. He looks right into the camera.

"Look after yourself."

He hangs up. I turn off the tablet. Shit. Shit. Shit. I just gave away a book my ex-boyfriend's dead sister gave him. I have to get it back.

Chapter 31

How Not to Do Things the Easy Way

Alitalia flight AZ1780 Milan: Tuesday, 1:46 p.m.

I'm on a plane, on my way to Milan. The events and conversations that transpired to put me here, in seat 14E, thirty-eight thousand feet over Italy, sipping a tomato juice with lime, still seem like a highly blended cocktail of excited panic, ridiculous ideas, and dubious choices. Whether a love potion or a Molotov cocktail has been created remains to be seen.

After my desperate phone calls to the number I'd been using to exchange flirty song lyrics with Frantonio went strangely unanswered, I called Regina and spilled my guts. She told me Frantonio was famous for his moodiness and games, so it didn't surprise her that he was playing it cool. Just last week, at her villa, he had relentlessly coerced her into being his date for a charity masquerade ball he was hosting in Venice this Friday, but he had yet to call and give details. *Presuntuoso!* Did he think she had costumes of every sort, just standing by? (In truth, she had her personal dresser in Milan on standby, but that was beside the point.) Without a moment's hesitation, Regina decided that I should go to the ball in her stead. She had Piero #2 booking me a flight before I could blink.

"Go see Sheela first, in Milan. She'll get you decked out in something fabulous. Then, you go to the ball in Venice, get your book and whatever else you want from him. *È Perfetto, carina.*"

"Wow. That's definitely one plan. Or another plan could be, I know this sounds crazy, just get him to FedEx me the book," I say, laughing.

"Why would we do that?"

"Because, he's expecting *you* at the charity ball, Regina, not me."

"My dear, his ego wants me there. His penis would prefer you." I hoped she was right.

"Who is Sheela in Milan?"

"My stylist. She dresses me for all my events."

"Didn't you say this was a masquerade ball? I'll need a costume, not just a gown, right? She can help me find one?" I ask. At this Regina just laughs.

"I'll tell her you're coming. You'll stay with her a couple of days in Milan, then we'll get you a car to Venice. You're doing me a favor, Marina. I hate these functions. Surrounded by rich, non-creative people who just want my autograph, photo, or money. *Faticoso.*"

"Totally. I hate fattycosos. They won't want my autograph."

"Not yet, my *cara autrice.*" I can hear her smile. "Not yet."

"Regina . . . thank you."

"*Non è niente, carina.* Have fun. I want to read it all in your book."

"My travel blog," I laugh.

"*Meglio!* No editor to cut out the sexy parts."

Teatro alla Scala, Milan: Tuesday, 5:43 p.m.

No, I am not taking a tourist side jaunt to one of the most famous opera houses in the world. If the iconic sails of the Sydney Opera house or the ballerinas of Degas in the Paris Opera now jump to the front of your mind, it's because you're not a true opera aficionado. (Neither am I, but after a quick online search, I realized I was in for a treat.) In 1778 La Scala was the preeminent meeting place for the noble and wealthy. Puccini,

Verdi, and Rossini premiered their operas here. La Scala is the crème de la crème of opera.

"Tours are over for today," a man in a gray suit informs me. I tell him I'm there to see Sheela and his expression becomes indecipherable. Surprise? Fear? Pity? He lets me in and instructs an underling in a vest and ponytail to take me to the costume department. I follow her through a series of hallways, down a series of steps, down another hall, into the bowels of the ancient building. Everything smells old, and fancy. Dust and brass. Marble and velvet. As we reach the door to the costume department, the girl stops and just points. This is as far as she goes, I guess.

"Sheela works in there?" I ask. The girl cocks her head and peers at me sideways with contemptuous, narrow eyes.

"*Signora O'Shaughnessy è la capo costumista per* Aida." Her brow wrinkles and her ponytail wags. I want to reach up and pull it down like a doorknocker, to straighten her head.

"Thanks." She shakes her head and disappears. I stand outside the door, unsure. *Capo costumista?* I know *capo* means head. Head costumer? Regina's personal stylist just happens to be the costume designer for La Scala's upcoming production of the legendary opera *Aida*? And she's going to dress *me* for a charity ball? I digest this revelation. *Uhhhh. Fuck yeah.* I swing the door open with gusto.

Inside the costume department are people dyeing fabric, people sewing, people painstakingly working with feathers, leather, velvet, and metal. There's an entire room of women making and styling wigs. I gawk as I wander through the busy workshop. This is a peek inside the theatrical underbelly that is not on the tour. The machines are loud, but even louder there is Verdi playing from somewhere. Everyone is too busy to notice me. Finally, I see a door with an antique brass sign, *Capo Costumista*. Bingo. I knock, but there is so much noise, I'm certain nobody heard. I crack the door open and stick my head in. There is a middle-aged, stylish woman with red cat-eye glasses and 1960's mod makeup sitting behind a computer. Above her on the wall is the head of a fuzzy unicorn costume, mounted like a hunting trophy. Odd. I step inside.

"Excuse me, Sheela? I'm Marina Taylor. Regina sent me?" The woman looks me up and down and purses her lips. The unicorn above her stares at me vapidly with his black cheesecloth eyeholes. I think he likes me more than she does.

"Yes, we received her message," she says unenthusiastically.

"I guess, I need a costume for this charity thing she wants me to go to?"

"*Mais bien sur.* We are not busy designing an opera. We can drop everything to make a costume for an American girl to go to a party. *Oui?*" she says. French? Sheela O'Shaughnessy is French?

"So . . . that's a yes? You're going to help me with a costume?"

"No. I am not," she says. I'm silent. Completely thrown.

"Marie, are you being a bitch to our guest?" croaks a voice from behind me.

"Sheela is going to help you," says the French woman as I turn around. Behind me stands the living Medusa. Only, instead of snakes there is a writhing, sprawling, crawling, dangling head of dreadlocks. They're every color including her natural gray. She can't be less than seventy. The fullness of her face hides many of her wrinkles, but her neck looks like a tree stump covered with bread dough wearing more jewelry than an Egyptian corpse. She's wearing a simple black sheath dress, purple knee socks, and high-top vans. An unlit cigarette dangles from her lips.

"Get the fuck out of my chair," she barks at Marie. "I don't want it smelling like fettuccini farts." Her voice sounds like Lauren Bacall with a diluted Irish brogue. She's obviously smoked her whole life and worked all over the world.

"I had a salad!" Marie objects sharply as she gathers her stuff.

"Like hell. I may be seventy-six but I can still smell a garlic fart." With bright green fingers Sheela pulls the unlit cigarette from her mouth and smiles at me. "Please excuse Marie. She's got a fire poker up her arse, and she can be a bore, but she's more organized than a German watchmaker. I can't live without her." Marie exits in a huff, throwing me a withering glance. *Jealousy?* I wonder if their relationship is more than professional.

Sheela prods me over to a short pedestal in front of some mirrors. "Okay. Up you go. Let's have a look atcha." I obey and stand still as she puts the unlit cigarette back into her mouth with her green hand and studies me. "You're skinny as a post."

"Thanks."

"No tits. No hips. Yer arse is half the size of Regina's."

"Sorry."

"We've got eighty years of costumes here. What's the theme?"

"I have no idea."

"That's heaps of help. Maybe we'll just throw you in Marie's unicorn suit and be done with it." She jabs her unlit cigarette up at the unicorn hunting trophy. "One size fits all. The rest of it zips on, with real hoofs."

"That guy looks extinct." I stare at the hollow unicorn head with haunting eye patches and a twisted plastic horn.

"Marie mounted the head after a party where Luciano ran around sticking the horn into women's bums, loads of craic," she laughs.

"Wait, Regina told me the name of the event. I'll check online for the theme." I do a quick search. If Frantonio sees me in that unicorn costume I'll just die. Sheela crams the unlit cigarette into her mouth and whips out her tape measure. She wraps it around various parts of my body, making notes on her forearm, which is a light pink color. When she sees me staring at it, she explains.

"Fucking eejits in the dying room don't know carmine from crottle. I have to babysit them every day."

I shake my head in sympathy (as if I have a clue what crottle is). Then I find something on my phone. "Oh, this may be it. The Italian Cultural Institute's Gods and Warriors Battle Hunger in Italy. So, I guess the theme is gods and warriors? This chick's got a sexy Greek dress and a sword. And this guy is a samurai warrior."

"Gods and warriors? Boring but easy. Sexy Aphrodite?" she asks, rolling the unlit cigarette back and forth in her lips. I consider.

"Maybe something a little more kick-ass?"

"Like Kali?" She pulls a large book off a shelf, flipping through. "Hindu goddess and destroyer of demons. Dark mother goddess of creation and rebirth."

"Fantastic and original," I say, getting excited. "The last thing you want at a costume party is other people wearing your same costume." But then, Sheela shows me a picture. "Wow! That's . . . a lot of arms, and she's blue, and topless."

"But look at that headdress and all that bling! Fucking brilliant."

"How about a Celtic goddess?" I ask. Sheela smiles.

"I'm named after one. Sheela na gig," she turns pages in her book.

"That's awesome! Tell me more."

"Gig is from the Norse for deified female or giantess. Sheela just means girl. You can find her carved in stone on old churches. Sheela na gig is like a version of the ancient Earth Mother and associated renewal and afterlife."

"Is she sexy?" I ask. Sheela shows me a goddess with big gold earrings and long, flowing red hair cascading around her naked body. Her legs are spread wide open, and her hands are *pulling open her vagina*. I stare in shock. Speechless.

"Sexy enough for you?" Sheela snorts.

"Your mother named you after her?" I ask, surprised. Sheela holds up a pendant from the pile of pirate's treasure heaped around her neck and shoulders. What looked like a Celtic heart with a hole in the middle I can now see is clearly the image of legs spread, feet together, and hands in the shape of a vulva.

"I am the entire universe within the void," says Sheela. "Mam was sick almost her whole life. I was an accident. She knew she was dying during the birth when she chose the name. For mam, "tomb" and "womb" were linked. She wanted me to know she'd always be with me, even after death."

"Oh, that is really, sweet and sad . . . I'm sorry, I didn't mean to—"

"Forget it. My mam also had a terrible sense of humor. The bitch. How about the Egyptian goddess of power and protection?"

"Isis? Maybe not. Let's go back to Greek. Could you just make me an Amazon warrior princess . . . like Wonder Woman?" I ask. Sheela grins widely, revealing a gold canine tooth.

"Does the pope shit in the Vatican?" she asks with a wink. This is not a woman who drives ten miles under the speed limit, or listens to Garrison Keillor with her friends while knitting cat toys. Florida doesn't have oldies like Sheela, unless they're working as palm readers or fading off the biceps of Vietnam vets. She is fantastic.

Teatro alla Scala, Milan: Thursday, 3:14 p.m.

I'm waiting for my final wardrobe fitting. No messages from Frantonio in days. I desperately want to message him but hold myself back, not wanting to tell him yet that I'm coming. I hope he'll be glad. I flip through my journal, going over the notes I made during my days in Milan. Sheela was kind enough to let me stay in her large studio flat in *centro storico* near the theater, but kicked me out every morning when she left for work. "Too many things to see here to lie around all day like a dosser."

If by "things to see" she meant every pizzeria and gelato shop within a mile radius of her flat, I came, I saw, I conquered. There was a lot of walking, to make sure the ass she measured for my costume on Tuesday was going to match the ass I had to squeeze into my costume on Friday.

I saw the Duomo, Last Supper, a castle, and two palaces, but my favorite place was the *Museo Nazionale delle Scienza E della Tecnologia Leonardo Da Vinci*. In addition to a massive collection of Da Vinci's sketches and models of his inventions, the museum has examples of every form of transportation you can imagine. My favorite exhibit was about the mathematician Maria Gaetana Agnesi. Sadly, she was the only woman featured in the entire museum. Did I happen to miss the room filled with all the female Italian scientists? Or has the math and science patriarchy in Italy always been just as exclusive as it is in other parts of the world? I wonder.

NOTES ON ITALIAN WOMAN OF INFLUENCE: Maria Agnesi

1. Born in Milan in 1718, the daughter of a silk merchant, a child prodigy surrounded by tutors, modest and deeply pious.
2. Driven by family ambition, her father pushed her to learn French, Latin, Greek, and Hebrew and displayed her talents publicly in his evening salons.
3. She published a book on philosophy and physics at age twenty.
4. At thirty, Maria published a two-volume work on new differential and integral calculus, bringing it into general use.
5. The pope arranged for a faculty appointment at the University of Bologna that she never took. Instead she taught math in her home.
6. Maria wrote the first surviving mathematical handbook written by a woman, *Analytical Institutions for the Use of Italian Youth*. BUT, she is remembered for a mistranslation an English man made.
7. Maria studied a special curve, and her Latin word *aversiera*, "versed sine curve" or "that which turns," was confused with the Italian word *avversiera* for "witch or she devil," and this curve became known as the "Witch of Agnesi."
8. When she was thirty-four her father died and she turned to charity work, selling her possessions to create a retirement home for the destitute. She worked and died in this same house.
9. She is one of the leading pioneers of women in math and science.

I scribble down some of the math, even though I have no clue what it means. I'm mesmerized by an animation of the math concept. It shows a gentle, gracefully curved line rolling over the circle like a ball under a blanket. I watch it for five minutes.

Chapter 32

How Not to Wonder, Woman

Car to Venice, A4 Motorway: Friday, 9:36 a.m.

I wonder, in this traffic, if the drive to Venice will actually take only three hours as the driver promised. I'd offered to take the train, but Regina didn't want me having to haul the costume and my bags. Now that I'm carrying an Amazon princess shield, sword, and helmet, I wonder if they'd even have let me onto the train. As excited as I am about my first masquerade ball, I wonder, even now, if it's a good idea that Regina has still not told Frantonio I'm coming. She wants me to surprise him in full Amazon glory. Should I message him, just to warn him? He's one of the organizers of the event, so he's probably very busy, but hearing nothing from him makes me uneasy. Did I say something wrong? Had he tried to call when Will was on the phone? I wonder.

Car to Venice, A4 Motorway: Friday, 11:04 a.m.

I have just drifted off to sleep in the back of the car when a buzz on my phone wakes me. A text message! From Frantonio? No. It's Mike.

MIKE: Florida woman
simultaneously seduces
Sicilian mafia brothers

                ME: yesterday's news

MIKE: Where are you
now? I'm in Rome in
tomorrow!

                ME: In a private car,
                heading to Venice for
                a masquerade ball

The phone rings immediately. I pick up. "What time is it where you are?" "I have no idea," Mike admits. "All Marriotts look the same and I'm so exhausted I can't remember what country I'm in. The towels are super tiny so it's probably Japan. Who cares, it's not like I get to see anything but this hotel room, a bus, and the airport. But hello, masquerade ball in Venice? Why are you not posting this already?"

"I'm not sure how it's going to go. I'm Frantonio's date to some charity thing, only he doesn't know it yet."

"Surprise fancy dress date with French-Italian sexy photographer? This just keeps getting better. What's your costume?"

"The theme is gods and warriors, so I'm dressing as Wonder Woman."

"Linda Carter or Gal Gadot?"

"More like Xena, warrior princess goes American."

"Sexy badass."

"Exactly."

"Holy shit. A Venetian ball. You get to be glamorous *and* slutty, like Veronica Franco, the famous Venetian courtesan."

"Did you just compare me to a prostitute and call me slutty?"

"She was educated and classy-slutty. Every man wanted her. Like Helen of Troy but for real. *She's* a woman of influence for your book."

"Mike, I'm writing about mathematicians and poets."

"Veronica wrote poetry. She also started a charity for courtesans, their kids, and other orphans, so don't get judgy."

"A hooker with a heart of gold?" I laugh.

"Yes! Maybe that's where the saying came from!" Mike suggests.

Aman Venice Hotel: Friday, 12:47 p.m.

I can't believe I'm staying at the same modern and chic hotel where Amal married George Clooney. Having friends like Regina really has perks. I have arrived too early to check into the room that Piero booked me, the receptionist tells me, but she's happy to check my belongings if I'd like to walk around and enjoy the square. This sounds like a great idea to me, so I hand the bellhop my suitcase, backpack, and half a suit of Amazon armor including a thirty-inch sword. He looks appalled. Suddenly there is a room available. Do Amazon warriors always get perks like early check-in? What else do they get? Free coffee refills?

My room is by far the most elegant hotel room I've every stayed in. The queen-sized bed has a feather mattress pad that sinks a full three inches when I sit on it. I bounce on the bed a bit. Will I be alone in this bed tonight? I wonder. There is gold brocade fringe along the bottom edge of the bed skirt that matches the throw pillows, curtain pulls, and decorative hand towels. I take my shoes off and wiggle my toes under it for a full two minutes. I notice how dirty my feet are. There is something exquisitely beautiful about the crumbling, dirty decay of Venice, a web of ancient buildings clinging to each other with grasping bridges as it sinks slowly into the sea. But, flip-flops are not recommended and there's also a soggy, dank smell I can't quite figure out. It's not bad . . . but not good either.

In the shower I carefully shave all the appropriate bits of my body in anticipation of the night of passion I've been imagining for weeks. Thankfully my sunburned face has fully healed and my *figa* no longer looks like the cat from *Austin Powers*. Since my toes will be visible in my sexy warrior sandals, I decide nail polish is non-negotiable. I pop down to the hotel gift shop and return with a twenty-euro bottle of bright red nail polish so small I wonder if it's going to be enough for all twenty of my digits and decide to strategically paint the tiny toes last. I've never been good at painting my nails, and by the time I'm done I've got crimson smears on my wrist, neck, knee, and elbow—don't ask. I have no idea. Of course, they were out of remover so I make a mental note to stop at a pharmacy on the way to the event so I can clean myself up a bit in the bathroom before my grand entrance. While I'm waiting on my fingernails, toenails, wrist, neck, and elbow to dry, I power up my tablet and read about Veronica Franco. Mike has piqued my interest.

NOTES ON ITALIAN WOMAN OF INFLUENCE: Veronica Franco

1. Born 1546 in Venice to Paola Fracassa, a courtesan.
2. Educated alongside her brothers by private tutors.
3. From her mother she also learned the profession of *cortigiana onesta*. These were the educated, honored courtesans to rich and noble men.
4. Married off to a doctor, but separated from him soon after, requesting her dowry returned.
5. Worked as a courtesan, gaining fame and eventually consorting with famous nobility, including the king of France.
6. Tintoretto, the famous painter, did a portrait of her.
7. Wrote two poetry books, *Terze Rime* in 1575 and *Lettere familiari a diversi* in 1580, in which she asserted opinions on male behavior and upheld the educated courtesan virtues of fairness, wisdom, and reason.
8. Forced to flee during the plague, she lost much of her wealth.
9. Defended herself against witchcraft charges brought by the Inquisition (common against courtesans), and was acquitted due to her connections to Venetian nobility.
10. Took in orphans as she grew older and founded a charity for courtesans and their children. But sadly, she died in poverty.

Wow. I guess she didn't get the *Pretty Woman* ending she deserved. But what a life. Clearly she had figured out very early how to command the sexual gaze and harness that power, much like Regina had. Perhaps it's playing with fire?

At last it's time to get dressed. Sheela's wardrobe fairies helped me during the fittings—this time I'm on my own. After forty-five minutes I've managed to lace up the leather bustier, fasten all the buckles on the leather bicep and shoulder guards, tie the straps of the sandals, position the fur cape around my collar bone and under my arm, and yank the rayon skirt back out of my sturdy leather panties so my golden lasso isn't knocking against my bare ass. Did Amazons really wear uncomfortable leather panties? I wonder. Just as I squeeze out the special "glue" that Sheela gave me onto the back of the metal tiara and press it firmly to my forehead, my video rings. Frantonio? I can't let him see me in costume, he'll know! With one hand I fish out my tablet and am relieved that it's Mike again. I click the camera icon to answer his video call.

VIDEO CALL
Call- Mike Ford—6:32p.m.

"Sweet baby Jesus! You look amazing! Wonder Woman, Amazon warrior princess, ready to conquer mankind—or at least one man."

"*Grazie!* That's the plan," I grin.

"Why are you holding your head?" he asks. "Is your tiara giving you a headache? It looks uncomfortable."

"I'm gluing it on."

"Gluing it? Like with theater makeup spirit gum?" Mike looks skeptical. "You know you need special spirit gum remover to get it off, right?"

"Seriously?" The sudden panic on my face causes Mike to break down in hysterics. I look in the bag from Sheela—nothing. Marie's had her revenge.

"Trust me, I learned that lesson the hard way too, the Halloween I went as Wolverine. I managed to pry a few of the claws off but Michael made me sleep on the couch so I didn't slash his Brooks Brothers pajamas."

"What am I going to do?" I can already feel that it's stuck fast.

"Lean into it! Keep the sword on too and tie his arms with your lasso. He'll think it's a dominatrix game." Somehow this seems like a good idea.

"You're a genius, I love you!"

"I know!" he smiles.

IF YOU: ever find yourself heading for a charity event in Venice dressed like a super hero, DEFINITELY DO NOT:

1. Stop to take photos with tourists. Even if they start to play the *Wonder Woman* song on their phones and offer you money.

2. Encourage a small crowd to form by imitating moves you saw Robin Wright do in the movie.

3. Assume the *carabinieri* also want selfies with you.

4. Lasso one of the *carabinieri* as the crowd applauds.

5. Take your fake sword out and pretend to fight the *carabinieri* when they write you a ticket for unlicensed street performing.

6. Drop your ticket into the canal as you're trying to unbend your aluminum prop sword, which the officer bent into a pretzel.

7. Get onto the ground, leaning over to fish your ticket out of the filthy canal, knocking your shield over the edge with your knee.

8. Lunge to catch your shield, nearly going into the canal yourself.
9. Scream and flail as a large German tourist grabs you by your left sandal and sturdy leather panties (is this why they wear them?) to keep you from falling into the disgusting black water.

Ca' Rezzonico, Grand Canal: Friday, 7:58 p.m.

I am late, but I'm finally here. I'm wearing my shield, now slimy and stinky, but miraculously saved by an amused gondolier. I also sport my re-straightened aluminum prop sword and red nail polish that I've not been able to remove from my wrist, neck, and elbow. I've decided it looks like blood, so part of the costume.

At the entrance to the gorgeous, eighteenth-century Venetian palace, complete with three columned stories of arched windows, a woman dressed as a butterfly searches for my name on a list at the reception desk, and gives me an odd smile as she checks me off. Regina has called ahead.

"Are you alright?" she asks.

"Yes? Why? Oh, this. *Si, grazie.* I'm fine it's not blood, it's nail polish. Goes with my costume, right?" I smile and unsheathe my sword. "Badass warrior princess."

"The party is in the grand ballroom." She's still looking at me funny as I walk inside, down the red carpet. Several paparazzi turn, realize I'm not a celebrity, but then, laughing, decide to take my photo anyway. I pose with my sword.

"*Fanculo le regole, eh?*" they laugh and give me a thumbs up. I smile and nod, unsure. Doesn't *fanculo* mean fuck? I get a funny feeling in my stomach as I keep walking. A Hare Krishna passes me, wide eyed. (How did he get in here?) At the door to the grand ballroom I meet (appropriately) St. Peter, wearing a white robe and a big golden key on his belt.

"*Ce n'è sempre uno,*" (there's always one) he says. He shakes his head. What does he mean? The feeling in my stomach gets stronger. He leans down and opens the door. "Try not to start any wars, Americana." As I step inside the stunning ballroom with frescoed ceilings and magnificent

chandeliers, my stomach drops, and my mouth hangs open like a surprised skeleton. A silk banner overhead reads:

Italian Cultural Center Celebrates the World Peace Initiative
Welcome Creatures of Peace

There are angels, monks of every sort, two Martin Luther Kings, a cupid,
a handful of Mother Teresas, more butterflies, a Benazir Bhutto, heaps
of hippies, several Gandhis, Nelson Mandela, at least six Jesuses, and *lots*
of unicorns. Fucking unicorns! In the vast ballroom, swimming with a
hundred fantastically costumed creatures of peace, there is only *ONE*
heavily armored, bloody, Amazon warrior princess. *Merda.* A wave of
heads turns my direction, and my feet freeze to the ground. It's the spec-
tacular entrance I've fantasized about—for all the wrong reasons. As
the last head turns, there, by giant gilt cages of doves decorated with
white poppies, "Bono" pulls down his sunglasses. It's Frantonio, and he
is horrified.

Chapter 33

How Not to Spew the Hooch

Library, Ca' Rezzonico, Venice: Friday, 8:13 p.m.

"*Tu te fous de ma gueule, là!* You cannot be content with ruining my photo shoot and embarrassing me in front of my friends? *No?* You must come to Venice and humiliate me in front of my patrons and colleagues? *Pourquoi?* Why would you sabotage me like this? Where the hell is Regina?"

"She sent me in her place. She thought you'd be pleased."

"Pleased!? I'm so fucking pleased, I could toss you in the canal."

"I didn't mean to embarrass you!" I force back tears.

"You're dressed as an Amazon warrior! You have blood on your face. I guess you couldn't find a Hitler costume?"

"I looked up the event online and I saw gods and warriors!"

"That was last year!" he barks. I reel as the realization hits. *Of course.* They wouldn't have had photos from *this* year on the site yet. Shit.

"I'm an idiot." The tears fall.

"Yes," he says sharply. This stings. "The theme is *peace.*"

"Yeah, which is just weird! I thought Venetians were known for wild parties. Who wants to get drunk with Jesus, or grind on Gandhi?" I fire back, through my tears. Really I'm just mad at his reaction, and hurt that he's yelling at me.

"With the violence that's been happening in Europe the last few years, the committee decided it was appropriate for this year's charity ball to benefit the World Peace Initiative. But maybe that's hard to grasp for an American."

"Hey! We've all had our Mussolinis and Napoleons, pal," I retort. Then, under my breath, "I'm glad I didn't go with Isis."

"What did you say?"

"That . . . it's not a crisis. That's what I said." I wipe my nose on my cape.

"For you it's just another embarrassing episode at which you're quite well practiced."

"Thank you—"

"But I helped organize this event!"

"I know. Good job. Really. The doves were a nice touch." We both fall silent. He takes a deep breath. Reaching into his pocket, he pulls out a familiar handkerchief. This time he hands it to me. My heart lifts a little. He picks up his guitar from the chair behind him.

"*Allora*. I'm going to go back out to my guests, and you're going to wipe the mascara off your face, come back in when you're ready, and stay as far from me as possible." He puts his sunglasses back on and walks out. I stare at the door. How can I go back in there? How do I always fuck everything up so badly? I nervously play with the golden tassels on the ends of my lasso. I start to cry again.

"*Scrollatelo di dosso, bella*," says a soft, warm voice. I look up. "Shake it off." One of the Gandhis is standing in the doorway. This version looks twice as old and twice as heavy as the real Gandhi. He walks slowly over to me as I dry my face. The brown eyes behind the round wire-rimmed glasses are kind and gentle. "A true Amazon's strength comes from within, this is how she wins."

"Win?" I sniff. "I think this is a lose/lose situation, Mahatma."

"You win by going back in there and enjoying yourself."

"My date doesn't want me here. I should go."

"My nephew's temper is driven by his ego. Please forgive him."

"You're his uncle?"

"And talent manager. True talent is often not easy to manage."

"I think it's he who won't forgive me."

"'Forgiveness is the attribute of the strong,'" he says with his best Indian accent.

"Is that a Gandhi quote?"

"I memorized ten of them, I want to use them all tonight." His eyes sparkle. "Go on. Don't pass up your chance to attend a true Venetian masquerade ball with all of these fascinating people."

"I'm dressed like a trained killer," I say.

"So you'll have no trouble starting a conversation." All of his wrinkles smile at me simultaneously as he extends a hand.

Grand Ballroom, Ca' Rezzonico, Venice: Friday, 9:41 p.m.

Standing by the chocolate fountain, I am nursing my second glass of wine with a very tall, handsome Leo Tolstoy, whose costume consists of a blousy, white peasant shirt, a Russian hat, a long gray beard, and a copy of *War and Peace*. True to his costume, he's got a sharp writer's wit. As Leo cracks jokes about everyone in the room, I laugh so hard I almost start crying again. His Māori accent is magical. He's sexy, yes, but there's something goofy about him that makes me comfortable.

"Tolstoy was a pacifist?" I ask, ignorantly. He looks surprised at the question. "Well your book is called *WAR and Peace*," I point out.

"Have you read it?"

"What? Like three times," I lie transparently. "Hasn't everyone?"

"Then you know heaps of it is philosophical discussion."

"Obviously."

"Tolstoy's writings had a big influence on Gandhi and Martin Luther

King. He took the teachings of Christ literally. He's like the father of non-violent resistance movements."

"Golly. Now I'm not sure you should be seen even talking to me, Leo. After all, I am a supernaturally gifted fighter."

"Everyone deserves a shot at redemption, Wonda Woman," he laughs. "Even that Susan B. Anthony over there who looks more like Ebenezer Scrooge in drag." This cracks me up. "It's true," he continues. "Specs hanging off her nose and a lace curtain 'round her neck." He does a stern librarian voice, "Give us the vote, or we'll smack your knuckles and suspend your library card! Equality! In the eyes of God all of us are equally wretched rats—oh, could you pass me another antipasto skewer, *per favore*? The bocconcini are lovely, and the sticks are useful for keeping this dead possum of a wig on my head."

"Stop, please!" I beg. "I nearly snorted wine up my nose."

"I'm a pretty funny guy, huh?" he asks, proudly. "I also do magic. I'm here in Venice studying art history, but my real passion is magic-comedy."

"Magic-comedy? Is that a thing?"

"It's difinitely a thing." His squeaky sweet accent is a charming contrast to his large, masculine build. "Maybe you just haven't got it in America yet. Want to see a trick?" he asks.

"*Perchè no?*" I smile and shrug. He picks up a napkin, turns around, and writes something on it I cannot see.

"Do you know what I wrote?" he asks.

"Uhhh . . . no," I say, puzzled. He smiles, turns the napkin around. On it is the word "NO." I look at him. "That's not a magic trick," I groan.

"Tough customer. Here's one of my favorites. He pulls a box out of his pocket, turns away and takes something out, replaces the box. "Hold out your hands." I do. He drops a dead fly into my hand. I'm so startled I nearly drop it.

"What? Gross!"

"No, wait. I'm going to bring it back to life." He closes my hand gently and then breathes warm air into my hand. "Abra-cadaver!" He winks.

"Just look now!" I open my hand, but the fly is dead. I drain my wine glass and drop the bug inside.

"I think your whole routine needs some work, Leo. Just like your costume—that beard makes me want to tell you if I've been naughty or nice."

"You? Naughty. No question. It's my mate Alfonso's costume, he works at the embassy. He was invited but got pissed at a different party last night and spewed the hootch, so I got his invitation! Lucky break. Hey?"

"Spewed the hootch? Is that a Kiwi thing?"

"It's from my magic-comedy show. You know, like screwed the pooch, but funnier." Leo examines the fly in the glass. "Maybe I said the wrong word." The song ends and I see Frantonio take the stage and the microphone. He looks ruffled and handsome in his Bono costume. Why did he have to be such a dick to me? Why did I come all the way to Venice? For a book?

"Ladies and gentlemen, it's time for our This or That Auction. I'll ask my co-chair, Paolo Renaldi, to join me." An older Italian man with a gray beard walks up with a large fishbowl. Inside are pieces of paper. "Each of you put your name into the fishbowl when you checked in. When we call you, you have the opportunity to buy one of our donated items: This." He gestures to the right. "Or that." He gestures to the left. On one side of the stage, a scantily clad model carries a large, wrapped basket. Frantonio reads from his notes. "Gorgeous Giulia is carrying a basket of age-defying Rinnovo products from Milan." The second scantily clad model holds a handbag. "Sexy Silva is modeling a Dolce & Gabbana, Sicily leather top handle satchel in peacock blue." Paolo reaches into the fishbowl and fishes out a name.

"Cariddi Giuseppina," he announces. A woman in the back raises her hand excitedly and moves to the stage. She looks at the bag and the basket.

"I forgot to mention the handbag is used," Frantonio says. People laugh. "By Bianca Balti!" he says with a charismatic smile. The woman's eyes widen.

"I'll take the bag for four thousand euro," the woman says eagerly.

"Four thousand euro for the World Peace Initiative!" announces Frantonio. Holy shit! Four thousand for a used bag? I realize now the woman checking me in must have been too distracted by my costume to take my name for the fishbowl. Thank God. A round of applause as a third scantily clad model on stage lights up part of a giant screen, showing the fundraising goal. The top of the screen says two hundred thousand euro. Frantonio continues with more items as the woman follows the model off stage to the green room to purchase her four-thousand-euro used handbag.

As the fundraising continues, I can't take my eyes off Frantonio. I've seen him working a photo shoot, but his relaxed confidence speaking to a crowd is impressive. He cracks jokes, warming up the guests, getting people into the game of outbidding each other. Usually when I find myself the center of attention, it's some small catastrophe I've created. Every second I watch him, I'm less angry with him and more determined to make things right between us. Imagine the stress he must have already been under, planning this event, and then I show up looking like a Comic-Con reject. But it's too late now. This last fight was the nail in the coffin. Our brief, romantic love affair is deader than Leo's fly in my empty wine—I look at my empty wine glass. To my utter amazement, the fly is crawling around inside!

"I don't believe it!" I interrupt Leo, who is talking about a junior magician competition he won in Melbourne when he was twelve.

"It's true," he says. "The rabbit died of a tooth infection from eating a rotten mango so I had to use a lizard instead."

"No, Leo! Your fly is alive!" I say excitedly.

"Why'd it take so long? I paid heaps for those frozen flies," he mutters. I choose to ignore this last, focusing on the obvious metaphor in front of me. My love affair with Frantonio is not dead! It's alive, and . . . drinking wine? The fly is definitely drinking the last drop of red wine in the glass. I take this as inspiration.

"I'm going to get another glass." I leave Leo with his zombie fly and walk over to the bar. There is a stressed exchange going on between the young bartender and a cocktail waitress behind the bar. The bartender breaks off and flashes me a forced smile. "Red wine please," I say. There's a flash of something on his face, but it's so fleeting I cannot decipher it. He takes the bottle the waitress is holding and pours me a glass. This one tastes much better than the last. "*Grazie!*"

"When I suggested you use my invitation, I didn't think you'd get me banned from the event for life." I turn to find myself face to face with a radiant Pax, the Roman goddess of Peace. "But now I'm realizing it was a stroke of genius." Regina looks amazing wrapped in flowing white organza and silks, embroidered with golden olive branches, holding a golden scepter. Her hair is perfectly coiffed around a golden cornucopia that adds another eight inches to her already imposing height.

"Regina! I thought you weren't coming."

"Couldn't handle the guilt. And I'm hoping to grab a photo of Minister D'Angelo with his mistress, so I can blackmail him to reexamine his political position on large game hunting trophies. Besides, I still had this get-up from when I was crowned goddess of peace at the Pax Romana festival eight years ago in Rome." Of course she does. "And there I was thinking I'd never wear it again," she winks.

"I'm sorry to embarrass you. I looked at last year's invitation."

"Clearly," she laughs. "But never apologize for looking fiercely beautiful," she smiles. I blush, relieved and flattered. "How are things going with our host?" She watches Frantonio on stage, as he waits for a man to choose between one of Frantonio's framed photographs and a donated Gucci watch.

"Not well," I admit. "I've humiliated him and stressed him out even more." The man on stage picks the watch. Frantonio visibly bristles but masks his bruised ego with a charismatic smile. "He doesn't want me here."

"He's an idiot, with a fragile male ego," Regina says as I watch him put his hand on the naked back of one of the models. She sees me self-consciously adjust my bustier. "Why are you wasting your time and energy on him?"

"I don't know . . . . It's like I keep hearing part of a song, the same stanzas over and over. I can't get them out of my head, and I just need to hear the end of it," I try to explain. She smiles and nods. She gets it.

"They mostly end the same way, my dear. But, I understand. *Allora*, if you want him, you must retake the sexual gaze." This sounds familiar. I watch her take another sip of wine, elegantly tilting her neck back ever so slightly like a swan. A man at the table behind us is staring. Not at me.

"I'm not as good at that as you are, Regina. And I think he's better at it too." I glance back up at the stage, but this time Frantonio is looking at *us*. He's relieved to see Regina. Maybe her unexpected appearance is helping my cause.

"Perhaps. But he wants you, my dear," she says. "That's easy to see. Let's have a glass of wine." I follow her to the bar where the bartender's hand visibly shakes as he pours her another glass of red. "I cannot believe they're serving a *Sandrone Barolo* at a fundraiser. Italians." She shakes her head, laughing. I take a sip of mine. Wow, this wine is incredible. Regina watches Frantonio on stage. Strutting, putting on a show.

"I think your Mr. Darcy is too proud. And you my dear, are smitten, but too prejudiced. If you want the man, you must forgive the ego. In order to command the gaze, you must first submit to it." She gives my shoulder a gentle squeeze and then spots someone across the room. "And now, please excuse me for a bit, I have political blackmail to engineer." Regina glides elegantly across the ballroom until a Mother Teresa stops her for a photo and autograph. Submit to the gaze. Humility is not my strong suit. But, my strong suit clearly wasn't working and it's leather panties were getting itchy. I take out my phone, do a quick search online for songs about apologizing, and impulsively I send him a message. It's a link to the video for a Bryan Adams song, one of his cheesiest, but a favorite: "Please Forgive Me." Maybe he'll come around.

"There you are, mate. You try the Bickies yet?" Leo walks up with a plate of cookies. I realize I've had a lot to drink and little to eat. I take one. Then another.

"Ladies and gentlemen," announces Frantonio, "we are over halfway to our goal and it is time to bid on our prized donations: the vintner's choice from the top vineyards in Toscana, Veneto, Piemonte, Bordeaux, Champagne, and Provence," he smiles. People applaud and whistle. "As if you weren't already drunk enough." People laugh.

Frantonio looks to the right, but the girl standing there is empty-handed. Over by the green room, Paolo argues with another man. Something is clearly wrong. I see hints of distress wash over Frantonio, but no one else does. His smile is firmly fixed. "First, an intermission." He looks to the DJ stand but it's empty.

"The DJ's in the handicapped bathroom with one of the cocktail waitresses," Leo volunteers loudly. People laugh. Fumbling frantically with equipment he doesn't understand at the DJ stand, Frantonio finally gets a song going and dashes off.

"I hope everything's okay," I say, concerned.

"Everything is difinitely not okay," says Leo, pointing to Paolo, who is now dragging the young bartender by his collar to the green room. "Bet the wine's gone missing. Reckon somebody stole it?" he asks. I suddenly realize what's happened. I taste the red in my glass. Yep, pretty amazing. My friend Nadya isn't here, but I'm pretty certain it's one of her kings or queens of the Italian wine aristocracy.

"We're drinking it," I whisper. The gravity of this huge mistake sinks into my brain as Leo laughs.

"Seriously? That's fantastic, I'm going to get another glass. Maybe two," he says. I cringe inside. If I'm right, Frantonio is fucked. As the song ends, no new song starts. The DJ is still gone. Murmurs in the room. Leo returns within moments. "No more wine just a crying cocktail waitress serving warm beer. Pretty sad. People are starting to leave."

"Leo, the host is my friend," I say. "What can we do?" He thinks.

"Magic-comedy!" says Leo, "I'll do my one act."

"We want people to *stay*," I say. Suddenly, I have a flash of inspiration. I make my way quickly to the DJ stand and plug in my phone. "Imagine" starts to play, and I race over to the last model standing awkwardly on stage and whisper in her ear. She smiles and takes the microphone.

"Ladies and gentlemen, we will like to invite all John Lennons to the stage for a lip-synch contest." Laughter and applause from the crowd, as the various Johns make their way up. I notice Regina smiling at me. My confidence boosted, I stride quickly to the green room with my cloak billowing out behind me. Wonder Woman is here to save the day.

Chapter 34

How Not to
Expose Yourself

Green Room, Ca' Rezzonico, Venice:
Friday, 10:28 p.m.

Inside the green room my Amazon sandals come to an abrupt halt. A waitress sobs in a chair. An older man pops heart pills. Frantonio roars into his phone in French. Paolo argues with the bartender in Italian. Five scantily clad models in sequins and ridiculously uncomfortable stilettos huddle by their makeup station like frightened gazelles. Uncle Gandhi is seated quietly in the corner, praying? Frantonio hangs up and throws the phone across the room, swearing angrily. He glares at his uncle.

"What's happened?" I ask.

"The fucking wine we are supposed to auction is gone," Frantonio barks. "They poured it at the bar!" He runs his fingers through his hair over and over again, trying to calm himself. How could a mistake like this happen? I walk up to Frantonio, who is staring into space, trying to figure out what to do. As I put a hand on his shoulder, he just looks at me, shell-shocked.

"How can I help?"

"You have eighty thousand euro, Wonder Woman?"

"If I did, I'd totally give it to you. Talk about brownie points, I wouldn't have to go to church with my mom for a year." I smile, but he just puts his head in his hands. He's sweating, looking sick to his stomach and a little lost. The last time I saw him flailing like this was in the library at Regina's. My heart tightens in my chest. Despite our ups and downs, I want badly to help him, to see that handsome smile again.

"We'll think of something," I say softly. He glances up at me, his big brown eyes full of despair and embarrassment.

"What? We have nothing left to sell." I pace, thinking. Surely there's a creative way to get these wealthy people to fork over a measly eighty thousand.

"It's a charity fundraiser. Can't we just ask for the money?" I ask. Paolo laughs without amusement.

"Rich people don't like beggars," he says bluntly.

"I'm afraid he's right," Regina says. All heads turn toward her. "This is Italy my dear. Even worse, it's Venice. These people expect a show. You have to dazzle them, coax the money out of them."

"What about a photo with you?"

"Sorry, I've been giving them out for free for the past hour," she laughs. One of the men arguing with Paolo leans over and says something to him quietly in Italian. Paolo smiles.

"We could sell dates with the models," suggests Paolo. Regina frowns but doesn't seem surprised. Frantonio looks at the girls quietly, thinking.

"What?" I ask. I *am* surprised.

"Auction off dates with the models. It will get us at least fifty," Paolo explains.

"This is not a human trafficking fundraiser," says Regina indignantly.

"It's not sex, Regina. Just a date," says Frantonio. I glance at him, disappointed. "We won't force them and we'll pay them." I look over at the girls who are staring at us, with blank, wide-eyed expressions. They don't understand English but they can tell we're talking about them.

"Pay them? What, a hundred euro to be auctioned off like a cow?" Regina asks. She turns to the gazelles and translates. A ripple of surprise and shock flashes through them, but none of them say anything. They're too scared to object.

"They're not going to say no to you," I say. "There are rich, powerful people here and these girls work as baristas, cleaners, and shop clerks," I say.

"I'm leaving. I'm won't watch rich old men bid on the dignity of young girls," says Regina hotly.

"You're overreacting, Regina," Frantonio objects. She flashes him a glare of disapproval and walks out. His sudden confidence fizzles. He seems worse than before.

"We have to sell them something," Paolo grumbles. My mind races as I nervously play with the tassels on my lasso. I look down at the golden tassels in my fingers, run my hand along the lasso. That's it!

"We can sell them *their own* dignity!" I announce boldly. And then, having already practiced it thirty-nine times in the hotel room, I sweep my cape up in a flourish as I turn on my heel and stride purposefully through the doors.

Ballroom, Ca' Rezzonico, Venice: Friday, 10:39 p.m.

On stage: the worst possible scenario. Leo has the microphone and is now performing his magic-comedy tricks.

"Knock knock!?" he says with a smile. The audience looks unsure.

"Who is there?" various people answer from the crowd.

"Wiser," chirps Leo.

"Wiser who?" shouts an American man in the middle of the crowd.

"Why's her wallet in my ear?" he laughs as he reaches behind his "ear" and pulls out a billfold. He points to a lady in the crowd. "Madam, I believe you lost this!" he says triumphantly. She opens her handbag and holds up her wallet.

"No, mine is here," she says.

"Bugger. Whose is this, then?" Leo rifles the billfold in his hand. "Olivier Thomas? Terrible photo on your license, hey?" He shows it to the crowd. "But everyone takes bad photos on their licenses." A man walks up to reclaim his wallet. "Oh, that's what you actually look like. Bad luck, mate. And your condoms are expired I think. Little wonder."

My heart racing, I grab my sword and shield and stride up the steps to the stage. I try to take the mic from Leo. "But I still have the big finish where I release all the doves from their cages."

"Do that when we hit two hundred," I suggest.

"Fantastic! Yes!" He relinquishes the mic and hurries off stage to prepare. Suddenly I find myself alone, holding a microphone, facing a ballroom full of important people from numerous countries, all staring at me. I realize my hand is shaking. My idea, which seemed brilliant moments ago, now seems less shiny. In fact, potentially humiliating.

"Hello," I say nervously. "You're probably wondering about my Wonder Woman warrior costume, since our theme is world peace." People murmur, some laugh. "But, superheroes do fight the bad guys for peace."

"Typical American," snipes someone from the crowd. People laugh. I'm losing ground as Frantonio emerges from the green room.

"Tonight, I'm not an American. I'm Wonder Woman, an international symbol of feminine strength and power. Most people don't know this but, Wonder Woman was created by a man living with two women." This gets a whistle of appreciation. "Two very strong women: his wife and the niece of one of the most important feminists of the twentieth century. I did my research." I see Frantonio moving toward the stage. "The man, Dr. Marston, was a psychologist, fascinated by feminine power, but it was his wife who insisted his new comic book hero should be female. The character Marston created was his ideal for a new type of role model. Super strong, intelligent, and loving. Marston believed the world of man was one of war. But a world controlled by strong women— this would be a world of peace." The women in the room applaud. I get a few shouts of "*Sì!*" Frantonio, now at the foot of the stage, stops. He doesn't climb the stairs. He just watches me. My confidence is bolstered.

I struggle to unsheathe my slightly bent sword. "My sword shows my strength. And my shield protects the things I love." I lay both of these down. "But neither is my most important tool. Dr. Marston AND his wife Elizabeth helped invent the lie detector. They were obsessed with truth. So, Wonder Woman was given a golden lasso of truth." I hold up my lasso. "Truth is our most valuable asset." I pause for effect. "Shall we see if it works?" People clap and cheer. "*Allora*," I smile.

"Minister Luca Mancini," I read aloud from the fishbowl as Frantonio watches with curiosity. "Please come to the stage for This or That." More cheers as a rather drunk politician makes his way through the crowd and up the stairs. There are hoots and hollers as I wrap my lasso of truth around his chest. "Minister Mancini, you will be asked two questions and get to choose which to answer truthfully. My first question is simple. Minister, how much will you be donating tonight to help us meet our goal?" People clap. Luca snorts a laugh. "The second question will be from the audience," I announce. Luca's smile drops. "Any question they want to ask you." People cheer.

Someone immediately shouts out: "Who did you vote for in the election?" There is a ripple of delight and laughter. Then, everyone falls silent. All eyes on Luca. Phones come out. People are filming, ready to post on social media. "Well minister, this question or that one?" He stares at me, not amused. I hold my ground. He looks at the phones pointed at him.

"I'll be donating five thousand euro." Everyone cheers. Some people boo. Frantonio leaps onto the stage and lights up another five grand on the screen. He is beaming. I remove the lasso and hold it up. "This young lady will escort you to the green room to make your donation." I turn back to the crowd and hold the lasso over my head. "It works!" People laugh. "Shall we see who's next?" The crowd cheers. Frantonio walks over to me, puts his hand in the fishbowl, and gives me the smile I've been waiting to see. A warm feeling radiates through me. For once, I didn't screw things up. I fixed things. I feel Wonderful.

"*Grazie, bella,*" he whispers.

"Who needs wine when you have Wonder Woman?" I wink.

THINGS YOU DON'T WANT TO BE ASKED IN FRONT OF A CROWD:

1. Have you ever done any hard drugs?
2. Where were you last Tuesday night?
3. Did you ever cheat on your taxes?
4. Do you love me?
5. Did you sleep with my sister? (Or brother?)
6. Have you ever used Viagra?
7. Are those real?
8. Have you ever been arrested?
9. How old are you really?
10. Who is the better kisser, Bruce Willis or Al Pacino? (This was for Regina, who has starred opposite both and chose to make a donation instead of kiss and tell.)

Portego, Ca' Rezzonico, Venice: Friday, 11:59 p.m.

I unbuckle my leather Amazon sandals one strap at a time as I sit in a cushioned chair, waiting in the *portego*. Leo is out front, getting us a water taxi. He's invited me three times to visit New Zealand when he goes home. I've taken him up on his offer to drop me at my hotel, knowing he's hoping for at least a kiss. He's very charming, but I'm very drunk, my feet hurt, and I've decided to enjoy my king-sized bed and fancy hotel room solo. I wiggle my toes on the carpet that's probably over a hundred years old and rub my new blisters. That's what I get for dancing like a fool. Regina had slipped out much earlier in classic "leave-them-wanting-more" fashion.

"You were a true Wonder Woman tonight, *chérie*. We surpassed our goal." Frantonio smiles as he squats beside my chair, sets a bottle of

Brunello down, and picks up my right foot. "This was the last bottle of the donated wine. I saved it for us to share at my hotel," he winks as he rubs my foot with his soft, warm hands. Wow, that feels amazing. Frantonio looks spent, but somehow still very sexy in his Bono costume. He's lost the leather jacket and just wears the T-shirt, leather cuffs, and fake tattoos. The scruff on his face seems to have grown in the last few hours. At least, grown on me. But . . .

"I'll have to pass," I say with great difficulty.

"It's eight hundred euro a bottle, Marina. We'll have it for breakfast."

"I meant, your hotel. I'm exhausted." I can't believe I'm saying this and neither can he, but the truth is, I'm still a bit stung by his behavior tonight. His smile melts. The best foot rub I've ever had stops abruptly. A moment ago he was tired but elated, now he looks confused. He puts my foot down and runs his hand through his hair.

"Really?" he asks softly.

"You were going to auction off helpless models. It was kind of a libido killer," I say.

"We were desperate. It was a bad idea. You saved us from ourselves."

"Wonder Woman!" calls Leo from the front door. "Our water chariot awaits." Frantonio looks from Leo to me with shock.

"Marina, you're not going home with *him?*" Frantonio asks, incredulous. I know I should tell him I'm "difinitely" not going home with Tolstoy but truthfully, I'm enjoying his jealousy.

"He's the world's greatest Russian author, and Santa beards are sexy." I pick up my sandals and stand. Frantonio reaches out and gently but firmly grabs my elbow. Suddenly I find myself in a nearby alcove standing in the shadow of a marble statue. Frantonio's face is inches from mine. He pulls off his glasses.

"Put those back on," I say weakly.

"I just want to talk to you," he says. I didn't want to talk to him. He was too good at talking and . . . he's been working all night, how does he smell like warm butter and leather? Okay, he's been wearing a leather jacket, but come on! He leans in closer so I try not to breathe through my nose. Now I look like I'm panting. *Perfetto.*

"*Chèrie*, please. I said stupid things when you arrived, but I was already a nervous wreck. And then, I saw you, dressed like this!" He looks down. My panting is causing my breasts to heave up and down in my corset like I'm in a Jane Austen film. I hold my breath. They stop moving. He looks deep into my eyes. "When I saw you, I was thrilled, embarrassed, totally turned on, but angry. And, the truth is, I was terrified." He was terrified by his feelings for me? By my strength and beauty? "I was terrified that you'd turn the whole event into one of your little catastrophes." Oh. Right. That's not quite the same. Somehow, I'm still holding my breath. "But, instead, you saved it *from* catastrophe. You were brilliant and brave and beautiful, and I was a complete ass. I needed you tonight. I need you now." His face is tortured and utterly sincere. I stare at him. "*Please forgive me,*" he whispers. This last is my undoing. The Bryan Adams song I texted him earlier. All the air goes out of me.

"*Basta.* Enough talk," I say. "*Tienimi stretto,*" I whisper. He pulls me to him, and I melt into his arms as his lips close around mine.

Chapter 35

How Not to Talk

Frantonio's Suite, Belmond Hotel Cipriani, Venice:
Saturday, 1:13 a.m.

FIRST: Everything is a hot, fantastic blur

His jeans pressed against me. My fingers in his hair. His tongue in my mouth. I can't get enough of that sweet, soft mouth—sucking me in, drinking me. The shield on my back clangs against the door as he presses against me. I tear it off and toss it wildly, hearing something break, but neither of us stop. He unties my cloak and it drops to the floor at my feet. He slips his fingers into my hair and pulls my head back, gently biting my earlobe, my neck. My tiara stays on. It's not going anywhere.

The scruff of his beard sends tingles through my body. My fingers slip under his T-shirt, my hand grabbing his taut abs. So fucking sexy! His palm on my breasts. His fingers frantically prying into my corset from the top. I gasp for air as his lips slide down my neck to the tops of my moving breasts. His hair smells like coconut oil. I inhale deeply.

My hand slides down his chest to his belt. My fingers fumble desperately at the buckle. He grasps my ass, his fingers spread, holding me tightly against him. I feel his hardening cock through his jeans but cannot get his belt undone. I whimper in frustration. He presses his cock against me. Harder and harder. My heart pounds in my chest. Faster and faster. His hand still struggles with the corset, and now he moans in frustration. My breath catches as his other hand finally finds the strings on my leather panties and tugs at them desperately. My wet *figa* aches for the touch of those fingers I remember from Amalfi. But he can't undo the knot. Fucking leather panties, I think.

"Fucking leather pants!" he cries. I laugh.

"Wait, I'll do it," I say, but suddenly his hands are on my hips and he quickly twists me around, bending me over the desk. I grab it for support as he spreads my legs. He flips my skirt up. His fingers pull the laces from the panties and he yanks them off. Free! The muscles in my throbbing *figa* contract with anticipation and I brace myself on the desk. I wait for the jingle of his belt. I long for the thrust of his cock inside me. But, instead, with a flash of surprise I feel the stubble of his beard on my bare ass. I turn my head. He's on his knees behind me. His thumbs tickle the outside edge of my *figa* as his hands pry my inner thighs further apart.

My head spins as his face slides underneath my ass. Then, lightning flashes through my body as his whiskers graze my soft, wet insides and he plunges his tongue deep into me. As my knees buckle, I grab the back of the desk, sliding the lamp over, resting my forehead against the cool wood. Stuff falls to the floor as the desk shakes, and I moan loudly. My body trembles with pleasure as his lips and tongue move against my *figa*. There is no tender tickling. There's only hungry passion as he presses his face further into me, his tongue deeper, sucking and demanding. The lamp crashes to the floor. Darkness as my back arches and I climax, inhaling deeply. Every muscle in my body is frozen; I cannot feel my legs. I cannot breathe. I only pulse. I cry out.

THEN: Everything slows down
I feel myself being guided into the chair next to the desk. It's as if the world is in slow motion. As the blood returns to the far corners of my body, bringing a tingling sensation with it, I watch him put his glasses back on and carefully examine the tiny latches on the front of my corset. I smile.

"You are beautiful with your glasses," I whisper. He smiles as he unlatches the first buckle on the corset . . . and then the second and third. My breasts now half popping out, I try to finish the job, but he stops me, moving my hands back to the chair. He kisses me sweetly.

"Leave it on." He traces a finger down my neck, over my chest, to my now exposed nipple. Tracing small circles around it, he leans in, caressing it gently with his lips, then more firmly. His other hand gropes my other breast. His breath is hot on my skin. His teeth find my nipple. I can feel his body against my leg, his hard cock pressing into my thigh, his jeans still on. My eyes fall on the sword, on the floor.

"Stop," I say. He stops. "Stand up." He does, looking confused. Leaning down, I pick up the sword (it's bent) and point it at him. "Take off your clothes." He smiles and pulls his shirt off quickly, tossing it onto a chair. "Slowly," I command. He slowly unclasps his leather wristbands, tossing them too. Watching me watch him, he now unbuckles his belt, slides his jeans to the floor. His cock is practically bursting out of his tight black jockey shorts. He bends, removing them. His gorgeous body is perfect in the pale light of the room. He just stands, waiting. Transfixed, I stare—at his stomach, his strong shoulders, his magnificent erection.

"Yes, Amazon princess?" He waits. Oh right. I'm directing. I point the bent sword towards the bed.

"Sit," I say. He does. Remembering my prize of the night, I suddenly toss the bent sword down and take the golden lasso into my hands.

"What are you going to do with that?" he asks nervously.

"Not ask you questions," I smile. Sliding my fingers along the cord, I stretch it out. My hair tickles his back and my breasts graze his face as I lean over him, wrapping it once, twice, three times around his bare chest and arms. "Put your hands behind you." I wrap the cord once around his hands, and then deposit the rest in his open palm. "Don't worry, I'm not a knot-tying type of girl." I smile, pleased at my clever double entendre.

I kneel in front of him and slowly slide my lips around the head of his cock, tickling the tip of it with my tongue. Pushing his knees apart the same way he'd spread my legs, I slip my lips down over his erection. The largeness fills my mouth. I slide up and down slowly, sucking and teasing him, stroking him and massaging him with my tongue. He groans softly. Reaching around the outside of his legs, I hook my hands onto his thighs to find leverage. Now moving faster, my lips close around him and I suck harder. His groans grow more intense. And then, I stop and stand.

"Condom?" I ask.

"My case, there," Frantonio says, out of breath. He tries to point but he's tied up. I fumble through his suitcase and quickly grab a condom, ripping it open. With both hands I slide the condom slowly, slowly, ever so slowly down onto him. He looks me in the eye. "You're torturing me. *Chèrie* please, just fuck me," he says. I smile. Putting one knee on the bed, I swing my other leg over him, straddling him. Holding onto his shoulders, I hover over him.

"Say it in French," I tease.

"*Baise-moi, s'il te plaît,*" he says.

"Now Italian," I say.

"*Fottimi, per favore,*" he begs.

"You're right. French is sexiest," I agree. With that, I slide my *figa* down onto his waiting, throbbing cock.

"*O dio,*" he whispers in ecstasy as I grip his bare shoulders and ride him up and down. He leans his head back, breathing hard. I feel his hands on my bare ass. He's dropped the lasso. I let him. Who am I kidding? I'm no dominatrix. He pulls me up and down on his cock, grasps me by the hips and ass. In one fluid move, he flips me onto my back. The feather duvet sinks under me as he presses his naked, sweaty body against mine.

He thrusts himself deep inside. The muscles of my *figa* tighten again and then I'm coming a second time. I cry out with pain and pleasure as he pushes into me over and over again. Then, as my whole body shakes and tightens, with a final massive push he comes too. My toes and fingers curl against the soft, clean cotton of the cool sheets as he collapses onto me. His heart beats through the leather of my half-on corset. I smell his hair against my cheek. I breathe in deeply and drift into bliss.

Frantonio's Suite, Belmond Hotel Cipriani, Venice: Saturday, Dawn

The clean scent of lemon blossoms is carried in from the garden by a breeze off the canal, and it almost but not quite masks the soggy, moldy, dank smell of Venice. This smell is strangely starting to grow on me. There is something surprisingly satisfying about it. All the fine and foul folded into one. You can smell the years. Venice *smells* like a dusty attic or damp basement *looks*. Overburdened with boxed up memories and forgotten lives, these places give you a solid sense of being. You can see, smell, and feel the past, present, and future. And by sensing it, you are part of it. Time feels tangible. Like the ridges on a tree stump, you can feel the years.

As I lie here, blinking slowly in the unfocused light of dawn, breathing in the comforting smell of sixteen hundred Venetian mornings mashed into one, I realize for the first time that a person is also this. A person is a compilation of millions of moments, thoughts, and experiences. Of actions and reactions. Of choices, dreams, adventures, encounters, and emotions. You are a living, breathing, tangible record of your life. A Collection of Being. If you are a child, this is a very short collection of stories. And if you are like me, in your twenties, your collection of stories may require a shelf or two. But if you are like Regina, Bob, Sheela, Uncle Gandhi, my mother, or even Ruby of the Vegan Goat Farts at Miami International Airport, your collection is a vast library.

Why has it taken me so many years to see this? To respect it? Because these same people ask loud questions during movies, walk slowly in front of you despite highly engineered orthopedic shoes, tell the same stories over and over, and use cell phones like ham radios. But, are not the years they wear like permanent scout badges—and these badges actually tantalizing hints of what still lies ahead for me? They are promises of the collecting I still have left to do. This is both daunting and thrilling. Or at the very least, surprisingly satisfying.

I feel a warm hand move over my waist, slide up my belly and between my breasts. Speaking of satisfying . . . I close my eyes again and smile. Frantonio's chest rises and falls against my back, and I think for a moment that he's still asleep. Then his thumb and forefinger begin to tickle my nipple. His lips on the back of my neck are soft, but his whiskers rake my skin and I begin to squirm.

"It's barely light out," I complain. But he can hear me smiling.

"*Perfetto,*" he whispers, deep and sexy. "Time to nap after." He rolls me over. This will be our third time. If Piero #4 was sexercise, Frantonio is more of a sexathon.

Frantonio's Suite, Belmond Hotel Cipriani, Venice: Saturday, 9:12 a.m.

A knock at the door wakes us. I open my eyes and immediately realize it's much later. Bright sun floods the balcony, spilling into the room and onto the bed. By the third knock, Frantonio is out of the bed, wrapped in a fluffy, white hotel robe and swearing as he answers the door.

"This better be important," he says harshly.

"I'm sorry. Your mobile is off and Mr. Barton needs to move his appointment up to ten because he's taking an earlier flight home." I recognize Uncle Gandhi's soft, melodious voice as I burrow deeper into the sheets, hoping he can't see me.

"Who the fuck is Barton?" Frantonio's sharp tone startles me. A far cry from the sexy whispers of his sunrise seduction.

"The curator from Soho."

"Dammit."

"I'll have the car brought around while you're gone and load every-thing up for the drive home."

"Good. Then you can look for a new job," Frantonio says bluntly. My eyes widen. *What?*

"*Per favore, nipote.* What happened last night was a simple mistake."

"What happened last night was unforgivable and a public relations nightmare. It could have cost my reputation. If you can't see that, you're either a moron or too old for this job. Which is it?" Fantonio asks. Uncle Gandhi, perhaps knowing someone else is in the room, retreats deeper into the hall and to his native tongue.

"*Per favore non parlare così,*" he says quietly. "*Tutti fanno degli errori.*" I think the conversation is over when I hear the door close, but quickly realize Frantonio has stepped into the hall to berate his uncle. I hear his shouts in angry Italian, through the door. I sit up, feeling awkward, won-dering what to do with myself. I cringe as his voice gets louder.

Remembering his uncle's caring words to me last night, I can't under-stand how Frantonio can treat him this way, even if he screwed up the wine auction. Didn't it all work out in the end? Suddenly my phone vibrates next to the bed. I pick it up. One new message . . . from Frantonio? I stare. This isn't possible. I look around the room and see his phone, lying next to his leather jacket on the floor. Bewildered, I click open the mes-sage on my phone:

I cannot forget but I forgive you, I do
Like a stone in your shoe my heart beats for you.

More song lyrics? My head swims. What's happening? The truth hits me hard. This is not Frantonio. All the song lyrics, this whole time, they were sent by someone else. But who? I puzzle it out. The first message I got was a French number. I assumed it was Frantonio and that Yin had given my number to him. But she'd never actually confirmed this. My mind races through the conversations I had with him in my room at Regina's and in her library. *I'd* always been the one referencing the song lyrics, *not him.* But just last night, hadn't he quoted the Bryan Adams song back to me? Or was he just saying, "please forgive me?" I'm an idiot. I had assumed it was Frantonio because I wanted it to be him. I had seen what I wanted to see. The flirty, romantic, and mysterious exchanges I'd been having this entire trip had been with someone else entirely.

Chapter 36

How Not to Take the Wrong Ride

Frantonio's Suite, Belmond Hotel Cipriani, Venice: Saturday, 9:20 a.m.

"Je suis désolé, my dear," Frantonio says as he walks back in. I quickly stuff my phone under the sheet. "That was a rude awakening after such a lovely night." He leans over the bed and kisses me. "I hate to run but I'm late for a meeting about a show I'm doing in New York." He heads into the bathroom, turns on the shower. "Please say you'll come to *Firenze* with me and let me show you my city."

"Florence?" My hand tightens around my phone under the sheets. I feel unsure of everything. All the romantic, late night exchanges I thought I'd been having with this man had been with an entirely different person. And the man yelling profanity at his elderly uncle moments ago on the other side of that door also seemed like an entirely different man from the one I'd just made love to three times. My dawn musings on age and experience now sit in my stomach like a lead milkshake. Suddenly I want to be in my own room, alone. I need to think. Frantonio's robe drops to the bathroom floor and I'm once again staring at his gorgeous naked body.

"Oui chèrie. Florence is where I live. Where my studio is," he winks as

he walks back over to me. "Maybe you'll let me shoot you in my studio?" He gently pushes me back onto the bed, his muscular chest leaning over me, the graceful curve of his neck lit by the sun. "Just the two of us?" He smiles. "No fountain or Roman *carabinieri*?" He leans in and kisses me deeply. My lower half wakes up. The steam from the now hot shower drifts into the room. He stands. "See, only one kiss and you torture me." Standing there naked, back lit, with steam billowing behind him, Frantonio looks like Michelangelo's David in a porn film. "My little red car is downstairs, *chère*. Maybe you'll accept my offer of a ride this time?"

Belmond Hotel Cipriani, Venice: Saturday, 11:15 a.m.

I have packed up in my own hotel room, left my costume at the front desk for Sheela's courier, and returned to Frantonio's hotel swiftly. I'm no longer part fish, I'm all shark. I must keep swimming. If I stop, I'll start to wonder if Yang was right, if the French-Italian photographer of my dreams who fucked my brains out last night and now wants to drive me through Tuscany in his vintage convertible is actually an egotistical ass. And I will sink.

Wheeling my roller board bag toward the front steps, I see Frantonio's car in the valet area and Uncle Gandhi . . . *unloading bags*? I wheel over and greet him with a smile, hoping he's recovered from Frantonio's earlier outburst.

"Good morning!" I say.

"*Buongiorno,* Wonder Woman. You are in your human disguise, I see."

"But always ready," I smile. "Why are you unloading?"

"These are just my bags. I'll take the train," he smiles. I stare at the car and realize there are only two seats. Frantonio has chucked his elderly uncle out of the car, for me. My inner shark stops swimming and I sink rapidly. I am again part fish. Floundering.

"I can't take your seat."

"Don't worry, dear. I'd probably be on the train anyway. He's fired me again and he's in one of his moods."

"Fired you for what reason?"

"I told him last night was my fault. I just couldn't let that bartender and waitress lose their jobs." Uncle Gandhi can see my distress. "Don't worry. He fires me once a year at least."

"And then rehires you when he feels guilty?"

"He can't find anyone else to do the job," Uncle Gandhi laughs. I'm glad he's got such a good attitude about it. I'm struggling. He takes my bag and wedges it into the tiny trunk, putting a few more items into the car, like the eight-hundred-euro bottle of wine we never drank last night. "He'll be here soon. They have a lovely bar in the lobby, please have a coffee, relax." I force a smile and walk inside, but my head is spinning.

At the bar, I've put three sugars into my now lukewarm *café latte* without realizing it. My phone buzzes and I look down. This message is from Mike. Just seeing his name on the screen makes me smile. I miss my friends.

MIKE: Florida Woman Wows Crowd with Wonder Wit?

ME: Florida woman realizes she's fucked a dick.

MIKE: Hello? Straight girls fuck dicks.

ME: Okay I fucked an asshole.

MIKE: That's my job lol. We'll talk about it in Rome. See you tonight?

ME: He wants to take me to Florence.

MIKE: What? Fuck that asshole!

ME: Already did.
Pay attention.

MIKE: Come to Rome!
Michael got me a room at
the De Russie for my birthday!

Shit! Mike's birthday, I forgot. A familiar voice turns my head. There, at the front desk, Regina is checking out.

"*Ciao*, Wonder Woman," she smiles. "I didn't get to say good night, or tell you what a fantastic job you did saving our host," she chuckles.

"Thank you," I blush. A driver in uniform walks up and takes her bags.

"No, thank *you*. I've spent my life seeing women taken advantage of in this country . . . well in every country I've lived in. It's hard not to just feel overwhelmed, like your own small actions never make a difference. But you reminded me we can make a difference if we keep trying. Things are changing so slowly."

"That means so much coming from you."

"How did things go after I left? Did you get what you wanted? Did you hear the end of Frantonio's song?" she asks with a smile.

"Yes," I say.

"And did the song end as you expected and dreamed?" she asks.

"*Sì*, and no," I admit.

"It seldom does, my dear." She laughs and snaps her designer purse closed. "*Allora, I go*. I'm already late leaving. Tomorrow I fly to London for a meeting with a film director so we're driving to Roma today. Would you like a ride?"

"Frantonio has invited me to his villa in Tuscany."

"Well, that sounds like a lot more fun. Perhaps there is a verse left in his song that you haven't heard yet." She gives me a kiss on both cheeks. "*Buon viaggio e buona avventura, cara*." As she walks through the elegant hall, heads turn. A verse I haven't heard yet. I wonder to myself: is there?

"Regina! Wait . . ." I call. She turns.

Outside, I see Frantonio's car parked at the edge of the valet, over-looking the lower garden and pool. Maybe I can slip off without having to see him. I'll call him. Or send a text. It's a total guy move, and not very nice, but somehow I think he'll get over it before lunchtime.

"Give me one minute," I ask. I hurry outside to reclaim my bag. But the trunk is locked. Damn! Uncle Gandhi is nowhere in sight. No valet either. Where is everyone? I look over and see Regina's driver loading up her luggage in a black town car. Shit. I don't want her to leave without me.

IF YOU: ever find yourself in this situation, DEFINITELY DO NOT:

1. Try to pop the trunk lock with a paper clip from your purse.
2. Bounce on the trunk with your butt trying to spring it open.
3. Try to fold back the convertible canopy, which is also locked.
4. Stick your arm deep through the open vent window to reach that lever you think will open the canopy.
5. Fumble blindly because your head is forced the other way and yank the gearshift out of park by mistake.
6. Panic as you realize your arm is stuck, throwing your full weight against the little car, trying to pry your arm out.
7. Scream as the car now begins to roll downhill toward the pool, dragging you.
8. Grab onto a small sculpture as you roll past, pulling it over to the ground.
9. Realize you can turn the wheel and steer the car away from the pool.
10. Run over a lounge chair as you steer the car . . . into a small fountain.

"My next trip, I'm going somewhere with no fountains," I groan from the ground as Uncle Gandhi helps me pry out my arm and opens the car door. I rub my arm as I stand up. That's going to hurt later. I stare at Frantonio's front wheel in the fountain. That's going to hurt more. I look up and find Regina and her driver both staring at me from the valet area. Shit.

"My dear, are you okay?" she calls, concerned.

"I'm okay!" I call back. "Just moving the car into the shade."

"I think you'd better come with us now dear," calls Regina. "Frantonio loves that car more than his own mother."

"Go," Uncle agrees. "Quickly. My nephew is on his way."

"But, the car!" I object. "He'll blame you."

"What's he going to do? Fire me?" smiles Uncle Gandhi. I kiss his cheeks goodbye and thank you. I reach into the back seat and grab the bottle of Brunello we didn't drink last night.

"Good move," Uncle Gandhi smiles. Turning, I start up the hill toward Regina. Suddenly, I stop. Shit! Will's book. I had to get it back.

"Uncle, could you help me with one last, little thing?"

Road to Roma: Saturday, 1:43 p.m.

For the first part of the ride Regina is on the phone, making arrangements for her upcoming trip and meetings, but after we stop for coffee she asks me about myself. It is way too easy to talk to her, and now I find myself babbling about my Roman holiday, my capers on Capri, the brothers Sicilian, my book, my blog.

"You've had quite the Italian adventure," she laughs. I nod, and find myself wondering, for the first time since I've been in this country, how much longer I'm going to stay. One of the reasons the airline buddy pass was so appealing was the open-ended return. I could leave (or *try* to leave) whenever I wanted. But was I ready? With a twinge of guilt I realize I haven't video chatted with my mother in a week.

"Yes. Maybe enough adventure for one trip. You know you're getting homesick when you actually miss talking to your mother," I quip. Regina chuckles.

"I miss talking to my mother every day," she says. I cringe.

"Sorry, I didn't—"

"*Non è niente, cara.* Everyone complains about mothers. They are the universal constant. They pull when you push. They give when you take. Nobody wants to be like her mother until she becomes a mother and realizes how great her own mother was. Then, we change our minds," she smiles.

"You're a mother?" I ask. It never dawned on me that Regina might have kids.

"*Sì!* I have two grown sons. One is a lawyer in New York and the other is at university. And neither call me."

"Was your mother like you? My mother and I are so different."

"We were alike in the most important ways, like the way we connected with others. Our love of giving and sharing. Our capacity for joy. These are the things she taught me. You may feel different from your mother because you want different things. But, you are who you are because of her." Regina pats my leg in motherly fashion. Suddenly, I miss Rosalie very much.

"I should think about going home soon. But I have so much more work to do on my book."

"*The Influential Women of Italy*?" she smiles. "It's a big topic for a first book."

"I guess so," I admit. "I've never been intimidated by big goals. I just throw myself into it completely and stumble my way through. Discover things. Screw up as I go." I laugh.

"But see, *this* sounds like the interesting book. The discovery, the journey."

"That's what my friends say. They want me to write about my travels, my goof-ups, and the sex. But that's why I'm starting the blog. I just can't see how to fit the two ideas together."

"Reading about women who have accomplished so much will be interesting and inspirational, but also a little intimidating. No? They may seem too good to be true, unreal," she says. I see where she's going.

"So mixing in the adventures of a screw-up will be good contrast?" I smile.

"Contrast, depth, sincerity. Sharing your own experiences will connect more with readers, allowing them to enjoy your journey as you learned about these impressive women. And you, my dear, are also an impressive woman."

"Well, I make an impression. We'll leave it at that," I say, but my cheeks burn self-consciously with the praise. "I guess throwing an imperfect woman in with the perfect ones does shake things up a bit. Thank you." Regina smiles.

Mike's Room, Hotel de Russie, Rome: Saturday, 6:45 p.m.

"You hitched a ride with Regina Lombardi and didn't introduce me to her?" Mike berates me. He's still trying to decide what to wear to dinner and has changed twice.

"You weren't here yet, Mike."

"Stylish vest and button-down or sexy tight tee?"

"Exactly who are you trying to impress? Michael's at home."

"Exactly everyone! We're going to Alfredo alla Scrofa for dinner and then we're going to dance our asses off in Testaccio. What are you wearing? That's your bed over there. Unless you get lucky tonight!"

"Mike, honestly, that's the last thing I want." I open my suitcase and dig out my last clean dress as he changes his shirt again.

"You may change your mind after a few drinks when you have Mario and Luigi grinding you from both sides on the dance floor."

"As appealing as a Super Mario Brothers sandwich sounds, I just had a full night of amazing sex with a man I'd totally fallen for, only to realize he wasn't the man I thought he was after all."

"Who *is*?" he says.

"I still don't know," I answer.

"I was being rhetorical or metaphorical or something." Mike rolls his eyes.

"Well, I was being specific," I say. "I have no clue who I've been exchanging midnight texts with over the last few weeks. It's not Frantonio. It's a French number. Ernesto's number is Italian, but he was always running out of credit and texting me from other numbers. I doubt it's Tango. His musical education was limited to American pop and Italian opera. And the messages started before the brothers Sicilian. That's everyone on my romance roster."

"Not everyone," he says as he puts back on his vest.

"Regina's assistant doesn't count. That was a sympathy screw."

"Not the assistant, silly. You've been using Skype for years and never noticed when you message a phone number from your computer it uses a French country code? It's a French company."

"Crap . . . it could be anyone. Someone I don't even know."

"Or . . . someone who can't quite let you go," he says pointedly. "Back home."

"Will?" The thought stuns me like an electric jolt. Like the time I put my hand on my grandpa's electric cattle fence—the entire world freezes, flips, then starts up again slowly, leaving a sick, tingling feeling in my chest and stomach. Will knew more about music than anyone I'd ever met. Then I remember the last video call we had. I was naked in bed, in Sicily. Tired of the song lyrics from Frantonio (I thought), I had sent:

Serenades are lovely, but the words of others.
I wait for your real voice, under the covers.

And then . . . Will had called. How could I be so blind? With a terrible lurch I remember telling him I was expecting a call from someone else. I remember the hurt in his eyes on the computer screen. That was the last message for days and days, until yesterday, when I had apologized to him . . . accidentally. "Please forgive me," the Bryan Adams song title I'd texted him. And he had answered me . . . when I was lying (naked again) in Frantonio's bed.

I can't believe it. Even accidentally, I had somehow managed to hurt Will again. This was awful. I long to see him, to explain. But what? That I was sorry I'd left? I wasn't. Sorry I'd been with other men? Nope. That I still loved him? I didn't. Did I?

"I think you're right," I say to Mike.

"What are you going to do about it?"

"Nothing, now. I left home to research my new book, see new places, meet new people, have new adventures—and new relationships. And that's what I'm doing. I'm adding to the living, breathing, tangible record of my life. My Collection of Being."

"Florida Woman Fucks Italy to Find Herself," Mike announces with glee as he adjusts his hipster hat in the mirror.

"You completely missed my point. Sex is not the destination, it's the gas in your car along the way." I pull out the ridiculously uncomfortable stilettos I haven't worn since the pond incident at Regina's.

"You're wearing those?"

"I have to, because you look pretty damn stylish and handsome right now," I answer.

Mike beams. "You bet your ass I do! It's my birthday."

"*Buon compleanno, bello!*" I grin. "Neither of us is getting laid, but we *are* going to eat until we're sick, flirt until we hurt, and dance until we drop."

"Yes! I'll get the front desk to call us a taxi in ten minutes." Mike hurries to finish getting ready as I head to the bathroom, but my phone buzzes on the bed. I stop in my tracks and look back at the phone, then at Mike who is staring at me. I smile, leave the phone where it lies, and enter the bathroom.

TIPS FOR *NOT* GETTING PICKED UP WHILE CLUBBING IN ROME:

1. Don't wear stilettos. Or legs. Or breasts.
2. Don't tell them you date women. That turns them on.

3. Don't pretend your friend is your boyfriend because he's already flirting too, and this leads to ideas about three ways.
4. Don't wear earplugs even if the music is loud enough to make you feel like an old lady.
5. Don't nod and smile because you've got no clue what they're saying—you may be nodding yes to something you shouldn't.
6. Don't try to sit on the top of the trashcan even if you wore your stilettos and there is absolutely nowhere else to sit down in the entire club. It will collapse.

Bathroom, Club Caruso, Testaccio, Rome: Sunday, 12:25 a.m.

The garbage is now cleaned off my dress. I was wrong, there is *one* more place to sit down in the club. Covered in sweat, swollen feet throbbing, completely exhausted, I sit on a cold, germy toilet. I have now made it six hours and forty-two minutes without checking the message on my phone. It was Mike's birthday and my sordid love life was not going to take center stage. But now, it's after midnight. Not Mike's birthday anymore. I click open the message. It's a link to a music video for a song called "The Promise." I hold my phone to my ear and plug the other one so I can hear the song over the muffled din of the club. The notes and lyrics strike something deep inside me.

Maybe it's the four cocktails I've had. Maybe it's the fact that I've spent the last two hours peeling the hands of smelly, sweaty strangers off my body. Or, maybe I just know these lyrics are true. He'll always be there. My screen suddenly blurs as I fight back tears. I will not cry on the toilet in the most disgusting bathroom I've ever seen, as the girl in the stall next to me pukes. I will not. There is no toilet paper. *Perfetto.*

Someone bangs on my stall door. *"Fai la cacca a casa!"* I stuff my phone into my bag, fish out a used gelato cone wrapper, wipe, flush, wash, and escape. The flashing lights of the club pulse through me as the loud music bounces my brain. Across the room Mike is dancing in his own world. I find a dark spot under the stairs, ignore the couple making out to my left and the smelly garbage can (I just sat in) to my right, and I pull out my phone again to look up the song online. "The Promise" is by an English New Wave group called . . . When In Rome. Wow. Perfect. I read the lyrics to the song on my phone. The singer apologizes over and over for not knowing the right words to say, fumbling with the wrong words, but ultimately promises to make the listener fall for him.

It's definitely Will. And he knows I'm back in Rome? Not likely. But he's a cop. He's got ways of finding things out. Was he *tracking* me? I close my eyes and wonder if I should answer the message. And then it happens. As if my life were one of those silly romance movies Will used to make me watch, "The Promise" now begins to play in the club. Impossible. This was the difference between me and Will. I was an intrepid escapist hunting down adventure. Will was a hopeless romantic waiting patiently for his happy ending to come to him. Sure, I like romance films, but I watch them for the meet, the chase, and the sex. Not the über-sweet, implausible happy endings. Real life is never happily ever after. Right? But now, as I listen to the words of the song, I look up and see something that makes my heart leap.

Across the club, through the crowd, in the darkness I see Will's unmistakable straw cowboy hat. I blink, and he looks over at me. His face is shadowed. This is not happening. This cannot be happening. But . . . maybe it's just the sort of desperately romantic thing he would do? Jump on a plane and come find me? I take a step forward, but suddenly my hips are grabbed and I'm spun around. It's one of the many guys I've been dancing with tonight. He laughs, twirling me, and Will blurs. When I stop spinning, I look back but Will is gone. My dance partner pulls me close and I pry myself out of his sweaty grip. I see Will's straw hat, sandy blond hair, and broad shoulders headed toward the door. I fight my way through the crowd, around the bar, and finally, out the front door. The moonlight is dim. Cars are crammed into every corner of the lot. Kids laughing and smoking. In the neon glow of the club sign, I spot him by a tree looking away.

"Will?" The broad shoulders turn and a handsome American guy, much younger than Will, with freckles and a pointy chin, grins at me.

"Nope. But I wish I were," the guy answers with a thick drawl. "I'm Patrick. From Texas. You're the first American I've seen. These Italians sure like the music loud. I needed a break."

"Yeah," I laugh, trying desperately to stuff down my bitter disappointment. Of course it's not Will. What was I thinking? I'm drunk and tired, and—

"You solo?" Patrick asks.

"I'm here with a friend. Better get back." I feel the tears coming again.

"Okay then. Nice to meet you." He tips his hat the same way Will does, which breaks the dam. I turn away as the tears flood down my cheeks. Around the corner of the club, I pull my stupidly uncomfortable shoes off and sink my feet into the damp grass, leaning against a cool stone wall. The moon is a sharp crescent above me, stars blinking around it, despite the clouds moving in. A breeze cools the sweat on my dress, sending a shiver through me. I wipe my face.

Yes I'd left Florida to research my new book, see new places, meet new people, have new adventures and new relationships. And I had. My collection was growing. But Will was still part of it. He'd never not be. Somehow, the realization of this settles onto me like a warm, cozy blanket and I stop shaking. The moon sails through the patchy clouds like a tiny, glowing yacht cutting through a dark frothy sea. My fingers find the tiny gold star around my neck. Celestial navigation was one of the first things my father taught me. So I could always find my way back home. I look up at the stars above me. Maybe it was time now.

I wrap my arms around myself, close my eyes, and conjure up the texture of Will's favorite blue shirt against my cheek and forehead. I can hear his strong heartbeat, smell the salty sweet scent of his skin. Did I really miss him that much or was I just finally homesick?

"You okay, Marina?" Mike's voice pulls me back to the nightclub, the muted sounds of the pounding music, and misty cold of Testaccio.

"Yeah. I just want to go home."

"Okay, yeah. This club sucks."

"No, I mean . . . home."

Chapter 37

How Not to Choose Your Ending

Gate 34B, *Fiumicino* Airport, Roma: Tuesday, 11:05 a.m.

I have heard nothing from Frantonio and cannot say that I'm surprised. Clearly what we had was just another tryst for him, and maybe that's what it was for me. Now that our cat and mouse game was over, I was ready to move on. The airline's standby list for my flight is seven people long. I'm number one on the list and have chosen not to ask Mike what he had to do for the flirty gate agent to make that happen. Although the last name of the passenger listed just below me is Johnson, I don't make the connection until Ruby of the Vegan Goat Farts wheels her plaid grocery cart up to the bench and sits down next to me.

"Wow, this is a coincidence. We're both trying for the same flight on the same day, again," I say, forcing a smile. She looks exhausted.

"Not really," she says. "I've tried for all four flights to Miami for the last four days." I cringe inside. "So I've seen a few familiar faces. How was your trip?"

"Pretty incredible. You?"

"My great-granddaughter is cuter than any angel in the Sistine Chapel," she beams. "This trip has meant so much to me." She eyes the standby list. "Huh. In Miami, I was ahead of you on the list, but now you're ahead of me." I know it's because Mike's pulled strings. But this is all Ruby says. Maybe she's too tired to fight. Ruby pulls out a photo, a printed snapshot. "To add to my collection." I nod and smile. Her word "collection" sinks into me like a cold stone into warm water, dragging me down to thoughts I'm struggling to resist. Collection of Being. "The flight's oversold. We'll be lucky if there's even one seat. I had a great trip, I'm just really ready to go home. I've had enough pizza and pasta for a year," she laughs.

"Me too, but I could eat that caprese salad with the buffalo mozzarella, tomato, and basil every day."

"Speaking of Basil, my uncle once had a dog called Basil, he was British you see, and that dog, he was a border collie, they're very smart you know, he used to pull his own sled up a hill . . ." she goes on. This time, I actually listen to her story.

Mike's friend begins the boarding process. Newfound feelings of respect for age and experience scratch and claw at my conscience. Like me, Ruby of the Vegan Goat Farts is a compilation of her millions of moments, emotions, experiences, dreams, and adventures. She is a living, breathing, tangible record of her life. The years she wears proudly are promises of the ones I have left to spend. Doesn't that deserve a little consideration, if not homage? As they finish boarding, Ruby gets up to move to the next gate. "Good luck, dear." She smiles. I watch her walk away, crop dusting as she goes. I look over at Mike's friend, who winks at me.

"Passenger Taylor, Marina Taylor," he announces. I walk up to his counter. I look back at Ruby, who is trying to figure out a vending machine.

"I've had a change of heart," I say.

Passenger Pick-Up, Miami International Airport: Wednesday, 1:07 a.m.

Swimming my way through one of those special Florida monsoons, dragging my bag through pavement puddles turned into lakes, I reach our old, clunky van for the bed and breakfast. I climb inside.

"Hi sweetie! Welcome home." Rosalie smiles, way too chipper for this time of night.

I lean over and give her a big wet hug, which lasts a little longer than usual. She feels warm and squishy in my arms. She's surprised but brushes it off.

"Okay, don't drip on my purse."

"Are you nuts driving in this weather? I said I'd take the shuttle. It's the middle of the night."

"Pshaw! My only daughter isn't taking the bus at this godforsaken hour, in this godforsaken weather, after such a long trip!"

"Thanks. How long have you been waiting?"

"Not too long. An hour maybe?"

"An hour?"

"Don't worry, I just drove in circles until I got your text, so we don't have to pay for parking. It's so expensive here!" She smiles. Of course she did. I probably would have done the same thing.

"Want me to drive? Aren't you tired?"

"No! I brought two thermoses of coffee and had a long nap this afternoon! I'm just fine," she chirps. "You relax, honey. But don't put your feet up there," she says. I smile, take my feet off the dash, lean my chair back, and look over at my mother, a reflection of bright raindrops on her soft, round, wonderful face. It's really good to see her.

"Thank you."

"Of course, honey," she smiles. "I brought you a pillow if you want to take a nap. I'm sure you're exhausted."

"No way. I want to tell you all about my trip. I've got tons of photos and videos to show you later."

"Wonderful! It will almost be like I was there with you!" This surprises me. I didn't think Rosalie cared about traveling. I'd always thought she was content, or maybe even too afraid to venture out.

"One of these days I'll take you there, Mom. You'll love it." Rosalie's face betrays an earnest moment of shock and sentiment, but she quickly recovers, focusing on the road.

"I'd like that, Marina."

"The whole country is beautiful, but there's one place you'd especially love, in Naples. It's called Christmas Alley. The entire street is just Christmas shops year round." My mother's jaw drops and she gasps with sheer delight.

"Pure heaven! Did they have wire stars, you know, like I taught you to make when you were little?" she asks. I remember the multitude of Christmas ornaments I made as a kid. The aluminum stars were the predecessors to the tiny gold one I now wear around my neck. As Rosalie peppers me with excited questions, I realize my mother is and always will be the first woman of influence in my life.

WOMAN OF INFLUENCE: Rosalie Taylor

1. Practical southern girl, middle child of a Protestant, conservative family.
2. Lived in St. Augustine until her mother inherited money, bought a B&B, and moved the whole family to Key West. She was six.
3. After the move, her father died of a brain aneurysm, and her brother was diagnosed with schizophrenia. She's never been good with change.
4. Like her mother, she says what she thinks, and does what she says.
5. A pack rat, craft-o-holic, and prize-winning quilt-maker.
6. Takes the same "vacation" road trip every year with friends from church, driving through small Florida towns, antiquing their brains out.

7. Like me: doesn't mind cheap wine, can't carry a tune, doesn't follow recipes, is klutzy as hell, loves Bob Dylan, and grew up with a strong mother and absent father.

8. Unlike me: she consistently and graciously puts others before herself.

Regina's words about her own mother fade back into my mind as I think about Rosalie. I grew up always wanting to swim away so I didn't get caught in the net of normalcy. The same net that Rosalie did. I wanted to choose my own path. Despite this, I realize how much I am like her. I pride myself on being open to new people. She opens her home to new people every day. I tell stories on paper. She tells them through the quilts she makes. I will always be like her, no matter how far I wander. And maybe, this is okay.

Harbor House Bed and Breakfast, Key West, Florida: Wednesday, 5:03 p.m.

Fish scales flip into the air and stick to my sweaty cheek as the blade of my dull knife stutters down the slippery side of a snapper like a beginning skier on a bumpy slope. Despite the fact that my mother is thrilled to have me home, I am, within twenty-four hours of my return, once again cleaning the fish the guests caught. Right back where I started.

My phone buzzes and I eagerly put down my knife, wipe fish guts off my hands, and dig it out. It's a message but not from Will. I'm relieved. I haven't told him I'm back yet. Not sure why. Maybe I'm still trying to sort out our interaction while I was gone and what it meant. This message is yet another message from Leo, my odd Kiwi Māori friend from the fundraiser. He keeps inviting me to visit New Zealand when he returns in a month, and sending me photos of strangers' dogs in weird costumes. I'm not sure how this is supposed to convince me. This photo is a poodle dyed and shaved to look like Elmo, leaning up against Big Bird, also a dog. I am not kidding. Apparently people really do this to their pets.

I stuff the phone back into my pocket and pick up my knife. I've got two more fish to clean. My feet are back on Florida sand, but my mind is not fully here. It drifts back to Capri as I scrape off scales and cut off tails. Just as I'm remembering my fruitless struggle to "save" the octopus in the crab trap during my bold skinny-dip, the knife slips and I slice into my finger. Shit. As the blood oozes out, instinctually I put my finger into my mouth and instantly regret it. Spitting blood and fish slime onto the ground, I rinse my hands off. But I'm still bleeding. Squeezing my finger, I head back toward the inn for some first aid bandages.

Halfway up the little hill from the beach, I notice movement in the marina. It's Will, moving around on his sailboat. What's that doing here? He sailed it up to Miami months ago. As if he can sense my gaze he turns around and looks up at me. I instantly feel guilty for not telling him I was back. I wasn't sure what to say. What I would do when I saw him. I didn't trust myself. And now, staring at him in the truthful glare of the Florida sun, I know I was right not to trust myself. He tips his hat and my throat tightens. I smile. He waves. I break our gaze, looking down at my flip-flopped feet, covered in fish guts. Don't go down there, I command them sternly. They start walking anyway. There is really no part of me that's obedient.

Marina, Key West, Florida: Wednesday, 5:16 p.m.

Will drops a line, half-cleated, onto the dock, and looks at me with sunburnt cheeks and that adorable smile with his one slightly crooked tooth.

"Hi there, Cowboy. Inbound or outbound?" I ask.

"I was going to ask you the same." He smiles. Music drifts out from the cabin. The song is familiar but I cannot place it.

"I thought you moved your boat up to Miami?" I ask, trying not to notice the fact that he's obviously been working out the last few weeks and looks fantastic.

"Changed my mind," he says. "Thought I'd bring her back down. In case I needed her here."

"For?" I ask, remembering the countless nights we spent on that boat, tangled up in his small bunk together.

"Sailing," he says.

"Right. Of course."

"My mom still likes to go out when I can pry her off of eBay and Amazon."

"Addicts! Mine's up there right now at her sewing machine." I gesture toward the inn with the knife I'm still holding for some reason.

"Marina, what the hell happened to your hand?" he says with alarm. I realize my bloody hand looks like it wants to be in a Tarantino film. In two bounds he's up on the dock, examining my wound. "You've always been shit at cleaning fish. Come into the cabin." Inside, the music is louder. Now I recognize the Leonard Cohen song that made me cry on the ferry to Sicily. "A Thousand Kisses Deep." He reaches over and quickly skips the song. I'm grateful. Another song starts to play. I don't know this one.

"Sorry." He looks embarrassed and pulls out rubbing alcohol. "This is going to hurt."

"Try not to enjoy it too much," I say playfully. His eyes are covered by his hat brim, but I see his lips smile. My hand burns. He mops it off.

"Sit." He takes bandages out of the first aid box as I sit on the little table next to him. He stands in front of me, takes my hand, and gently wraps my finger. The song ends and we hear the first few notes of "The Promise." My heart melts. Will looks instantly uncomfortable. He reaches over to skip it. I stop him.

"I like this one," I say.

"The Promise," he says.

"By When in Rome," I smile.

"A playlist I was working on these past few weeks."

"So I noticed."

"Sorry about that." The brim of his hat again hides his eyes as he fidgets with the already finished bandage on my finger. The song continues.

"Don't be," I say, trying to sound more casual than I feel.

"I shouldn't have been texting you, Marina," Will says with effort. "You need your space to travel and do . . . whatever you need to do. I guess it was just driving me crazy that I was back here thinking about you and you were out there . . . not." He won't look up. I take my bandaged finger out of his hands and use it to push the brim of his hat back up. Now his hazel eyes look deeply into mine.

"I was," I say—or try to say. But my voice sticks in my throat and no sound comes out. He can read my lips and I see a light in his eyes. He gives me a skeptical look and starts to turn away, but I catch his chin gently with my fingers and nod. Suddenly, he is kissing me. Not just with his sunburnt lips but with his whole body, arms wrapped around me, hands behind my neck, in my hair. I kiss him back, leaning into his firm chest, drinking in the smell of his favorite shirt that I've missed so much. The notes and words of "The Promise" swim around us like a school of fish. I wasn't sure which of us had made the other fall. I'd known Will forever, and it was like we'd always felt this way, but were still figuring it out.

Will's hand finds the bare small of my back, sending a tingle through me, and I kiss him harder, knocking his hat to the floor as I grip his strong shoulders. I hear a soft whimper. Was that me or him? I feel his heart pounding out of his chest. Or is that mine?

I wrap my legs around his waist. He pulls my hips closer to him and lifts me effortlessly, still kissing me. My breath quickens as I wait for him to carry me to the small sleeping berth. But Will comes up for air, resting his forehead against mine, his eyes closed. My heart skips a beat as he carries me instead up the narrow boat steps to the deck and over to the edge of his boat. He buries his face in my hair, and we just hold each other. The song ends. He sets me gently on the dock.

I watch Will pick up the line and untie his boat as he smiles at me, takes a deep breath.

"Outbound." I answer my own question from earlier.

"Just a short one, maybe some sunset fishing," he says. I force a smile and reach my foot out, giving the boat a little shove. "Thanks."

"Catch me a nice one."

"You don't eat fish." Will's boat drifts farther from the dock. "You just catch them and toss them back, Mermaid." This stings, but it's true. I don't want him to leave.

"Wait, I have your book!"

"You read it?" he asks doubtfully. Damn. Why did he have to ask this?

"Not all of it," I admit. He knew I hadn't.

"Keep it," he says. "For now." He starts the tiny engine. The boat moves out of the little marina. My finger hurts. Everything hurts. I head back up the hill. The intrepid escapist watches from her mother's porch as the hopeless romantic sails out of the harbor, still waiting patiently for his happy ending. My phone buzzes. I quickly dig it out hoping it will be Will. But it's not. It's another dog photo from Leo. This one looks like Che Guevara, wearing a beret.

AT THIS POINT, IF: your heart aches and your fingers are cramping holding different places in your metaphorical *Choose Your Own Adventure* book, trying to keep your options open . . .

YOU SHOULD:

1. Finish cleaning the fish.
2. Go inside, look at your unpacked suitcase, your empty wallet, the quilted sea turtle pillow your mother made you while you were gone, and the journal of un-compiled notes for the book you haven't even started writing.
3. Take the bottle of eight-hundred-euro Brunello you brought home back down to the dock with two glasses and wait for that Key West sunset you swore you'd stop and watch.

DO NOT:

1. Buy a ticket to New Zealand.

Acknowledgments

Thank you the Michaels who always make me laugh and to Nadya, Alexia, Chiara and Philippe for their help with my egregious Italian and French.

Special thanks to the inspirational women in my life: Marie the artist, Sally the sage, Deborah the dancer, Donna the travel queen, Mary the explorer, Alexis the listener, and most of all, Virginia—my mother.